LOVE Lies

A PARANORMAL ROMANTIC COMEDY

USA TODAY BESTSELLING AUTHOR

CYNTHIA ST. AUBIN

Published by Oliver-Heber Books

0 9 8 7 6 5 4 3 2 1

To wild girls and willful women, wherever they can be found.

ACKNOWLEDGMENTS

Having your very own hot, tattooed, talented musical genius of a cheerleader/fiancé is pretty much the coolest thing ever. Thank you, Ted Levin, for believing in me even when all I believed in was crawling under my desk with a bag of M&M's and a bottle of whisky.

My undying gratitude to Kerrigan Byrne, my first reader, Emotional Support Human and Friend. Thank you for being the Gutter Bear to my Trash Panda. Thee and me.

My sincere thanks to Casey Harris-Parks, who was Team Abernathy and Team Crixus before it was cool.

Much love and endless thanks to Tanya Anne Crosby, writer and publisher extraordinaire, for being willing to take a chance on my silly little werewolf stories.

PROLOGUE

I couldn't breathe.

I couldn't move.

I couldn't scream.

It was neither day, nor night, but some hellish unidentifiable interval in between. Not light enough to see, not dark enough not to.

Something cold brushed the soles of my feet and began a slow, sinister journey upward. Gripping my ankles, stalking slowly up my calves, slithering up the insides of my thighs and over my hips.

Mute, suffocating, panicking, I couldn't so much as twitch as it licked its way up my stomach and settled itself on my chest. Faceless, formless, ancient.

Looking at me.

I felt its regard on my face like the tingling of a numb limb, knowing instinctively when it moved to my hair, my eyes, my mouth.

My throat.

A touch as light as the tip of a feather began at the indentation at the base of my throat and slowly slid upward, ending beneath my chin. There, it grew to the sort of gentle pressure a lover might apply to turn your mouth to theirs.

The chill sank downward, circling my neck like a scarf.

Then, tightening.

Beneath that inexplicable, deadening grip, my heart beat hard enough for me to feel it against my ribs, my oxygen-starved brain beginning to shrink my vision to a single darkening point.

Hot tears leaked from the corners of my eyes and ran down my temples. Pooling in my ears.

The scream I couldn't release vocally tore loose within my mind. I imagined it echoing off the rough stone walls like a singular, violent choral note as I sank deeper into the circling black.

CHAPTER 1

One week earlier...

"Ernest Hemingway, get out of my bathtub."

Hemingway's heavy lidded eyes met mine, his thick dark hair gone a little wiry at the edges from the steam. Defiantly, deliberately, he reclined further into water that could have boiled the flesh from his bones.

Turns out the vampires aren't so great at monitoring water temperature.

I mentally added this to the long and mostly horrifying list of discoveries I'd begun documenting in the previous months.

Discovery number one: *My boss is hot.*

Discovery number two: *My boss is a werewolf.*

Discovery number three: *If I bang my super-hot werewolf boss, I'll become a werewolf too.*

Why?

Enter, discovery number four: *Even though I'm not a werewolf, I am the female heir of a super old and infinitely powerful werewolf bloodline.*

Weird, right?

Hemingway cleared his throat, disturbing the bubbles anchored in the rugged shoreline of his chest hair. In one hand, he clutched a glass of amber liquid. In the other, a pipe.

"That had better not be the Balvenie Portwood," I said, narrowing my eyes at the cut crystal rocks glass clutched in his meaty palm.

Hemingway's eyes, the exact color of freshly turned earth, slid guiltily to the side.

"You can't even drink scotch," I said, my hands flying up in frustration. "You're a vampire!"

Hemingway took a sip demonstratively, then promptly spat it into the bathwater before squaring his shoulders and sitting up straighter. "Drinking the scotch is not the point. Only that I set out to drink it with honest intention."

"I honestly intend to drag you out by your nostrils if you don't get the hell out of my apartment immediately, if not sooner." Snatching the glass, I walked through to the kitchen and paused at the sink. For a brief moment, I considered just downing the remnants myself, but decided against it owing to probable undead cooties.

"Don't worry, I'm getting rid of him," I told Gilbert, Stewie, and Stella, my three feline roommates, as I slung the glass's contents down the sink. They sat poised like gargoyles on the kitchen counter, sniffing at the pear-scented tendrils curling out into the kitchen.

It had been the smell of my best bubble bath that tipped me off when I'd opened the door of my small studio apartment in a converted Victorian home in historic Georgetown, Colorado.

So much for an evening of Netflix and chill.

And cheese.

So. Much. Cheese.

Palming my Gunter Wilhelm butcher's knife, I stomped back into the bathroom, where Hemingway puffed at his pipe.

An impressive effort, considering vampires didn't actually breathe.

"Stop that!" I hissed, slapping the pipe from his hand. "You'll set off the smoke detector." Bits of charred tobacco flake floated on the water's surface like autumn leaves on a pond.

"That was altogether uncalled for." Hemingway sniffed, his impressive mustache tugging upward.

Feeling no particular need for ceremony, I angled the butcher knife's tip at his jugular. His borrowed blood would quickly make the bath a salty soup should the vein be severed.

"I'm calling for you to get out of here before I give you a second mouth," I said, pressing the blade into his skin just enough to create a tiny dart of flesh.

His chest ceased to rise. He'd been undead long enough that breathing was no longer a habit and died away under pressure.

"And before you explain to me why I should be honored by your visit and reveal the sacred purpose which brings you, let me save you some time by telling you the answer is *no*. And not just no, but *hell* no."

"I don't recall asking a question." Hemingway's thick brows drew together, creating a ponderous crease in the center of his forehead.

"You didn't," I said, "but you will. All the others have. Twain, Poe, Dickens, Fitzgerald..."

He sat forward in the bath, the water sloshing against the sides of my once-beloved claw foot tub. "They have been here?"

"Bro, I've had enough famous writers wander through here to make a tenured literature professor cream his starched boxers."

Hemingway's eyes took on the same kind of gleam I often caught in my own accidental reflection in a doughnut shop window. "Wilde said—"

"Oh, I *know* what Wilde said." A hot blue flame of irritation flickered to life at the base of my skull. "I know what he said because I *lived* it."

Hemingway opened his mouth to speak, but I retracted the knife from his neck, plopped down on the toilet lid and rattled on.

"There I was, minding my own business, schlepping around London looking for my 431-year-old werewolf boss, and *shazaam*! Oscar Wilde starts snackin' me down like I'm a triple cream brie croque monsieur. And if that's not bad enough, he's got to tell every damn vampire in his knitting circle I'm the sanguine equivalent of crack. Next thing I know, I've got a line of vampires around the block asking for *samples.* Samples! *'Oh just one little sip, Miss Hanna. I promise I won't try to eat your soul, Miss Hanna'.*"

"Well, I—"

"If you run into Oscar, tell him there's a dick punch coming his way," I said, pointing the knife's tip for emphasis.

"Might you be persuaded to cease waving your weapon in my vicinity?" he asked.

"Might you be persuaded to get your undead ass out of my tub?"

Hemingway appeared to consider this. "I might."

"Look, it's not like I don't understand your curiosity. I really do. I mean, shit. There's all *kinds* of cheeses I want to try. *Pule,* for instance. Never mind it's made from the milk of a genetically superior pack of Serbian donkeys. Speaking of, did you know that donkey's milk has sixty times the amount of vitamin C compared to cow's milk?"

"I can't say that I—"

"True story," I said. "And it only has one percent of its fat content, which is why Pule is so crumbly. Why anyone would want to pay $567 a pound for crumbly ass cheese is way beyond me, when there's such a thing as triple cream brie in the world. You follow me?"

Ernest Hemingway blinked.

"Okay, maybe not my best work metaphor-wise." Scooting forward on the toilet seat, I looked Hemingway straight in the eye. "The point is, I get it. But all the same, the answer is no. I know that as a werewolf heir, my blood is super tasty, but I'm kind of determined to keep it inside my body."

Hemingway folded his arms. The resulting wave drove the bubbles away from his groin. I looked away before I accidentally caught sight of his kibbles and bits. "Perhaps I could write you something. Something to express my *appreciation*," Hemingway suggested. And suggest he did. His eyes were mischievous beneath their straight, dark brows. His sensitive lips drawn into a lascivious curve, the masculine dimple like a thumbprint in his chin. He was younger than he had been when he died to the world.

This was the chief advantage to being a vampire, I supposed. Werewolves only continued the lives they lead before transformation. Vampires banished life, and all its skin-sagging, boob-drooping indignities, into retreat.

"I'm flattered," I said. "I really am. But I kind of already died once with Wilde, and I didn't really care for it."

"I understand," Hemingway said, setting his pipe in the soap dish and pressing himself upward. I jerked my head over my shoulder and shoved a towel at him. He scrubbed it brusquely over his body as I kept my eyes trained firmly at the floor.

When the tub voiced its final, gurgling protests, Hemingway pulled the curtain and set the shower running to rinse it.

An oddly gentlemanly gesture for someone who had come to guzzle my life's blood.

I shooed three furry cat bodies off Hemingway's clothes and tossed them in his direction.

The clothes, not the cats. Though the latter option would surely have ensured a quicker departure.

"Thanks for stopping by," I said. "I'd appreciate it if you'd never do that again."

He captured my hand and kissed it. The surface of his lips was warm from the bath, but he lingered long enough for me to feel the cold flesh beneath.

"I promise nothing." He bowed, and was gone.

CHAPTER 2

Mark Andrew Abernathy, my aforementioned 431-year-old werewolf boss, rolled in an hour late to the gallery he owned and I pretended to help him run. I say gallery, but really it was an oddities shop attached to an exposition space, where a ramshackle pack of werewolf artists routinely exhibited their work.

Though my official title was gallery assistant, my regular duties involved lint-rolling werewolf fur from Abernathy's custom made suits, scheduling appointments and gallery shows around the lunar cycle, and stocking a doomsday arsenal worth of Tide sticks and other blood removing chemicals.

Because that's totally normal.

Seated at my desk on the landing of the old wooden stairs that lead up to Abernathy's office from the gallery below—I was eye-humping a catalogue of office supplies when I heard the gallery door open. Abernathy's familiar warhorse-on-the-hunt gate thundered across the wood floor. He took the stairs two at a time—an easy task for a guy that busted the height charts at six foot five inches.

(Insert your favorite tall guy stereotype here.)

Standing a wobbly five foot eleven inches myself, his height often felt like a personal blessing. It's always an unsettling feeling to know that if shit gets real, your friends and family are likely to scamper behind your back for protection. Mark's back could shelter about three of me.

Four, if I laid off the French baguettes.

Unlikely.

I shoved my mouse to the corner of my Apple monitor and used the brief black flash before the screensaver descended to check my wild mane of auburn hair. Due to the previous evening's unexpected visitor, I'd had little sleep. Still, I managed to make it through an expedited makeup routine, complete with black cat-eye liner and matte pin-up red lipstick.

Mark, on the other hand, looked like hell.

Which is a complete reversal of roles for us, by the way.

I'm the one who flaps through life in a perpetual state of feathery panic. He, meanwhile, utilizes centuries of patience to glide from one situation to the next in his perfect dark-haired, dark-eyed, stony-jawed stoicism.

But not today.

Today, Mark was handsome's shadowed, stubbled, edgy cousin: dangerous.

I mentally stripped away his custom-tailored suit as he slogged up the stairs. To be honest, after seeing him naked a handful of times, it didn't require much imagination.

Though imagine I did.

Like, a lot.

Because although he was still my boss, we had pretty much leapt over the line dividing "employee" from "person you work for but also rolled around naked with" once upon a time.

But not lately.

Lately, we had reverted to a strictly paws-off, quasi-professional, fully awkward mutual denial that the naked rolling had ever happened.

Owing in part to the aforementioned consequences of bones-jumping.

Namely, I hadn't yet decided whether I wanted to complete my transformation to alpha werewolf female.

"You have got to do something about these fangers," I announced, borrowing a term introduced to me by Allan Ede, Mark's 1,000 year-old werewolf tailor.

I'd been the unwitting recipient of a couple pints of Allan's blood after my little run-in with Oscar Wilde. A curious side effect of my nontraditional transfusion had set me on Mark like a hunting dog on a ridiculously sexy fox.

That's how it goes when your blood donor has a penchant for Gucci specs, velvet jackets and well-muscled men.

"What about them?" Mark asked, pausing in front of my desk. If I had to describe the sound of Abernathy's voice and its affect on my lady bits, it would be something like: coffee, dark chocolate, and whisky have a sweaty, hours-long, back-breaking, bed-splintering threesome that ends in simultaneous orgasms.

Which is pretty much how I would describe the rest of him as well.

His hair was the dark chocolate. His eyes, the whisky. His deep-chested, long-limbed, hulking form, the coffee.

Scorchingly hot.

Definitely prone to making my nerves crackle and my blood burn.

"Do you know how many vampires have broken into my apartment since we've been back from London?" I demanded. "I might as well be running a blood bank."

"They're harmless." He shoved past the door to his office, a veritable man-cave of leather and wood, all of which I'd polished liberally with Murphy's lemon oil half an hour before his arrival.

"Smells like fruit," he grumbled.

"I believe *lemony fresh* is the term you're searching for," I said. "And don't you dare put your feet on the desk!" I leaned forward at my desk just in time to see the heels of his Italian leather shoes hovering in midair above the glossy surface.

I narrowed my eyes.

He let them fall back to the floor.

Rising from my desk on a wave of administrative victory, I followed him into his office and assumed my usual spot cross-legged on the leather couch opposite his desk. "What do you mean they're harmless? How do you know?"

Abernathy shucked his coat and slouched into his wide wingback chair behind his broad desk.

I bit my lower lip, unwittingly holding my breath as I silently begged the Universe.

Please roll up your sleeves. Please, dear God, roll up your sleeves.

Please dear God, baby Jesus and every feathery-assed angel...

Roll.

Up.

Your.

Sleeves.

When Abernathy reached down and flicked off his cufflinks, the aforementioned angels treated me to a mental performance of the *Hallelujah Chorus*.

A seasoned forearm ogler of old, I stole glances as Abernathy's oh-so-deft fingers (trust me on this) made quick work of the fine fabric, revealing the long, undulating muscles and thick serpentine veins.

Checking my lap for drool, I refocused my attention on Abernathy's face, which—I was alarmed to note—held a trace of tired amusement.

Busted.

"If the vampires hadn't been harmless, I would have stopped them," he said, his whisky in the sunlight eyes fixed on my twitchy face.

"*Stopped them*? You mean you *knew* they've been breaking into my apartment?"

He graced me with one of his patented maddeningly noncommittal nods.

"And you knew this how?"

"You've been under surveillance."

"You've been watching me? *Again?*"

"Not again," he said. "*Always.* But I don't pick any more fights than I need too. Particularly not with vampires."

"Since when have you backed away from a fight?" Even if I employed the assistance of every bony digit I owned, there wouldn't be enough to tot up the countless times I had seen Abernathy throwing fists or ripping entrails or generally just being all masculine and threatening *at* someone whose face he didn't care for.

"Since the world stood to be destroyed by an apocalyptic battle between our two species." On the heels of this announcement, he grabbed the pile of neatly stacked invoices I'd left on his desk and began leafing through them.

"I thought vampires and werewolves lived in a bliss of mutual ignorance. Isn't that what you told me?"

"Yes," he said. "We had an agreement. For close to a thousand years, the treaty held. No werewolf attacks on vampires, no vampire attacks on werewolves."

"Had?" I asked. "Why *had?* What happened?"

Mark dropped the papers and skewered me with his glowing amber gaze. "You," he said. "*You* happened."

"Me?" I blinked in what I hoped was an innocent and unassuming manner. "What did I do?"

"You got yourself attacked by Oscar Wilde," he reminded me.

The familiar ache of guilt spread in my chest. "It's not like I meant for it to happen. How did my getting attacked break the treaty? I'm not even a werewolf."

Mark shot me a look akin to *God hears the prayer of a craps table junkie begging to win back his rent money.* This debate had been the source of consternation between us since he'd informed me of my status as a werewolf heir roughly a month earlier. I'd sort of had a little problem accepting it at first. And by 'a little problem,' I mean flatly denied to the point of wrapping my head in tinfoil and crawling under my bed.

"Not a *full* werewolf," I amended. "I didn't think untransformed recessives like me counted, strictly speaking."

In case, like me, you are unaware of the term, *untransformed* is werewolf speak for 'not boinked by an alpha male.'

An alpha male like Mark.

Not that he hadn't offered.

Not that I hadn't nearly taken him up on it.

"You don't count," he answered. "But *I* do. Wilde attacked you," he continued. "I attacked him."

"Seems fair enough." I shrugged. "You were provoked. Doesn't that count for anything?"

"You'd think so," Abernathy hinted.

"But?" I interrupted.

"But what?" he asked.

"Please," I said. "There was totally a 'but' in your last statement."

A small smile worked at his lips. "But," he conceded, "vampires can't die. Which means they also can't heal. At least, not quickly."

"I would have thought that would fall under the realm of standard supernatural powers," I said. "Wilde seemed stronger than a normal human ought to be."

"Extra powers, yes. But our two species are diametrically opposed in this way. We have extra life, but we also feel extra pain, extra pleasure."

He let this word hang between us, boiling away the air.

"Our senses are keener, our body processes faster," he

continued. "They traded all of this for the one thing that matters to them."

"Immortality," I said, remembering Allan's early explanations on this topic.

"Yes," Abernathy said.

"You're saying Oscar Wilde is tucked away somewhere looking like a silk blouse put through a rock tumbler?" I reached down and adjusted the waistband of my classic black slacks, a burp of regret about my recent eating choices rising in my chest.

"Something to that effect. He'll be back to his dandy old self in oh…" He paused, consulting the ceiling. "A couple centuries or so."

I sank back against the couch. "Well, shit."

"Very not good. Now, his followers are all riled up, and have decided vengeance against werewolves is the only proper recourse. The werewolf community regards this as a breach of contract, naturally."

The puzzle pieces finally slid into their horrifying place. "So begins war."

"Bingo," Mark said. "Fights have been breaking out. Everywhere. It's making the papers, the news. Not just under the normal titles. They're using words like 'unexplained, mysterious, inhuman.'"

"That can't be good."

"Decidedly not," he said. "Once humans get involved, we're all fucked."

"Hey." I gave him a mock-pout. "What's with the anti-homosapien sensibilities?"

Darkness worked its way into Mark's features. "Human beings are among the universe's worst xenophobes. Let them discover they're not the only ones on the planet and watch how fast they reduce the world to scorched dirt and smoldering ash."

"You talk about this like you've had experience." I uncrossed my legs and tucked my feet beneath me, a gesture of protection against the harshness of his words.

"The Crusades, the Spanish Inquisition, the Killing Fields of Cambodia, the Holocaust, the Salem Witch Trials," he ticked off. "Humans slaughter each other wholesale over what to call a pancake. You really think they'd be okay sharing their planet with *other* species? They can barely share the planet with each other."

Chills danced across my skin. He had a point. He usually did, as much as I was loathe to admit.

"Secrecy is survival. For all of us." His words had the cold finality of a headstone.

I picked through the rubble of details trying to assemble themselves into some kind of sense in my head. "If there was a treaty, it had to be negotiated by some kind of governing body from both sides, right? Can't we just explain what happened? Can't everyone shake paws and make up?"

"It's not so simple anymore, I'm afraid." Abernathy leaned his elbows on the desk and collapsed over them, his shoulders sagging. This small movement produced a worried ripple in my stomach. In Mark, I knew this to be a sign of exhaustion or resignation. Neither seemed fortuitous given our current topic of conversation. "When the treaty was signed, the vampires were united under one leader. That is no longer the case. Theirs is not an empire built on bloodlines. All that matters is power, and who can seize it."

"Who has it currently?"

"Akhenaten. Though Nero's bid has become increasingly successful as of late. He's gathering subjects."

I blinked at him, my face resembling something like a heavily stoned carp. "Nero as in *Nero*? Batshit crazy Roman emperor of the ostrich tongue appetizers and the eunuch wife?"

"That's the guy."

"And *the* Akhenaten? The only monotheistic Egyptian pharaoh? Nefertiti's baby daddy? King Tut's father?"

"The same," Abernathy confirmed.

"He wasn't such bad guy," I reasoned. "He revolutionized Egyptian art. He humanized the stylistic canons. He—"

"Was murdered by priests, resurrected by a Bastet, and now treats humans like Hamburger Helper," Mark interrupted.

"That was downright snarky," I informed him. "I think I'm rubbing off on you."

"Not in recent memory." His eyes glowed with the eerie amber light that only seemed to wake when he was aroused or angry.

I couldn't decide which I preferred at this particular moment.

An answering fire burned in my belly. The memory of his naked chest pressed against my back as my knees buckled with waves of crippling pleasure he'd wrought still ghosted my thoughts like an unfinished melody.

But I wasn't ready to be a werewolf, and he knew it. Not to mention the tiny matter of fine print: werewolves mated for life.

I mean…For. Life.

No small disincentive to Mark, who I regularly annoyed with my ill-fated attempts to run his business, if not his life.

Boss and assistant was a much more comfortable configuration at present, despite our regular clashes over technology, organization, and cleaning products.

I forced my mind away from the innuendo he'd introduced and ham-handedly attempted to redirect the conversation. "You said the vampire empire wasn't based on bloodlines. Does that mean the werewolf empire is?"

He nodded once again.

"So who's the king?" I asked.

"I am."

It wasn't Mark who had answered.

Chills erupted over my arms and scalp, riding down my spine as I whipped around to find an unfamiliar figure standing in the doorway. Tall, broad, silver-haired. He had the face of a sea captain—tanned and weathered, creased like an intimately rendered map of adventure.

I knew his eyes. A shade of golden amber shot through with whisky.

"Joseph." Mark folded his arms against his chest and kicked his feet to rest on the desk, defying my earlier admonishment.

Joseph smiled, the action deepening the good-natured crinkles at the corners of his eyes. "Son."

CHAPTER 3

*S*on?

At second glance, this man was *absolutely* Mark's father. Though he was a few inches shorter than Abernathy, his build was nearly identical in a dark pinstriped suit and crisp, tailored white shirt. I suspected he, like his son, might be a customer of Allan's, as they were old friends. Looking at his face, I began to sort out what of Mark's features had come from him. They shared the same strong, straight nose, same hard-cut jaw. Mark's mouth was softer than his father's, though his eyes perhaps not as kind. Joseph Abernathy had the look of a man who'd spent more years laughing than fighting.

Not so for his Mark.

I took their extended silence as a personal invitation to insert my own questions.

"This is your *dad*?" I asked. "I thought he died in Germany."

"It would appear not," the man observed, directing a look toward Mark. "No thanks to my son." He massaged his jacket in the place above his heart.

"What happened in Germany was between you and Katherine." Mark answered.

Without particularly wanting it to, the details of our first international excursion returned to me. On my second day as Mark's assistant, we had flown to Germany under the guise of his meeting with a fellow antiques dealer. In fact, my boss had come to meet with his father, who had recently been stabbed through the heart with the silver spoon. A rather Freudian gesture on his sister, Katherine's part, I thought. Katherine was still first on the super-fun list I'd recently begun compiling titled: "People Who Want Me Dead." My ex-husband still occupied the third slot, the twatmuffin.

"Four hundred and thirty-one years old and you still have the manners of a meat goat." Joseph shook his head. "Perhaps you should introduce us," he suggested, his eyes flicking over me.

Mark sighed beneath the weight of the inevitable. "Hanna Harvey, this is my *father*, Joseph Abernathy. Joseph, this is Hanna."

Abernathy Senior's eyes were like kerosene lamps, alight with a sudden, vivid flame.

"Hanna," he breathed. "Hannelore Matilda Harvey. Of course you are. I would know you anywhere." He closed the space between us and took both of my hands in his. They were warm and smooth like well-worn leather. The pressure they applied to mine left me feeling surrounded, protected. His eyes read the volume of my face. "How you look like her," he whispered.

It took me a moment to recover speech under such intense observation.

"Like who?" I asked.

"Your grandmother. Marion Matilda Goebels," he recited. "The one you are named for."

Indeed, it had been my grandmother who had brought me into Mark's orbit by asking his father for protection when she was yet pregnant with my mother. According to Mark, the task had fallen to him, as his father was a useless wastrel who spent his time chasing human skirts.

And was very likely pretty damn good at, from the looks of him.

"You remember her?" I asked him.

"*Remember* her? My girl, I would challenge a man to forget."

On this point, I understood him perfectly. My grandmother had been a severe betty. Platinum blonde hair, bright green eyes she accented with jet-black liquid eyeliner, lips shaped by matte red lipstick. The posture of a queen. Every man in the seniors' group of her Lutheran church had tried, failed, and tried again.

"Of course, she was no admirer of ours," Joseph continued. "Particularly after what happened to your brother. We certainly could have done a better job with that."

This word, brother, still felt awkward within my vocabulary. I'd grown up as an only child, never knowing I had a brother until Mark revealed his existence to me under duress.

Amazing how being naked and handcuffed to a bed will motivate a man to talk.

His hesitance had been understandable. Revealing that my father had been murdered when I was eight years old, rather than dying in a car accident as I had been led to believe, was pretty damning stuff. Particularly since Mark had been there the night it went down and had facilitated the cover-up after his death. Admittedly, "Local Salesman Gored by Bloodthirsty Werewolves Set to Destroy Infant Heir" would have made a much more awkward headline.

"*We*?" Mark challenged. "What *we*? As I remember, you were slouching at a roulette table in Monte Carlo with a blonde 800 years your junior at the time. Had there been a *we*, I might not have had to do what I did."

"What you did was save the child," Joseph said, half yawning. "What more could be expected?"

"Turning an infant into a werewolf is an abomination," Mark growled.

Joseph looked at his son with a mix of confusion and amusement. "He's no longer an heir. Not now that his blood is no longer pure. That fact alone redoubles his safety."

"Few of our kind are so discerning," Mark said. "Should any of them learn he is still alive—" At this, he cast a meaningful glance at me.

I resented the ocular implications of mistrust.

He had forbidden me from revealing anything I knew to anyone, my brother included. Trouble is, my brother, Steven Franke, worked as one of the resident artists in Mark's gallery, and in the short time we'd known each other, we'd been through a lion's share of bonding scrapes. I saw him every day, loved him already, and yet, I could say nothing.

I hated Mark for asking this of me as much as I loved him for keeping my brother safe.

"You haven't *told* him?" Joseph asked. "He doesn't know he has a sister? And the mother? She doesn't know her son *lived*? Mark, you can't do this. You can't ask this of Hanna. The boy has a right to know who he is."

"I know, right?" I interjected. "Only he isn't so much a boy as he is a weird Peter Pan-like ageless eternal teenager."

Mark's jaw ticked. A vein rose in his temple and pulsed.

Battle stations! shouted the little voice in my head.

"I ask what I *must* ask." Mark's voice had taken on that particular bowel-loosening timbre somewhere between a whisper and rasp. "What I do, I do for their safety. Who are *you* to question me? *You* who failed to keep even your wife—"

A blur, a brief whiff of wool, and Joseph's hand was at Mark's throat.

It was only the second time I'd seen Abernathy surprised. But then, Theo Van Gogh was a hell of a bluffer.

"You will not speak her name." Joseph said through clenched teeth. "You know *nothing* of what happened."

"I know *enough,*" Mark choked, the bones of his knuckles white as a fish belly as he gripped his father's tanned wrist.

Seizing the moment, I wedged myself between the two muscly, testosterone-twitching male bodies and push a hand against each of their broad chests.

"Okay alphas," I said. "I think we need a time-out."

Standing between them felt like being in a sauna, heat blasting me as they verily shot steam from their nostrils.

"Joseph," I said. "Why don't I give you a tour of the gallery? I'm sure your son has plenty to do. Isn't that right, Mark?"

Saying his first name aloud still felt like pilfering a dark chocolate truffle from my mother's forbidden stash. I'd melted into it sometime after our flurry of naked near misses.

Anticipating Abernathy's oncoming objection, I fixed him with my best steely-eyed German hausfrau glare. Miracle of miracles, it worked.

Barely.

He took a single step backward, his shoulders still squared, his fists clenched.

Deciding this was my only shot, I laced my arm through Joseph's and tugged him toward the office door. Only, he wouldn't be tugged.

Time for plan B.

Leaning into him, I allowed my breast to brush his arm as I tried to achieve just the right mix of playful and sex-kitteny. "Come on, you."

A familiar grin slid across Joseph's lips. I'd seen it on a face very like his on a couple lucky occasions. "With such pleasant insistence," he said, "how could I resist?"

"First stop, Mission Control." I felt like a flight attendant, all contrived gestures and shiny teeth as we exited Abernathy's office and approached my desk. "This is where I take care of all the administrative details that keep this place humming. When I'm not making futile attempts at trying to keep your son organized and generally driving him crazy."

A fond smile spread across Joseph's face as he shook his head. "Always been a bit of a slob, my boy. You should have seen his chambers growing up. Looked like a band of marauders had been through there."

This revelation presented me with a rather novel idea. Abernathy had once been a boy. A long lashed, chocolate-haired little lad.

"Where *did* he grow up exactly?" I asked, making my way toward the stairs.

"He hasn't told you?" Joseph asked, looking genuinely surprised.

"He never tells me *anything*," I said, employing my favorite adage where Abernathy was concerned.

"Well, if he hasn't told you, he probably doesn't want you to know." Joseph's voice held a familiar stony note that morphed into mischief as we descended to the gallery. "But he isn't here now, is he?"

"Indeed not."

We crossed into the main gallery space, the walls blank and bare in anticipation of our upcoming show.

"Mark was born in a castle on the River Tay in Scotland. Not far from the village *Abernethy* in Perth and Kinross from which we take our name."

"I knew he was Scottish! I *knew* it!" I said, digging my fingernails into my palm to curb the urge to break into a cheerleader bounce. Okay, I hadn't so much *known* Abernathy was Scottish as I had vividly and repeatedly imagined him as the kilt-wearing laird on a never-ending mental series of bodice-rippers, but I was willing to count it. Speaking of those kilts..."You don't have an accent though. Neither does he."

He treated me to a boyish grin. "Aye lassie. It isnae wise to have an accent if you're aimin' to blend in."

My stomach made a sudden and unexpected pilgrimage toward my knees as blood rushed abruptly into my face. Thank *God* Mark had never busted out the brogue. I would have been a werewolf about eighty-seven times over by now.

"Right," I said, recovering my wits. "I could see that."

We paused in the center at the edge of the gallery's post-modern white cube where the building's exposed brick walls hinted at the structure's true age.

"This place has a rather rustic feeling," Joseph observed. "But then, old as I am, rustic can be a problematic term."

"How old *are* you? If you don't mind my asking."

"Eight hundred and thirty-one," he answered without hesitation.

"You mean, you had Mark when you were...*four hundred*?"

"To the day," he replied, eyes all a-twinkle.

"And when is your birthday?" I probed. Oh, someone was in big trouble, all right. Streamers, balloons, confetti—okay, scratch the confetti. I'd be the one cleaning it up, after all. Maybe a mariachi band? Cake.

Definitely cake.

"August sixth," he answered.

"A Leo. I so could have guessed that. No offense," I added.

"None taken." He smiled, and certain parts south of the equator decided that 831 wasn't necessarily *that* old. I mean, what's a few centuries when someone is serving up serious werewolf daddy energy?

"Is four hundred a normal age for werewolves to have their first children?" I asked, all the while telling myself this question had not one thing to do with the fact that I'd begun ovulating twice monthly since the inception of my work at the gallery.

"Perhaps a little beyond normal. Many mate within their second century. I've been at Mark to settle down for some time now. He's in imminent danger of becoming a confirmed bachelor, I'm afraid."

"Don't I know it." I had meant it as an acknowledgement of Abernathy's resistance to change, his absolute unyielding bullheaded stubbornness.

Joseph took it as something else entirely.

"If only there were an eligible young alpha female somewhere around." He turned to face me, his left eyebrow taking on a lascivious arch. "How I would love to hear the pitter-patter of little paws again. To have some grandpups to spoil..."

"So, this is where we conduct the gallery shows every month," I broke in with enthusiasm bordering on hysteria. "All our resident artists contribute pieces, and people come buy them, and we drink the wine and eat the cheese and—"

"That sounds festive," Joseph said, gracious enough to let me change the subject. "I have to admit, I'm surprised he stuck with it all this time."

"Stuck with what?" I asked, stealing a glance at the miraculous place where Joseph's starched white shirt met his tanned, smooth neck.

"Art. When he ran away to Spain to chase that Caravaggio character, I thought it was a phase."

"Not...*the* Caravaggio?" In vain, I tried to keep my face from assuming that open-mouthed gape that seemed to lower my IQ by several points.

"You know of him?" Joseph asked, seeming genuinely surprised.

"Do I *know* of him? Are you kidding me? He's like a Baroque god! I took an entire seminar on his work. It was an elective of course, which was totally not for credit and he really wasn't part of my thesis but—"

"You wrote a thesis?" Joseph paused, turning to face me in the hallway leading to the artist's studios. "I'd love to read it."

I glanced around the gallery, turning to scrutinize his face.

"Look, I know we don't know each other very well, but I feel it's only fair in the spirit of full disclosure to let you know that you are very near to inducing a full-on unadulterated geek fest on my part."

"I believe I'm up to the task." An exceedingly charming crinkle appeared at the corner of his left eye when he smiled.

"No," I warned him. "You don't understand. I'll, like, *jump up and down* and stuff. And probably emit a variety of high-pitched squeaking noises. I might try to hug you. Or hump your leg. I've knocked people over before," I confessed, remembering my unfortunate first encounter with the man I believed to be Vincent Van Gogh.

Long story.

"I could think of worse fates," he said.

"You say that now, but just wait until you're flat on your back wondering why your head hurts and what that buzzing sound in your ears is."

"That sounds remarkably like an evening I shared with Sarah Bernhardt." He laughed, filling the air around us with sound rich and sweet as melted caramel.

"See?" I said. "That's why I don't want to talk about me. You're far more interesting."

"You're very kind to flatter an old man," he said, offering me his arm once again.

"I don't think *old* is an adjective I'd use to describe you." My voice had dropped an octave all on its own. Totally the brogue's fault.

We stopped in the hallway that joined the gallery to the oddities shop, flanked by studios on either side. Two of the four doors were open and their rooms empty.

"These are the artists' quarters, I assume?"

"You assume correctly."

"Only two are occupied?"

"At the moment, yes." I briefly debated regaling him with the sordid story of how the occupants of two of the studios had met their untimely demise, but thought better of it when I realized that his travel-dicking his way around the world was mostly to blame. Wolves and bastards and geriatric half were-ladies, oh my!

"Well," he said as if sensing a dark turn in my thoughts. "I'm just delighted that you survived your scrape with Wilde in London. Mark would clearly be lost without you."

"You know about that?" A blush stung my face as I felt my ears go all hot and throbby. Truthfully, I'd begun to feel a little awkward about accidentally starting an epic cross-species war. And by awkward I mean *hideously guilty and ashamed.*

"Of course I know about it." Joseph treated me to a winningly reassuring smile. "Allan rang me up gushing liked a damned schoolgirl. I thought I just might need to come meet the infamous Hannalore Matilda Harvey myself. And here I am." He bowed, somehow managing not to make the move as douchebaggy as it would have been on any other being.

"You came here for me?" I asked.

"Among other things." He raised a dark eyebrow at me.

"Hold it, mister." I poked a finger into his chest. "You said 'other things.' I know about other things. *Other things* is Abernathy speak for really important stuff you don't want to tell me but that could probably get me killed."

Now I knew where Mark got his patented impenetrable enigmatic smile.

"And we were off to such a great start," I sighed, my heart heavy and my stomach growly (though the latter wasn't at all Joseph's doing). "You were agreeing with me, telling me things Mark didn't want me to know…"

"What things would that be?" Mark asked, appearing behind Joseph with startling swiftness. Extraordinary speed is one of those endearing little qualities that makes working for a werewolf extra-fun. Especially because it's paired with extraordinary stealth. In my first weeks of working for Mark, I had deeply considered investing in absorbent briefs, such was his ability to sneak up on me. In addition to: reasons.

Joseph waved a large, sun-bronzed hand at his son. “Nothing of importance, of course.”

“Nothing of importance,” I echoed, failing to convince even myself.

“I’m sure.” Mark folded his arms and narrowed his eyes. “Care to tell *me* something of importance?” he asked, fixing his father with a frighteningly intense amber-brown gaze.

“If I must.” Joseph’s body had lost some of its casual alacrity. He stood a few inches taller, still barely scraping his son’s height.

“I’d like to know,” Mark paused, his lips twitching between amusement and disgust, “why you have a decapitated vampire in the trunk of your rental car.”

CHAPTER 4

Levity returned to Joseph's pleasantly weathered features. "I don't believe I heard you correctly."

"I'm sorry," Mark said, sounding not sorry in the least. "Perhaps I should have been more clear, given your advanced age. There's a decapitated vampire. In your trunk." Mark said, exaggerating the pronunciation of each and every syllable.

The smile fell from Joseph's face.

"There's *nothing* wrong with my hearing," he growled. "Nor with any other of my faculties, should you care to find out." He made no move to back his threat, letting his words carry the weight of his challenge.

Mark stared unblinking into his father's eyes.

"The only thing I care to find out, is why you've brought a slaughtered vampire to *my* gallery," he said. His voice bore the dangerous calm of an ice-skimmed lake. I knew from experience that venturing onto it meant a swift fall into spinning cold.

But Joseph was intrepid.

He shook his head and dropped a hand on Mark's shoulder.

"Son, I would have thought at four hundred and thirty-one years old you'd know these ploys for my attention are quite unnecessary. Did I not hug you enough when you were a pup? Shall I hug you now?"

He made a move to enfold Mark in his embrace, but was shrugged off.

"Well, if the body in your trunk doesn't concern you, then perhaps I ought to just call the police and let them look into it."

This was a bluff on Mark's part, I knew. He would sooner sew his own leg back on with kitchen twine and a spoon shank than involve authorities of any kind. Not only this, but he employed a crack werewolf clean-up crew to handle just such situations. By my count, they'd taken care of half a dozen bodies without so much as a sniff in the local newspaper. What's a random body in a trunk compared to reconstructing half the gallery overnight after a run-in with a Mack truck?

"You are certainly welcome to do so, of course." Joseph's smile only lacked a few yellow canary feathers poking out from between his teeth. "But, in the interest of fairness, I should inform you that the car is rented in your name. Might make for a tense discussion given your frequent difficulties with local law enforcement."

I didn't need to look at Mark's face. The wall of hostility radiating off him made it difficult for me to breathe. But then, Mark's presence had that effect on me even under normal circumstances. Or whatever passed as normal around here.

"Why the hell did you rent a car in *my* name?" Mark asked.

"The same reason I purchased my airline tickets in your name. I thought it best that no one know I'm here. Given the escalating series of recent *conflicts*, my arrival could seem problematic, don't you agree?"

"Is that why you've come?" Mark accused. "Because I'm not doing *your* job well enough anymore? Am I making you look bad? Affecting your dates is it?" His rage brightened and sharpened with each successive question.

"Unfortunately," Joseph said gently, not taking the bait, "it doesn't matter what I think. The last months have been messy. First Penny, then Van Gogh, and now Wilde. The clans are talking."

"Let them talk," Mark spat. "It seems that's what they do best."

"Have you thought about what it would mean if they no longer accepted our rule? If they thought the line was broken?"

"Daily," Mark answered. "For the last four hundred years. And you?"

"Not so often as that, admittedly," the older man shrugged. "Son, I'm not here to lecture you. God knows you've done more than you had to in my stead." Joseph glanced away then, the light from the gallery's plate glass windows reflecting in his eyes' sudden sheen.

"Why *are* you here then?" Mark challenged.

Joseph searched his son's face and spoke slowly. "To see how you are. How can I hear of all that has happened and not worry if you're okay?"

Would this be the 'among other things' he had been referring to, then?

"Right," Mark laughed. "Which would be why you hauled up with a mangled vampire in your trunk. You want me to be okay? Leave."

At this, I slugged Mark in the arm. Didn't he see a tender moment when it was trying to happen? The regret etched into Joseph's face made my heart feel like it had been roped to an anvil. I'd heard enough.

"He doesn't mean that," I interrupted. "He would love it if you stayed. Wouldn't you, Mark?"

"No," Mark answered.

"See?" I said. "He definitely wants you to stay."

"You are very kind, Hanna," Joseph said. "But I didn't come to impose. It was lovely meeting you." He reached out and gave my upper arm a fatherly squeeze.

Turning, he walked toward the gallery door. I looked to Mark, who had arms folded across his chest, back turned to his father, chin hitched in the air, eyes gazing at the ceiling.

Stupid werewolves and their stupid wolfy pride.

"All right," I announced, stomping after Joseph and dragging him back by the hem of his coat. "I didn't want to have to do this, but you leave me no choice. Mark Andrew Abernathy, you turn around this minute, or so help me, I will file every paper in your office. *Without labels.*"

He didn't budge.

"And I'll *move* stuff," I added.

His shoulders lowered a fraction, his large feet scraped a grudging circle until he faced his father.

"Now hug." I stood back, arms folded across my chest, resting bitch face strapped on tight.

Mark shuffled a couple centimeters towards his father's outstretched arms, mouth set in the flat unamused line frequently associated with my presence. Clearly encouraged by this infinitesimal surrender, Joseph closed the gap, clapping Mark on the back with manly solidarity.

"This one is good for you son," he said, smiling at me over Mark's shoulder. "I trust you won't let her get away."

"This doesn't change anything," Mark muttered.

"Of course not," Joseph agreed, releasing him. "I'll have to earn your trust. I understand that. I'm only asking for a chance to do so."

"You'll do what you want." Mark strode toward the stairs, not looking back. "But get rid of the thing in your trunk."

"I will, son." Joseph watched Abernathy go and turned to me.

"This isn't going quite as well as I hoped." His heavy sigh filled my heart with rocks.

"You can't feel too bad," I said. "It's just his way. He keeps everyone at a distance." *Even me.*

Especially me.

"He has every right," Joseph said with a small, sad smile. "I wasn't the father I should have been to him. I always seemed to fail him in some way. I've known he was stronger than I since the midwife handed him over. He looked at me with these *eyes*," he paused, looking at the gallery wall as if it might hold a portrait of his infant son. "They were so old, even then. I suppose I was intimidated. Isn't that ridiculous? To fear an infant?"

His disarming smile had returned.

"No," I said, "it's not ridiculous." In fact, I had heard similar sentiments from my mother's mouth on several occasions. I felt a pang of sorrow for the solemn little boy Mark must have been.

"Well," he sighed, "I better hop to it. I'd hate to fail my first test."

"I would offer to help," I said, "but, I really have no desire to see a decapitated vampire. I've had enough of them wandering through my life as of late already."

"Oh?" he asked.

"Indeed. Wilde blabbed, apparently, and now I'm the flavor of the week."

"That sounds decidedly inconvenient."

"Tell me about it, mister. I damn near had to share a bath with Ernest Hemingway last night." A shudder rippled through me at the memory of bubbles and chest hair.

Confusion creased his handsome features. "I wouldn't have thought Mark would allow such a thing."

I shrugged. A gesture far more casual than my real feelings on the subject. "He says they're mostly harmless. The ones that have been dropping by to see me, at least."

A sly, conspiratorial smile tugged one corner of his mouth. "I'll make some calls."

My cell phone buzzed in my pants pocket. Glancing at the screen, a small knot of irritation tightened in my chest.

"Shit," I muttered. "Defensive driving." Thank God I'd remember to set a calendar reminder two weeks ago. I'd have totally spaced it otherwise. "I better get going or the judge will probably re-issue my arrest warrant. Between you and me, I'm in no hurry to get hauled down to the pokey again."

"You?" he asked. "Marion Goebels' granddaughter was arrested?"

"On a totally a trumped up charge," I said. "The detective had a man-grudge against your son, and he had to drag us in together when we got back from London. The unpaid speeding ticket was the only thing he had on me. Fucking Morrison."

Who I sort of slept with a few times.

"Anyway, the charges against Mark were dropped after Detective Morrison beat the snot out of him during their interview, and a very nice judge said if I went to defensive driving class, he'd wipe the ticket off my record."

"Wouldn't it be easier to just pay it?" he suggested.

"And have a mark on my record? Are you mad?"

Now I was treated to the full wattage of his pearly whites. "You *are* your grandmother's granddaughter."

"Sounds like we both have important business to attend to then." He leaned forward and took my hand in his, bending down to brush a brief kiss across my knuckles. "Thank you," he said.

"For what?" A draft from the gallery's windows caressed my blood-warmed cheeks.

"Mercy," he answered. "First and foremost. And for being so kind to me. Undeserving as I am."

"We've all made choices we regret," I said. Like my ex-husband, for example. And that Quarter Pounder with Cheese I ate at midnight. "I'm not here to judge."

"What a rare woman you are," he observed. "Rare, and beautiful."

He gave me his second bow of the day, and left the gallery to dispose of the dismembered undead.

CHAPTER 5

I have this theory.

It goes like this: the universe hates me.

Arriving at my defensive driving class my standard ten minutes early, I sat myself in the shameless nerd-approved front row table and I took the time to arrange my effects: cell phone, two pens, notepad, iPad, and a bag of cheese crackers.

If I was going to spend the next four hours with my ass in a plastic chair, cheese needed to be in the equation somewhere.

My fellow students shuffled in over the course of twenty minutes, a buzz of discontent building when the instructor hadn't shown at ten minutes past the appointed start time.

A full twenty-eight minutes late, he shuffled through the door. I knew his smoky, scotchy smell as well as I knew his hard hewn but handsome face.

Morrison, my clever-tongued and dexterous detective.

So, *this* is what they did with cops on suspension.

His brown sugar fudge colored hair hadn't been washed this morning, the granite cliff of his jaw was begging for a shave. The lids over his hazel eyes seemed heavier than I remembered, wanting sleep, and more. The white button-up shirt stretched over his chest looked like it might have been resurrected from the bottom of a laundry basket. Ditto, the pants, which radiated resurrected from the floor energy. The body beneath the fabric appeared softer than the whole and vibrant image in my mind's eye. Dulled by time or beer.

He saw me at once.

I felt the small pop of recognition, but not the usual spark of hunger that generally attended it. His eyes darted not to my face, or my breasts as was their custom, but to my wrists and neck.

Checking for bruises, no doubt.

When I had deplaned after my meeting with Oscar Wilde in London, I'd had plenty. Only Morrison had assumed Mark had put them there. I'd argued as much as I was able without revealing that whole *werewolves and vampires are real* thing, but it hadn't been enough. Detective James Morrison had exacted justice by way of a fist, leaving due process to see to his suspension. I hadn't seen him since that night.

Satisfied that I'd sustained no further injury, Morrison refused to look at me for the rest of the class—even when mine was the only hand raised to answer the questions he posed.

Which was often.

I sat through all four hours, ignored and ignoring, resenting everything and everyone, and generally just wanting to throat punch someone.

Morrison's voice still resonated with the unrelenting edge that had ripped confessions from murderers and rapists alike and closed a record number of cold cases within the Georgetown Police Department. He was wasted on this class, and its bored, blinking occupants.

Well, most of its occupants.

I caught hungry gazes from my fellow female classmates lasering at Morrison's ass when he turned his back to the class to scrawl on the whiteboard.

And, damn him, he'd turned and *smiled* at them. Every single one of them.

Except for me.

You think he's flirting with you? I wanted to shout. Well I've ridden that man like a mechanical bull on nickel beer night, you smug eye-humper. Put that in your Juicy Couture sweatpants and smoke it.

After class, Morrison snapped his battered briefcase closed and was out of the room quicker than a greased pig. I packed up my notes and wandered out to the parking lot where my metallic flake blue 67 Mustang hunkered like a wolf at the herd's edge. The white racing stripes reflected the day's waning light in a dull gray.

Behind the wheel, I cranked the key over, and was met by a rhythmic choking.

"Aww, come on," I pleaded. "Don't do this to me. Not now."

I waited for the caravan of minivans to disperse before giving it another go. The engine sounded weaker this time, a patient in the last stages of vehicular emphysema.

I thunked my head against the cold steering wheel, worn smooth long before the Mustang had come to rest at my curb.

The horn gave an abrupt little beep, reminding of the first time I'd honked the horn of Mark's old Rolls Phantom. He had been in front of the car at the time, an unfortunate happenstance for us both. Me, for the new pair of underwear I required, and him for punching a dent in the car's hood that cost a nifty ten grand to replace.

Only it wasn't Mark in front of the car now.

It was Morrison.

He had my hood popped before I could get the car door open.

If that wasn't a metaphor for our entire relationship, I didn't know what was. Taking a blood pressure lowering breath, I levered myself out of the car.

Morrison leaned over the exposed engine, hands planted on the chrome grill. I had often thought that Morrison looked more like a boxer than a cop and glancing at his profile in the sun's dying light did little to change my mind. A strong nose that looked like it might or might not have been knuckle-adjusted at some point. The stony jaw capable of absorbing full force haymakers. Only his lips offered a hint of sensitive vulnerability.

"Hi," I said.

"Battery's dead." He thumbed greasy dust off the battery's terminal.

"Think so?"

"You left your lights on again."

I began to protest and then remembered. Checking the clock radio, wanting to be in my seat at least ten minutes before class started, I had squealed into the parking lot on two wheels. "I *might* have forgotten to click them off," I admitted.

"You have jumper cables? The Vic's parked over there." He shot his chin the direction of a Gold Crown Victoria a few rows behind us in the mostly empty parking lot. I'd once made the mistake of needling Morrison about the woes of police-issued vehicles, only to discover he owned it personally. I'd learned too slowly that the man liked his cars like he liked his women: easy to slide into, fast on the gas, and requiring little more attention than the occasional oil change.

Only managing two out of three meant I was a little too much for him to handle most days.

"Do I have jumper cables?" I scoffed. "What kind of girl do you take me for?"

This wrought the specter of his uneven smirk.

I pulled open the driver's door to retrieve the keys and swung back to unlock the trunk.

Where I found a decapitated body hunched around the Mustang's spare tire.

A dark suit ending in a ragged red stump, matching like a morbid puzzle piece: the head it belonged to at an impossible angle, the neck pale against drying blood. The copper clamp of one cable poked from the gory space between head and neck, looking like a failed mechanism for attachment.

Somewhere deep in my gut, I felt the spreading calm of a woman who had seen too much bloodshed. A woman who had seen scores of mangled bodies. A woman who had been bitten, beaten, and betrayed. A woman who met violence and death with the grace of eventuality.

But that was my gut. To my great regret, my gut didn't control my gross motor functions.

Nope.

That would be my brain. My panicky, neurotic, anxiety-addled brain.

I shrieked like a banshee, slammed the trunk closed, flapped a frantic circle, and slapped death germs off on my jeans. It's possible that I indulged in a full body shudder before I remembered Morrison, now staring at me in sudden squinty-eyed suspicion.

Shit. The cop face.

I'd fallen prey to its impossible scrutiny more times than I cared to recall.

I could show him. After all, he was a cop. He could find the bad guys that did this. They might even let him back on regular duty if he called this in. He'd be grateful. He might even forgive me.

Right, the ever-present cynic critic in my head said. You'll just let this cop who is convinced Mark is a murderer check out this sweet body in my trunk. I'm sure he'll know I was completely innocent of any wrongdoing and everything will be sunshine and rainbow-colored unicorn poop.

There was only one option open to me, and I knew it. I needed to get this mess back to Mark.

"Dear God! The gorgonzola!" I said, blurting out the first lame excuse that sprang to mind. Fortunately, it was also believable. "How did I forget?" Fanning my nose, I bent at the waist and retched. I could literally feel his gaze scorching the side of my face as he tried to decide if I was lying.

Either I was a better actress than I thought or he was feeling especially benevolent that day.

"I have cables," he offered. "I'll pull the Vic around."

His body's casual grace hadn't been compromised by the forces that drove him from his usual routines of measured control. He moved across the parking lot with the purposeful stride of a man who didn't attach conscious effort to the movements of his own body. Morrison's energy, as always, turned inward to the constant engine of his mind, processing details, calculating, determining.

He slid behind the wheel with a practiced gesture and the Vic roared to life. Morrison shot across the parking lot, spraying gravel in his wake, and swung around nose to nose with the Mustang.

"You didn't buckle your seatbelt," I teased, as he came around to clamp cables between our two vehicles. "I'm pretty sure you could be ticketed for that."

"You want my help or not?" he grunted, reaching over the Mustang's guts.

"Someone pee in your Cheerios this morning?" I asked

Anger flashed in the blue-brown vortex of his hazel eyes and I saw how close to the surface it lived. In that moment, I knew I could push him into a fight. One more carefully placed prod, and he'd scald me with the rage he'd been bottling since our last meeting. I'd know the whole of his ire, and we could begin rebuilding.

I let it pass.

He pushed his sleeves to his elbows, baring the forearms I

had admired as they'd pinned my wrists to the wall, on occasion.

What can I say? I happen to be a brachial musculature enthusiast.

I reminded myself that I shouldn't be staring as he thrust his hips against the car's body to rock himself backward without the aid of hands. Nor watching the way his fingers worked the cables' length to secure the connection before he ducked back into his car to rev the engine.

Morrison clearly wanted to be out of here as soon as possible, and I didn't blame him.

"Try it now," he ordered.

I gave him a salute and leaned into the driver's seat. Bucky's engine roared to life on the first turn. I was equal parts elated and disappointed.

He hopped out of his car, disconnected the cables, and tossed them onto the carpet of discarded fast food wrappers in his back seat.

"Thanks!" I called out the window.

He slammed his hood and sped away, leaving the acrid aroma of burnt rubber and unspoken words in his wake.

I indulged in a forlorn sigh dredged from the depths of my hopelessly romantic heart.

And then remembered the headless thing in my trunk.

"Why couldn't I have majored in something safe and boring, like accounting?" I asked the universe. "If I hadn't majored in art history, then I wouldn't have lied my way into this job, and if I hadn't lied my way into this job, I wouldn't be a werewolf's assistant, and if I weren't a werewolf's assistant, I wouldn't have a headless body in my trunk!"

I mentally added this to the growing list of "Reasons to Stay Human" I had been compiling. Probably soccer moms didn't have to deal with finding bodies in their trunks.

Not that minivans had trunks.

I gunned the Mustang out of the parking lot and aimed it back toward the gallery. My phone chirped in it's dashboard holster. I glanced at the name and scowled.

Maybe I could ignore it.

But then, I'd already been ignoring it for the last three weeks. It was only a matter of time before the cops were called, and I'd had enough trouble explaining my life as of late.

No. I would face this resolutely. Like an adult. No more avoiding the inevitable.

I clicked the answer button when I reached the stop light and put it on speaker.

"Hi, Mom," I said.

"Hanna!" she shrilled. "Oh God, Hanna, is that you?"

"No Mom," I answered. "I'm a robot clone that's been assigned Hanna's phone number in order to keep up appearances since the alien hive mind has assumed control."

"What?" she asked. "Is this Hanna?"

"Yes, Mom. This is Hanna."

"Oh! Thank goodness! I've been so worried. I left messages, but I guess you haven't been getting them."

"Sorry, Mom," I said. "I've just been busy." Avoiding vampires and assassination attempts by Theo Van Gogh, among other things.

"Oh, of course," she said. "Working full-time now and going to school. Even if you don't have a husband to take care of anymore." This last, she slipped in with just enough disapproval to set my eyelid twitching.

"No, Mom. I graduated, remember? I got my Master's last year."

"Your Master's?" she asked, familiar confusion clouding her voice. "But I thought you were working on your PhD?"

Irritation swarmed down my spine like an army of insects. I swerved around a Honda puttering in the fast lane and gave him the finger.

"No. No PhD. Just the Master's," I said, stomping on the gas. When the engine roared, I reminded myself about the body in my trunk and decelerated rapidly.

"Well, isn't that lucky then, that you found a job as a secretary in that art store."

"It's a *gallery,* Mom," I corrected through clenched teeth. "And I'm not a secretary. I'm an *assistant.*"

"An assistant? You're an assistant?"

"Yes, Mom."

"Who are you assisting?" she asked. "Is it a man?"

Sometimes. When he's not tooling around on all fours fending off vampires and rival werewolves.

"Yes, mother. He's a man and his name is Mark Abernathy," I said, already knowing her next question.

She didn't disappoint.

"Is he married?"

"No," I answered.

"Divorced?"

"No."

"Well, I'm sure he won't mind that you are," she said. "You're a very pretty young lady, when you don't wear too much makeup."

I made a mental note to buy slut-red lipstick and false eyelashes.

"I'm not planning on getting married again anytime soon," I said.

"That's okay," she said. "Lots of women are having babies out of wedlock these days. Even at your age."

Breathe, Hanna.

"Mother," I said, "I am *not* having a baby."

"Not yet," she said, her voice gone singsongy and hopeful. "But you could be. You know that checker at Save-Mart? The one whose line we always went to?"

"The one with three divorces, a smoker's cough and a boob job?" I asked.

"Yes! She's forty-one and *she's* pregnant."

"Mother, I'm not sure how this escaped your attention, but I am not forty-one years old. In fact, I'm not even thirty."

"I know. But you don't want to wait too much longer. A woman's most fertile years are—"

"When she's slouching around a hippie commune sleeping with random strangers?" I shot back.

"Hannelore Harv—" she gasped.

"Don't," I said. A one-word damn between the thoughts in my head and the mutiny they would cause if they left my mouth.

The unwelcome knowledge of my childhood burned in my chest like hot coals banked beneath unassuming ash. What about my father? What about my brother? What about my history? Your history? How can you pretend you don't know what I am? What *you* are? How can you sit here and pile guilt upon me while you hide a pack of lies?

"You got to choose your life," I said. "Now I'm choosing mine."

"Maybe I should call back," she suggested. "You sound like you're in a hurry."

"That's because I have a dead body in my trunk." I glanced at the rear-view mirror, half expecting to see flashing red and blue given the way this day was already unfolding.

"What was that?" she asked.

"I've got to go, mom."

"I'll call you later," she promised. "I love you."

"Love you too, Mom." Most days, that was true.

CHAPTER 6

"That's Rudy Valentino," Joseph Abernathy said, rolling the head to face us. A thin, dark dribble of blood worked its way down the gray flesh of a strong chin. Two pearly white points protruded between his waxy, bloodless lips.

Rudy Valentino was a vampire. There was a decapitated vampire in my trunk.

"What is Rudy Valentino doing in my trunk?"

"Not much," Mark said, leaning in past his father to get a better look.

We stood staring down into the Mustang's trunk in the alleyway behind the gallery. A relatively secluded spot away from the eyes of tourist foot traffic of historic downtown Georgetown.

"Let me rephrase," I said. "*Why* is Rudy Valentino in my trunk?"

"Because someone put him there," answered Joseph.

Ugh. If there was anything worse than werewolf dad humor, it was *double* werewolf dad humor.

"You know," I said, "you two are exceptionally helpful. I can't tell you how much I appreciate your input."

Joseph scratched at the silvery stubble dusting his jawline. "Second decapitated vampire in one day. This is not a promising trend."

"Odd how it coincides with your arrival." Mark let the comment float like a fetid balloon on the air between them.

"You can't think *I* did this." Joseph glanced from me to his son, as if requesting my confirmation of his innocence.

"The timing seems suspect." Mark failed to look his father in the eye after this accusation, a sure sign it was designed to annoy rather than discern.

"The timing is incredibly suspect, which is precisely *why* you should be questioning it." Joseph's good natured voice had taken on a steely edge.

Abernathys tensed on both sides of my peripheral vision.

Round two.

"Who was in *your* trunk?" I asked in a pathetic bid to redirect the confirmation.

"I'm sorry?" Joseph answered.

"Your trunk. Rudy Valentino is in mine, who was in yours?"

"Ahh." A small, strange smile stretched across Joseph's face. "It seems someone has a sense of humor. Charlie Chaplin."

"Good hell. Vampire actors? This is a thing? In the same way artists tend to be werewolves?"

"Think about it," Joseph said. "The obsession with remaining eternally young and beautiful, the desire to live forever through books, or movies..."

"You have a point," I admitted. The weight of all I had yet to learn about the non-human world bore down on my shoulders. Would there be no end to feeling hopelessly lost and tossed? "I'm assuming this has something to do with the whole werewolves vs. vampires thing then?"

"Very likely," Joseph agreed.

"But why a decapitated vampire in the trunk? Why not a

werewolf? Wouldn't that be a more effective way at getting back at me? Or at Mark?"

"It would," Joseph pointed out, "if simple revenge were the motive."

"As opposed to?" I didn't like where this was going. Not one bit.

"Complete and utter domination and destruction of your soul," Joseph said.

"It's kind of a vampire specialty," Mark added.

A chill worked its way from my scalp to my sneakers.

The face seemed so peaceful—a pale white mask slumbering in the gloom. Words bandied back and forth between the two Abernathys but filtered to my ears through cotton batting. I leaned into the trunk until I could feel the pale, smooth flesh of Valentino's cheek against my hand.

It wasn't skin.

Skin had pores.

This was something else. Something perfect. And dead.

My thumb traced the cool, pale gray of his lip, meeting a hard bud of resistance where the painfully precise point of one pearlescent fang protruded from his silent mouth.

"BWAHHH!" the head bellowed.

I managed to crack my head against the trunk lid as I leapt back, shrieking in a key that could deafen dogs, connecting flailing elbows with both Mark and Joseph in my pure, blind, panic.

Mark caught me before I went ass-first down to the concrete. Next on the list was scrambling up a wall like Wylie Coyote.

It was a noise that stopped me.

Laughter. Mark's, specifically. Doled out with a miser's generosity, it was enough to give me pause.

When it was joined by the harmonic booming of Joseph's guffaw, realization finally arrived.

The head hadn't screamed. Mark had.

"You bastard!" Knowing full well I was hurting my knuckles more than his marble-hard bicep, I went after his arm like the kid in every training scene in every boxing movie ever.

"He's not." Joseph gripped his stomach, tears of mirth watering his cheeks. "I can attest."

"You should have seen," Mark cackled, fighting for both words and air, "the look on your face!"

So, I did the only reasonable thing available to an adult woman my age.

I kicked him in the shin. Hard.

"Hey!" he yelped.

"Serves you right!"

"That really hurt." The surprise on his face gave me a little thrill of satisfaction.

"How long has she been working for you?" Joseph asked, seriousness darkening his tone.

"Two months, two weeks and four days," I answered. Not that I had been counting.

Joseph's eyebrows raised as the last of the levity vanished from his face. "Two cycles?"

"What do you mean *two cycles*?" I quizzed. "Are we talking lady bits?"

Joseph turned to Mark, his face an expression of the confusion I felt. "You haven't told her about that *either*?"

Until this moment, I hadn't been aware *sheepish* was an expression my boss was capable of.

"What?" I asked. "What *else* haven't you told me?"

Joseph's glanced at Mark, not so much asking permission as declaring intention. Mark didn't argue.

"If an untransformed recessive is exposed to an alpha for extended periods of time, certain symptoms of transformation can be...*triggered*."

Oh, I'd been *exposed*, all right.

"*What?*" This wasn't so much a question as the unintentional sound of a tea kettle. "How is that possible?"

"Have you ever had female roommates?" Joseph asked.

"Yes," I said. "In college."

"Forgive me for being indelicate," he continued. "But did you *cycle* with them? That is to say, did your menstr—"

"Yes," I said, cutting him off. "I always regulated with whichever roommate I was closest to at the time."

"That's how it's possible." Joseph's eyes were kind as they met mine, making sure I'd taken his point. "Your body senses the alpha, and it begins to respond, mated or not."

I turned to Mark, my hand finding their now-familiar notch on my hips. "Is this true?"

He nodded.

"Are you fucking kidding me?" A solid vein of crazy lent my voice that oh-so-charming teakettle-like shrill. "How could you not mention this? What was all that stuff about refusing to take my choice from me?"

"Because I had no idea it would take you forever and a fucking day to decide!" His voice amplified down the alley, bouncing off the centuries old brick walls and startling a flock of pigeons skyward.

"Excuse me all to hell for being the tiniest bit hesitant about whether I want to sprout a tail and tear-ass around town on all fours every time there's a full moon!" I jammed my pointed finger skyward, where the barest ghost of the mottled orb already hung on the carpet of darkening blue.

"Now we're throwing around stereotypes, Miss *I have three cats and no boyfriend*?"

My face stung as if slapped. Abernathy's aim was as accurate as ever, hitting bone with effortless ease.

"You're hardly one to talk," Joseph argued on my behalf. "Mr. *I haven't been laid in a hundred and twenty-four years*."

Cue mental record scratch.

"A hundred and twenty-four years?" I blinked at him, incredulous. I had asked him this question one sweaty, naked morning and he'd dodged it with the skill of a Cirque d'Soleil acrobat. In the few months I had known him, there had been no shortage of beautiful female satellites in his orbit. I had mistakenly assumed he'd been screwing them all six ways from Sunday. But I'd been disabused of this notion as one by one, their platonic positions in his universe had been revealed.

Worse, the only service he'd been providing them was protection.

Mark's breathing was slow and deep, lending his words the dangerous patience of a stalking predator. "Following my cock around the globe isn't a luxury I have, Joseph."

"Psst!" I held hands up to silence them both. "If you're going to fight like this, it's going to be in front of Dr. Phil, not a headless vampire."

"She's right," Joseph agreed. "This conversation is getting us nowhere."

"Thank you," I said. These words were rare and precious in my world.

Mark's face crumpled in irritation. "What did you do with the last body?" he asked.

"I took care of it," Joseph answered. "Just as I will with Rudy."

"Two bodies in one day?" Mark asked mockingly. "Are you sure you're up to the strain?"

"I have twice your years and twice your stamina," Joseph answered.

"Good enough for me." I dug in my purse and handed over my keys.

Joseph snapped his hand closed around them and pushed by Mark, bumping shoulders with him as he passed.

I felt a pang of jealousy as he gunned the Mustang down the alleyway and shot around the curb, handling my car with an expert intuition of machines that far outstripped my own.

I told myself the Mustang still liked me more. And he'd better, after all those summer waxings in naught but a bikini and cut-offs.

Mark was halfway down the alley toward the gallery's back door and I jogged to catch up with him.

"Hey," I said. "We need to talk about this."

"About what?"

"About this whole syncing cycles thing."

"It's very simple," he said, opening the door and crossing into the main gallery space. "You can't work for me anymore."

This phrase and the casual way Mark said it stole the breath from my lungs.

"What?"

"You can't work for me anymore." He continued up the stairs to his office without looking back.

"I mean, do we really need to be so drastic? Isn't there some kind of pheromone blocker or something like that? Nose plugs! What about nose plugs?"

Abernathy didn't answer until he was planted in his familiar chair with an expanse of desk between us.

"The longer you're around me, the longer you're around the pack, the more you'll transform. Obviously you don't want *that* to happen."

I plopped down on the leather couch, crossing my legs beneath me. "I never said that."

"You didn't need to."

Previously, I thought I had gotten pretty adept at reading Abernathy's face. The subtle downward twist of his mouth or tick of an eyebrow that could signal the difference between boredom and irritation.

Now, Abernathy's face was completely and utterly inscrutable. Deadly flat and calm.

"It's not that I don't want to be a werewolf—"

"Then what?"

"You talk about this like you're so certain, but I have a very vivid memory of someone stopping short at the mention of marriage the last time we were naked."

Mark's eyes sought the display of first edition tomes on his gleaming bookshelves. After discovering some of them had been inscribed by the likes of Charles Dickens, it had been all I could do not to set up an altar and dance naked in front of them, seeking favor.

"I have no use for binding papers," he said. "Nor do I care to appear in human government records."

"Let me make sure I'm understanding you correctly. You're willing to make me a werewolf, thereby binding your soul to mine for the rest of your unnaturally long life, but you don't want to be connected to me on paper?"

"Yes."

This single word sailed a rock at the glass pane of my ridiculously squishy heart.

"Bonds are only as good as the men who make them," he said, as if this would somehow salve the wound.

"That's such an Abernathy thing to say."

"What did your marriage to Dave buy you, save more paper to undo it and a mountain of debt and regret?"

"You're just going to say his name like that? I've got a paper cut here." I held out my hand. "Wanna rub some lemon juice in it? Maybe some salt? Battery acid?"

"It's a valid question given the circumstances."

I really hated it when he was right.

"It didn't buy me anything," I said. "But that's not the point. Marriage is an outward symbol of an inner commitment."

"Symbols?" Abernathy raised an eyebrow at me. "What about me says I'm a man who needs symbols? I do what I want, when I want. The show, the display, they're for everyone else."

"What's so wrong about wanting everyone else to know?" A

familiar, sinking feeling spread in my belly. The sure and sudden knowledge that I was losing ground, sliding backward.

"Why does everyone *need* to know?" Abernathy asked. "Who are you trying to convince?"

"It's not about convincing anyone." My scalp prickled in that special way that only Abernathy-directed irritation could produce. "It's about making it official."

"According to whom?" he asked.

"According to...to everyone!" Even as I heard myself say it, it sounded lame and pathetic. Which, to be honest, was the way I almost always ended up feeling after a verbal tussle with Abernathy.

"How did that work out with your ex-husband?" The corner of his mouth quirked up into his *I am totally winning* smirk. "Making it official?"

"I really don't like your face right now," I said. "You know that?"

"Your body..."

"Fine," I agreed. "Marriage aside, are you saying you're ready to be bound to me for life?"

"Yes," he answered without hesitation.

It's possible my heart stopped. Or my soul left my body. "Really?"

Abernathy's eyes moved from my body up to my face like fire licking up a trail of gasoline. "Hanna, I have to be with you."

My heart thundered in my chest. "You do?" I asked.

"Yes." He hesitated, glancing down at his desk then back up at me. "It's the only way to keep you safe."

The fluttering bird of my hope ran smack into a windowpane.

"You, sir, can fuck all the way off," I said.

"Is that an offer?" His eyes flashed with dangerous hunger.

"It's a suggestion for self-improvement," I said. "I'm not your project."

"I didn't say you were."

"You didn't need to." A total brat move, stealing his earlier statement, but I wasn't exactly feeling at the height of my emotional maturity at that precise moment. "I have work to do," I said, pushing myself up from the couch.

No sooner had I settled at my desk than the sound of a gasp and a sob echoed through the gallery.

Shayla.

I erupted from my chair and tripped down the stairs toward the oddities shop attached to the gallery through a door beyond the artists' studios. I found her bent behind the counter clutching the plastic-lined wicker basket I'd designated as the trash bin on my first day as Abernathy's assistant.

Her back arched as a fresh wave seized the curving cage of her ribs and racked the contents of her stomach upward from her scooped waist.

My hands found the damp strands of her cobalt blue hair and drew them back from her face and lifted them off her burning neck.

The hair, like the brilliant green eyes set against the reddening flesh of her face, were natural.

Which is completely normal if you're a Nereid.

She drew a deep breath and set the basket down, resting her forehead against the cool wood surface of the shop's counter. The rainbowed tapestry of her tattooed arms curled around her head.

"Honey," I said, handing her a paper towel to wipe her mouth. "Are you okay?"

"No." She lifted her head just enough for me to see her watery green gaze. "I'm pregnant."

I blinked at her, disbelieving. "Say what?"

"I'm pregnant," she repeated.

"Are you sure? Steve makes some pretty odd food combinations—"

"I'm sure," she said.

"But, but..." I sputtered, searching for words. "You and Steve have only been dating for a month."

"Believe me, I know," she said.

"How did this even happen?"

"I'm pretty sure you're familiar with the process." Fine red slits puffed at the sides of her neck. Poor Shayla was green around the gills.

Literally.

"What I meant was, didn't you guys use protection?"

"I was on birth control." She pressed her eyes closed tighter and moaned. "This wasn't supposed to happen."

"Is everything all right?" Joseph had materialized against the backdrop of shelves stuffed with the odd array of objects Mark had collected or purchased over his centuries on the planet. I wondered exactly how long he'd been lurking there. Stealthiness ran in the family, apparently.

"Shayla," I said, "this is Joseph Abernathy. Mark's father." I followed this statement with a meaningful glance of the *we will totally dish about this later* variety.

"Dude," she said with her characteristic bluntness. "Weren't you dead?"

"It seems to be the consensus," Joseph said. "I must say I am vastly grateful that seems not to be the case."

Shayla offered Joseph a clammy hand, which he took, and kissed. She shot me a side-eye of the *this here is a whole-ass daddy snack* variety.

I covertly nodded my agreement.

"You wouldn't, perchance, be dating a werewolf?" Joseph asked.

"She would, as it happens," I answered on her behalf.

"Ahh." He nodded, a knowing smile fixed on his handsome face.

"Ahh *what*?" Shayla blinked.

"Traditional birth control methods are somewhat ineffective against…em…" Joseph hesitated, presumably searching the air above his head for a polite way to say *werewolf jizz*.

"Were-spunk?" I asked.

Shayla stifled another gag.

"Sorry," I said.

She waved a hand, as much to silence me as to ask Joseph to continue.

"Hanna is correct," Joseph said. "although it's not necessarily the substance in question that's the culprit. Regular proximity to a werewolf often proves a powerful stimulant to female reproductive systems."

Didn't I know it.

"My mother warned me against dating non-humans." Shayla groaned.

I sure wished mine had.

"Hey fine people, what's shakin'?"

Steven Franke, my long-lost brother and Shayla's significantly odd other, hitched up the plaid pants covering his bony thighs and snapped his suspenders for emphasis.

Joseph looked at Steven's face, then to mine, comparing. I nodded, confirming what he already knew.

He had sprouted past my proportions, the male expression of my long limbs protruding from the black Def Leppard t-shirt just as his feet stretched the mint green boats of his Chuck Taylors. He'd inherited our father's fine blond hair and thick sable brows rather than the auburn mop I'd drawn from our mother's side.

Joseph, Shayla and I all exchanged nervous glances.

"Whoa," he laughed. "Why do I feel like the guy that baked an air biscuit in the middle of the party?"

"How could you not tell me?" Shayla accused, punching his upper arm. "What were you thinking?"

"Look, Nicholas Cage's career has been over for a long

time," Steve said. "I didn't exactly think it was a secret." His face took on a boyish cast that could disarm the Roman legions.

"Don't even start with the jokes," Shayla warned. "Not this time."

"What?" He looked honestly alarmed now, his face innocence incarnate.

"I'm pregnant," she said.

I watched Steve's face for signs of shock, but found only pure, uninhibited wonder.

"Slap a trout and call me daddy," Steve exclaimed. "No shit?"

"No shit," Shayla said.

"Me?" His long, bony fingers pointed at his own bony sternum. "I'm gonna be a dad?"

"You." Shayla pointed a red-lacquered nail at him.

Steve let out a whoop and galloped across the space between to scoop Shayla up and swing her in a circle.

"Stop!" She begged, laughing. "Do you want me to yark again?"

An unfamiliar expression crossed Steve's usually playful face as he looked down into Shayla's eyes. "You wanna get hitched?"

"What?" The features of her face curved like a question as he set her down.

"You. Me. With the ring and the thing and forever," he said.

"You're out of your mind!" she insisted. "We've only been together for a month!"

"In the physical realm, perhaps. But in here," he paused, tapping his skull. "We've been together always."

Shayla shook her glossy blue bob, her Betty Page bangs sticking to her forehead above the slim silver hoop piercing her eyebrow. "You don't want to marry me. You're just trying to be all honorable and shit."

"I don't?" he asked, dropping to one knee. From the back pocket of his skinny jeans, he pulled out a velvet ring box.

Shayla looked at it goggle-eyed, disbelieving. "How did you —but you didn't know—when did you—"

"I was gonna propose at the gallery show tonight, but, under the circumstances..." He snapped the box open, revealing a gleaming white gold band with diamonds winking around a sapphire bluer than the ocean's depths.

"You planned this? Even before—" she glanced down at an abdomen that had not yet begun to swell.

"I've planned this since the moment you shoved a menu at me and told me I was wasting your best table," Steve said.

My heart ached with the memory of our first meeting, ages ago, it seemed, on my first day as Mark's assistant. Before she'd run the antiques shop, Shayla had been a waitress at The Dusty Dahlia, a nearby tearoom Mark and company frequented. Owing to her ass-grabbing letch of a boss, Shayla had marched into the gallery and informed Mark he'd be hiring her to run the shop. It hadn't occurred to him to argue.

Now here she stood, my brother on one knee before her and a life changing proposition to consider.

"Okay," she said.

"Really?" Steve asked, his eyes like sun-lit emeralds.

"Really." Deep dimples appeared at the corners of Shayla's mouth as she broke into a wide grin.

Steve slid the ring onto her finger and shot up from his knee, crushing her in a hug once more.

In my peripheral vision, I saw Joseph's dark eyes scanning my face. "I'm not crying," I said, dabbing my leaking nose with a wadded tissue. "You're crying."

Joseph began to applaud, and I joined him, feeling the heat as I slapped my palms together, clapping with all the excitement I couldn't express.

"I'm going to regret this," Shayla said.

"Not a day in your life." Steve drew a cross over his heart and winked.

"Okay," Shayla said, seriousness drawing her features tight. "If we're going to do this, it's going to be before I'm all fat and bloated."

"Fine by me," Steve said. "The sooner the better."

"Where will you have the ceremony?" Joseph asked.

"I know you wouldn't think it," Steve said, glancing to his worn Chuck Taylors, inscribed in blue ink with his best ideas and favorite quotations. "But I've been saving for years. We can get married anywhere you want. Rome, Paris—"

"Here," Shayla said. This unfailing practicality of hers was the perfect complement to Steve's whimsical impulsiveness.

"I can take care of the food," I said. "The caterers we use for the gallery shows would leap at the opportunity."

"I'll do the invitations," Steve insisted. "I've had them drawn up for a while."

"How long is a while?" Shayla asked, her artfully shaped eyebrow arching.

Steve shrugged. "A year or so?"

"Okay, you know that's super creepy, right?" Shayla's face flushed a sudden vibrant pink, the thin blood-red slits at the base of her jaw rising. "Did I even have a choice?"

"Of course you did," Steve said. "But *I* didn't. I'd met the girl of my dreams. I gave you my heart a long time ago. The rest," he said, flexing one long noodle-like arm, "is just a bonus."

There was more affection in Shayla's eye roll than some people manage in a full body hug.

"Well, we have invitations and food sorted," Joseph said. "What about the date?"

"That one is all yours, doll," Steve said.

"March 21st," Shayla said without hesitation. "Spring Equinox."

"That's less than two weeks away." Joseph pulled a cell phone out of his pocket and opened the calendar app. Clearly, he had been a more eager adopter of technology than his son, who had been known to gnaw gadgets out of frustration. "We have a lot of work to do."

"We?" I asked, surprised and pleased to have a willing accomplice.

"Call me a dyed-in-the-wool romantic, but I love a wedding," Joseph said. "I hope you won't object to my helping you plan. In addition to certain…contacts."

"Oh," I asked. "What kind of contacts might that be?"

"A decorator, for example." He turned his eyes to the gallery's void. "It's raw, of course. But the gentleman I have in mind could do wonders with this space. If, of course, you are amenable to this suggestion?" Joseph looked from Steve to Shayla. "The bride has final say, of course."

And then he winked at her.

"Oh yes," Shayla said, perhaps a shade too eagerly. "I am *very* amenable."

Steve cleared his throat. Though he was no alpha, I could scarcely imagine any male not being at least mildly threatened by Joseph Abernathy.

"Good. If you'll excuse me," he said with a polite nod. "I ought to make a couple calls. Time is short."

Shayla and I watched him beat a path out the gallery's front door and down the sidewalk.

"Welp." Steve snapped his suspenders by way of punctuation. "I'll just finalize the invitation design then. Should probably get them printed sooner than later." He shuffled off toward his studio, only to be arrested by Shayla's hand in his back pocket. Reaching a hand around his neck, she pulled him down to plant a kiss on his lips.

"You make me happy," she said, then gave his narrow rear end a swat. "Now get working, mister. This wedding isn't gonna plan itself."

"Speaking of invitations," I said, "do you have any ideas about the guest list?"

She exhaled a breath and her shoulders sagged. "Oh gods," she groaned. "This is gonna get ugly."

"Ugly?" I asked. "How?"

Her gaze rose to meet mine. "Let's start with the most basic question. Who would be first on the list?"

"Your mother and father, I would think."

"Right," she agreed, giving me a meaningful look.

I blinked in confusion, utterly failing to catch her meaning.

"I'm a *Nereid*. Which means my father is a primordial sea god that predates Zeus. We'll need to invite him too, of course. He gets real jealous about that kind of slight."

"Zeus, like *the* Zeus?"

Shayla nodded.

"With the..." I mimed throwing, my mind suddenly a desert bereft of words.

"Lightning bolts?" she said.

"Yeah, those."

"Yep."

"And the..." My hand drew a path from my shoulder to the opposite hip.

"Toga?"

"Toga! Right."

"No!" She laughed. "Are you kidding? No one wears those anymore."

"Huh," I mused. "But your father is a god?"

"I mean, kinda? I guess it depends on how you're defining the term."

"What do you mean?" I asked.

She seemed to consider this as we returned to the shop where she gingerly tied up the plastic bag in the wastebasket and held it at arm's length. "Walk with me?"

We strolled down the hallway where I held the door that opened on the alley. Shayla tossed the bag of barf into the nearest bin and ducked into the newly built restroom to wash her hands. I congratulated myself once again on insisting upon its construction. Before my arrival as Mark's assistant, they'd gone God knows how long without a bathroom in the building.

My legacy: a toilet.

"The god part depends on what you believe, I suppose," she said. "If you were a human being living in ancient Greece and you ran across a guy that could occasionally control the tide cycles, what would you call him?"

"A god, I guess," I said.

"Exactly." She dried her hands and flipped off the light. I followed her back into the shop where she grabbed a dust rag and some lemon oil. "Does that make him a god, or just a letch with a few bonus skills?"

"Good point," I admitted. *Bonus skills* was a concept I was becoming increasingly familiar with, whether they be the odd transformation into a canine, the ability to suck life through a couple neck holes, or command water through a wiggle of the fingers—this last being one of Shayla's quirks.

Exceptional organization was another.

In the time since she'd taken over running the oddities shop, she'd changed it from a hoarded junk room to a boutique befitting even an upscale shopping district.

Between the two of us, we'd managed to beat back the tide of clutter and put some order to this patchwork colony of males.

"You have a lot of work to do for tomorrow?" Shayla asked from behind a row of shelves. The flash of her blue hair was visible through the glass case housing a collection of delicate animal bones.

I sighed, reviewing the list that stretched out between me and the upcoming gallery show.

"Cleaning the gallery, setting out the furniture, helping the caterer set up, and then, there's hanging the paintings, of course."

"Damn, lady," Shayla said. "You're making *me* tired. At least there's only Steve and Scott showing now. That's got to ease the burden, right?"

"Wrong," I said. "Ever since Kirkpatrick hooked up with Helena, he's been painting like a wild man. He sent twenty canvases over to be framed."

Once upon a time, Helena had been hot to trot on Mark, but had accidentally got herself killed by a geriatric half were-lady with a blood-grudge against Abernathy. Somewhere in the process, she'd been turned into a werewolf and slept with Scott Kirkpatrick, the gallery's resident misanthropic ginger munchkin, to wheedle information about Mark's whereabouts. The "mated for life bit" had been an unintended consequence.

"Twenty?" Her almost feline eyes widened in surprise. "I haven't even seen him around here lately," she said, polishing a bell jar that held a withered human hand.

"Where the hell has he been painting?"

"Best I can tell, somewhere beneath Helena."

Shalya shuddered. "What the hell she sees in him, I'll never know. Are they coming tomorrow? No pun intended."

"I don't know," I said. "And thanks, by the way. That's a visual I totally needed."

She wiggled her eyebrows at me around a display of 19th century wigs.

"Hanna!" Mark's unmistakable baritone rattled through the gallery. "Get up here. I need you!"

"How true that is," Shayla said.

I shot her the stink-eye as I turned toward the stairs.

CHAPTER 7

"We're pregnant!" Helena stood before me, irritatingly even more gorgeous than I remembered. Her eyes, the exact shade of melted milk chocolate, were bright with the joy of her news. With her flushed cheeks and glossy curtain of black hair she looked exactly like Snow White, freshly roused from restful nap on the forest floor.

Kirkpatrick stood behind her, beaming like a squatty redheaded lighthouse. Patrons milled around them, pausing in front of paintings like hummingbirds arrested by pops of color that might be flowers.

I handed her a heavy vase I'd been wrapping. "Do me a favor?" I asked.

"Of course!" She agreed with chirpy brightness.

"Hit me," I said. "Hard."

"Hit you?" she asked. "Why on earth would I do that?"

In earlier days, she wouldn't have hesitated at such an invitation for the space of a gnat's fart. Mostly she had called me names and tried to ruin my life.

"She's not feeling well," Shayla said, taking the vase from Helena. "She doesn't mean it."

"Oh!" Helena laughed. "I thought you'd gone batshit."

I laughed too. A high-pitched, edgy sound that did more to confirm her amateur diagnosis than deny it.

Kirkpatrick scrutinized my face.

"Congratulations," I said through gritted teeth. "I'm so—" I paused and swallowed a gag "—happy for you."

Helena surged forward and crushed me in a hug. "Isn't it wonderful?"

She bounced up and down, shaking me like the martini I badly needed, then darted across the gallery to Mark, who was surrounded by the usual conglomeration of adoring female satellites.

I watched as Helena delivered the news.

Mark glanced across the crowded gallery space and found my eyes, then looked away to shake Kirkpatrick's hand.

Shayla finished wrapping the vase for me, then slid it into one of the brown paper bags she kept under Mark's antique cash register. The very pregnant wife of a young husband reached across, grabbed it, and thanked her.

"How are we doing?" Shayla asked after they were gone.

"Great," I answered without hesitation. "Fine. Excellent. *So* good."

She laid a hand against the back of my neck at the precise moment I sank to my knees.

"Breathe," she said, pushing my head toward my knees.

"Babies." My lungs remained stubbornly flat as I desperately tried to drag air into them. "Everyone's having babies. They're everywhere. I'm not...I can't, my mom—"

"Shhh." She rubbed a hand over my back in reassuring strokes.

Everything in my field of vision took on a sudden brown patina while a thousand needles scrambled across my scalp.

"But I'm going to be twenty-eight and all I have to show for my life is three cats and a mild cheese addiction."

"Don't do that comparison shit," she said. "You're under no obligations to follow a prescribed path. Just because—"

My chest hitched anew, conjuring darkness to the edges of my vision.

"Good Christ. Are you okay, Hanna?"

Glancing upward from my humiliating station on the shop floor, I met the amber eyes of Joseph Abernathy.

"Of course she's okay," Shayla said. "It's just ridiculously hot in here." She tugged me to my feet and Joseph caught me mid-wobble, strong hands gripping my biceps.

"I heard," he whispered, a shade too close to my ear.

"I'll be fine, I promise. I just wasn't prepared I guess."

"Well it is spring, after all," Joseph said. "Breeding season and all that."

"Yeah, for like mice, and birds, and deer and shit. But—"

"Wolves?" he asked, beating me to the punch.

"Hey," I said. "Wolves are people too. Well, some of them. Sometimes."

"And people are animals too," he pointed out. "Most of the time."

A high, feminine cackle sliced through the white noise of conversation filling the gallery.

"Speaking of animals." I scanned the gallery to see if I could identify the human responsible for the eardrum bloodying cackle.

Several bodies stumbled forward, shoved asunder by an unseen source. And all at once, there she was. Tinkerbell, but with a boob job, a bad blond weave, and enough alcohol on board to float a trash barge. In her Lucite six-inch stripper heels, she might have been about five-eight. The skin-tight sweater slouching off one spray-tanned shoulder barely managed to cover her jegging clad-ass.

"Oh my God!" she slurred, swaying toward one of Steve's paintings. "Iss that a duck? Pfft! I could paint that!" She sloshed a half glass worth of the cabernet sauvignon I'd ordered onto the wood floor as she tried, and failed, to bring it to her over-glossed lips.

I sincerely hoped she wasn't really a fairy, because I was gonna feel real bad about curb stomping a Disney character's veneers into the gutter.

Joseph gave me a wide berth as I came around the counter.

"Excuse me," I said. I wove through the crowd as swiftly as I was able, all ready to add drunk bitch bouncer to my list of regular job duties. Perhaps a little less gently than I could have, I tapped her on the bony shoulder. "Hi there."

"Babe!" she shrieked, ignoring me. "Babe! Commere! You gotta see what they're charging for this shit!"

Babe stumbled into view, disheveled and equally shit-faced.

Detective James Morrison, my former bed buddy.

Someone had dropped a brick onto my stomach, and I didn't have the air to form words. Generic, predictable questions sprang to my mouth. *What are you doing here? Who is she?* and the like. But the answers didn't matter, though I knew them all.

Morrison looked at me, then slid a hand around Tinkerbell's ass. "How much, baby?" he asked, not looking at the painting.

"More than that knock-off Juicy Couture bag," I answered for her. "And I don't think *babe's* got that much left in the beer fund, cupcake."

She squinted and swayed as she tried to get her eyes to focus on my face. Or faces, I suspected. Mascara crumbs fell down her cheeks as she blinked with the effort.

"What?" she stammered. "Babe, did you hear what she said to me?"

Whispers bred around us as the other patrons turned their attention from the art to the impromptu reality show. It was only a matter of time before Mark saw Morrison, and this turned from a schoolyard scrap into a four-alarm shit-storm.

"Leave my gallery," I said. "Now."

"Not your gallery," Morrison cast an antagonistic look in Mark's direction. "And we have every right to be here."

"Yeah," Tinkerbell repeated. "Every right!"

Joseph sidled up to my elbow. "May I be of service?"

Morrison sized him up, his hand moved to the phantom weapon snugged against his rib cage. I guessed they'd relieved him of his duty piece when they'd relieved him of his badge, but I was nothing like certain he didn't have another one tucked somewhere else. A sinking feeling set itself down in my stomach as I envisioned several simultaneous ends to this standoff.

"No," I said, trying to work calm into my voice. "I'm sure *Detective* Morrison would be happy to be reunited with a few of his old friends if things get out of hand. Though I'm not sure if that would hasten his reinstatement."

The unmeasured flash of hope in his eyes at this word sent a little rush of relief into my chest. So he still wanted it, then.

Good.

"Come on, Jess," Morrison said. "Let's see if the food's any good."

It was a low blow, and he knew it. My food choosing abilities were superlative and all of Georgetown and the greater state of Colorado knew it.

"Or you could stagger down to Denny's for a drunk dish to yark onto the linoleum floor along with your self-loathing," I mumbled under my breath.

"Whas that?" Jess froze in place, eyeing me with pure dislike.

"Enjoy your evening," I said, coating each syllable with as much syrupy insincerity as I could manage.

"How long were you seeing each other?" Joseph asked.

Conducting a quick scan of the gallery to track their path, I was relieved when they joined the line at the catering tables as promised. "How long were we—what?" I peered up into Joseph's face to find it bright with amusement.

"He looked at you the way a man only looks at a woman when he's been inside her," he said.

Blood flooded my face. Way to make it awkward Daddy Abernathy.

"We weren't seeing each other," I informed him.

"Casual fucking, then," he smiled. "I can respect that."

"It wasn't like that," I said. And it was the truth. What Morrison and I had lived somewhere between combative friendship and championship naked wrestling. And doughnuts.

"Hey," Joseph said. "I'm not here to judge."

"I know that," I said. "But it's important to me that you know."

"You said *Detective* Morrison," Joseph answered, changing the subject. "Is this the man who's been investigating my son?

"Yup."

"Unsuccessfully, I'm guessing."

"As of yet," I added.

"And he was suspended?" Joseph pressed.

"Also yup."

"What for?"

I drew a deep breath, as memories flooded my brain. "I looked a little rough when we got back from London," I said. "What with being attacked by Oscar Wilde and nearly having my life sucked through my neck and throttled to the ground and whatnot. Only, Morrison seemed to think your son was responsible."

"I see." Joseph nodded.

"And then there were the murders," I said. "Which Morrison has been convinced Mark committed. When it turned out to be *not* Abernathy, I think it kind of bent him."

"He senses something," Joseph said. "He just doesn't understand what it is."

"His instincts, are pretty damned impeccable." Boy were they ever.

"Those sort of humans can be exceedingly dangerous." The creases at the corners of Joseph's eyes deepened as he frowned.

"Very much so," I said.

"So," Joseph said. "This detective with impeccable instincts has stumbled upon a pack of werewolves who have been associated with multiple murders, and is now suffering from a rash of decapitated vampires. And he has a blood grudge against the pack's alpha male, is in love with a werewolf heir the alpha male is sworn to protect, is hell-bent on uncovering the truth, and is now a rogue on the outside of the law. That about sum it up?"

"I don't know about the 'in love' part," I said.

"My dear." Joseph dropped a fatherly arm around my shoulders. "Pheromones don't lie."

My heart thumped at the revelation. Did Morrison love me?

Joseph rubbed the flat expanse of his palms together and grinned. "This is going to be good."

"Maybe not," I said. "Maybe everything will just work itself out. Like on the Brady Bunch. Half an hour, and the world is peachy. Problems solved."

"Mr. Brady wasn't a werewolf," Joseph pointed out.

"But he was gay," I insisted. "That counts for something, right?"

"Maybe in 1964."

"Fuck a duck." I fell back against the gallery wall, letting it absorb my weight.

Joseph's Cheshire Cat grin dropped away from his face. I followed his gaze, expecting to discover some new conflict with Morrison and the intolerable Jessica.

What I saw instead sent ice slithering into my spine.

Two unnaturally beautiful men walking in concert through the gallery. Pale, perfect.

Undead.

Faces turned toward them as they moved through the crowd, dragging a current of chilled air in their wake. The grace of their movements belied their origin from an earlier time when the world was darker, quieter, and bodies could move through it unremarked, if they chose. Now they belonged to every century and none.

The taller of the two spoke first. His perfectly-shaped lips formed words slowly, like a masterwork of Greek statuary moving reluctantly from eternity to life.

Vampires.

"Where are they?" His voice had a metallic rasp from age or disuse.

"Where are what?" Joseph asked.

An expression of delicate regret moved across the vampire's impossibly beautiful face, drawing his sleek, dark hairline downward. He might have been mourning the death of a butterfly.

Canvases and statuary shoved into my memory. All the history of art at my disposal, yet never before had such perfection been naked to my eyes.

"*Who*," the vampire corrected. "Not *what*. And don't ask questions you already know the answers to. It's predictably animal."

I half wanted to say "your mom's an animal," but I suspected this might be lost on a centuries old bloodsucker.

Mark was behind me. I registered his arrival as a heat at my back seconds before his familiar scent of European-made soap and expensive cologne filled my nostrils.

"Gentlemen," he said.

Something passed over both sets of eyes, a brief flicker of recognition in their jeweled, iridescent depths.

"Wilde's blood still stains your hide, *beast*," the shorter, fair-haired vampire hissed. A delicate network of veins became visible beneath his skin, rage moving borrowed blood through flesh that couldn't blush.

"I gave as good as I got," Mark said.

"And yet you are recovered, and he is broken," the taller, dark-haired vampire added.

"Being an *animal* has its advantages," Joseph said.

Mark shot his father a warning glare.

"They're coming for you, you know." The expression on the fair-haired vampire's face couldn't be defined as a smile. A smile requires the cooperation of facial features. This was pure, unabashed anticipation of bloodshed shining like joy from lifeless eyes. "I only hope they'll let me watch when you're made to pay for what you've done."

"I'll do it again," Mark growled, shoving his body in front of mine. "Wilde came after *Hanna*. What I've done is nothing to what I'll *do*. Touch her, come near her, threaten her, *breathe* at her, and I won't stop until all that's left of your kind are piles of smoldering ash and heaps of rotting blood and bone."

Why vivid threats of violence on my behalf created a sudden rush of dampness in my panties, I couldn't say.

But I liked it.

Those unsettling diamond-hard gazes fixed on my face.

"Heir or no, she remains *human*." The vampire spat the word like a cockroach on his tongue. "She's fair game, and we both know it. Wilde did nothing wrong."

"Whoa," I said, snapping out of my stunned, wordless silence. "Humans are fair game? Since when? According to who?"

"Since forever," the fair-haired vampire answered. "There are no rules governing the slaughter of livestock. This was agreed on by both our kinds millennia past."

I turned to Mark and felt his attention shift to me, though he wouldn't relinquish his eye contact with our unwelcome guests. "Hanna, we'll talk about this later," he said through gritted teeth.

"The hell we will," I said. "So, what? Humans are like cattle for supernatural consumers?"

"More like pork, actually," the fair-haired vampire offered helpfully. "There's a lovely sort of sweetness—"

His companion cut him off with a sharp look.

"Apologies," he said, his gaze dropping to the floor.

"In any case," the dark vampire said, "it is protecting our own which brings us. There are three of our kind who were expected by the council yesterday, and never appeared. We'd like to know what you've done with them."

"Council?" I asked. "What council?"

"Maybe you should check the appetizers," Mark suggested. "Someone picked the aged cheddar off the caramelized apples and—"

"Don't you bring cheese into this," I warned.

"What about the register?" he asked, dark eyes shifting over my shoulder. "Shouldn't someone be ringing up the transactions?"

"Shayla's got it." I fixed him with a smug smile.

"I don't suppose just asking you to leave would be at all effective." A familiar look of tired resignation overtook Abernathy's features.

"Has it ever been?" I asked.

"About the council—" Mark began.

"I'm afraid I have some bad news," Joseph cut in.

The wide, winged muscles of Mark's back tensed beneath the starched white fabric of his tailored shirt. I felt an echo in my own gut. Where was Joseph going with this?

"Your colleagues stopped into town," Joseph said, "but when they learned I was here, they lit out of here like a couple of fireflies."

"What distinction do you own that would disrupt them so?" the dark-haired vampire asked, his eerie emerald eyes narrowed.

Joseph held his hand out in invitation, though neither of the vampires seemed the handshaking type. "Joseph Abernathy," he said. "Pleased to make your acquaintance."

The blond vampire's eyes widened as he grabbed his

companion's wrist. "Do you know who this is?" he whisper-hissed.

"The Big Bad Wolf, at your service," Joseph said, executing a perfectly posh half-bow.

I wasn't sure who was more shocked in that moment. Me, or the dark-haired vampire. Our mouths sat agape in mirrored expressions of wonder.

"Are you saying Little Red Riding hood was a true story?" I asked when I could manage words again.

"Some of it," he said, his eyebrows lowering in a conspiratorial expression. "Though they left out the best parts."

"Like what?" I asked.

"Like how Little Red Riding Hood and I—"

"Enough." Mark said. "This isn't the time or the place, Joseph. Hanna, I need you taking care of our customers. Go."

"But I—"

"Go," Abernathy repeated. His eyes had gone as dark and hard as petrified wood.

"Fine," I huffed dramatically. "I guess I'll be going."

The vampires acknowledged my departure with a nearly imperceptible nod.

Pushing my way through the jostling crowd, I looked for some way to make myself useful among the chattering herd. It still amazed me how utterly oblivious most human beings were. Here in this small gallery, two supernatural species were within a hair's breadth of ripping each other limb from limb, and people were discussing potty training and patio color themes.

I'd been one of them, until recently.

Someone grabbed my elbow and I whipped around, expecting to encounter another undead visitor.

"Whoa! What's with the crazy eyes, sis?" Steven Franke asked.

"What did you call me?" I asked, my heart thumping a sudden erratic rhythm against my ribs.

"Uh, sis? Isn't that what all the cool kids are calling their lady friends these days?" he asked.

"Right," I laughed. "Of course. I knew that. What's up?"

"You look all pale and twitchy," Steve said. "Something twisting your tail?"

"Not *some*thing," I said. "*All* the things. Between Morrison and his crotch jockey sleazing around the gallery and the vampires over there looking for a body that was in the trunk of my car earlier, I pretty much want to slam my head in a door until the lights go out."

"Why don't you go take a break?" Steve suggested. "Just tell me where to find the receipts and I'll take care of the register."

"Shit," I said, remembering that I had meant to stop by the office supply store before I'd been derailed by the dead (re-dead?) vampire in my trunk. "Are we out?"

"A little," he admitted. "There's just a couple customers waiting. It's not a huge deal. Seriously. I can just write something up."

"No, I think I have another roll hiding somewhere. Just give me a sec." On the way to the supply closet near the artists' studios, I cursed Mark for insisting on keeping the brassy antique monster that squatted stubbornly on the oddities shop desk. Its abominable presence meant Shayla and I still had to write up receipts for every purchase by hand.

Like that was even a thing that people did anymore.

Opening the door to the crowded closet, I hopped back as an avalanche from the top shelf heaved toward me. The floor rattled as what sounded like a bowling ball dropped at my feet.

"What the hell?" I reached up and yanked the string for the single, naked bulb that illuminated the closet, and glanced down at a severed head, grinning up from my feet.

CHAPTER 8

"Why so jumpy?"

Morrison's voice sent a jolt of adrenaline singing through my veins. I barely had time to register the slim, headless body folded up like a lawn chair at the base of the shelves before I quickly toe-punted the head back into the closet and slammed the door.

"Why so wasted?" I asked.

"What was that?" Unfortunately, his habit of answering my questions with questions of his own hadn't been washed away by alcohol.

"What was what?"

"What you kicked into the closet."

"Kickball," I said. "Steve likes to play sometimes. Just to loosen up." This was the chief advantage of having a brother of whom even the strangest things were believable. It came in remarkably handy when explaining away the even stranger truth.

Morrison seemed to weigh this for a moment, then sagged against the wall, looking more like a wilting vegetable than a man at ease.

"It wouldn't kill you to lay off the sauce," I said. "Just a thought."

The slackened muscles of his face struggled to arrange themselves into something like indifference. "Would you begrudge an officer a few drinks while he's on leave?"

"I've heard of people doing that while they're on vacation," I said. "Not necessarily when they're on leave."

"Never took vacation." He swiped a hand over his jaw, the sound of stubble against his callused palm was oddly loud in the abandoned hallway. "In twelve years with the department. Never once. And now? Now I figure, what the fuck. I can't work. I might as well drink."

As if to punctuate this statement, he reached into the pocket of his leather jacket and withdrew a battered silver flask.

"Cheers," he said, tipping it back for a swallow.

"A flask?" I said. "Really?"

"That sounds like judgment," he said, having considerable trouble with the 's'.

"Not judgment," I said, leaning back against the closet door for extra insurance. "Concern."

"Now that's touching." Morrison slid the flask back into his jacket and took a couple faltering steps toward me. "Hanna Harvey, assistant to a murdering fucktard is concerned about *me*."

"She's also concerned about your dating life."

A savagely smug expression twisted his features. "Don't like her?"

"That would be putting it mildly." I moved to escape down the hall, but Morrison was fast, even when dulled by alcohol. He had my shoulders pinned against the supply closet door before I could exhale. Knowledge of the closet's secret occupant pushed against my back through the wood like the fuzzy sensation of a sleeping limb.

"Stay," he said. The stubble of his chin pushed against my

throat as he dragged his mouth to my ear.

Until he was ripped away and thrown against the opposite wall like a sock monkey.

"You will *not* touch her." Mark's voice filled the hallway with a potent, vibrating rage.

Morrison chuckled weakly from where he'd slid to the floor. "She's never seemed to mind before."

"Mark," I said. "Don't—"

He turned to me then, and I saw how thin the thread holding him to his humanity had grown. His amber eyes had gone molten copper, his nostrils flared, his muscles jerked. Every cell of his massive body warred against his mind, wanting to transform into the iteration that would better serve his revenge. My interference would only make it worse.

I slid back against the door and was silent.

Morrison struggled to his feet and took a couple steps toward Mark, squaring his jaw, straightening his spine. "So you're letting this cocksucker make your decisions for you now?" he accused, circling Mark but looking at me.

"Get out of my gallery," Mark said, a predator's stillness pushing unnatural calm into his voice.

"Or what?" Morrison challenged.

"Or I'll break you." The knuckles of Mark's hands were bone white as they flexed at this sides. "Don't mistake patience for weakness, James. Just because I haven't yet ripped your intestines from your ass and made you wear them like a necktie doesn't mean I can't. In fact, it would give me great pleasure." A small, angry smile curved Abernathy's lips as he mentally pondered this image.

I cleared my throat and tried to speak as calmly and serenely as possible. "I would really prefer that we leave everyone's internal organs where they are for the remainder of the gallery show, is all I'm saying. The guests are hard enough to clean up after as it is."

If either Abernathy or Morrison had heard me, they gave no outward indication.

"Remember that time in your apartment," Morrison said, completely ignoring Abernathy to turn to me. "When I bent you over the couch—"

Morrison's question ended abruptly with Mark's hand closed around his throat. Which was deeply problematic, as milliseconds earlier, he'd been across the room next to me. I'd never seen Abernathy so much as hint at any of his powers with a human present as it was a whole-ass no-no within the paranormal world.

Against my better judgment—if I could be accused of having any—I crossed the room to them and put a gentling hand on Abernathy's back.

"Mark," I said, hoping to bring him back to his wits. "Morrison is shit-faced drunk. Maybe we should wait to have any *serious* discussions until he'll actually remember them?"

"I remember how you taste," Morrison said, completely eradicating my attempt at brokering peace.

Abernathy's hand tightened on Morrison's stubble shadowed throat. "Say another fucking word and so help me I'll—"

"Kill me?" Morrison croaked out.

"You'd like that, wouldn't you?" Mark asked. "Maybe then you'd actually be *right* about me for once."

"I was sure right about your assistant." Morrison attempted a grin, which quickly vanished with the blur of Abernathy's fist and the sickening sound of teeth clacking against teeth. A thin line of blood worked its way down Morrison's chin as he looked around, wild-eyed and disbelieving.

"What the fuck *are* you?" asked through bloodied teeth.

"You'd better hope you never have cause to find out." Abernathy's lips pulled back, revealing his own sharp snarl. He released Morrison as quickly as he'd grabbed him and stepped back, clearing a path for flight.

Morrison refused to give him the pleasure. Instead, he met Mark's eyes with a clarity he hadn't managed all evening. "Whatever you're hiding, I'll find out. And when I do, I'm going to burn your entire fucking world to the ground."

With this, he turned and shuffled back toward the gallery, presumably to collect his tipsy, tottering Tinkerbell twat of a date.

"That went well," I said, hoping to ease the tension billowing in the air like smoke. When his shoulders lowered a fraction, I breathed a little deeper.

"You couldn't have listened to me when I told you not to get involved with him."

"Excuse me?" I turned to face him, my hand fixed in its usual position on my hip. "When did you ever say that?"

"Well, maybe I didn't say those *precise* words," he admitted.

"Damn right you didn't. I mean, when you think about it, you're the one who practically shoved me into his arms in the first place."

"The hell I—"

I held up the Shushing Finger. "Who was the one being all obscure and creepy when there was a murderer tear-assing around town ripping out women's throats? Who was the one who was all *Hanna, you don't know what you're talking about but I can't tell you anything. Hanna, I've got this book full of dead women's pictures but I'm totally not a murderer."* My neck cramped from bunching my shoulders up by my ears, trying to look bulky and sound monotone and morose.

"I do *not* sound like that," he protested, perhaps a little too quickly.

"Whatever you say, boss," I teased.

"Really?" The same voice I had been mocking moments earlier dipped into its huskier registers, dropping the room's barometer by several points. Abernathy stepped closer to me, body heat and the delicious scent that was his and his alone permeating my senses. "*Whatever* I say?"

Stepping backward to preserve my sanity, I was alarmed when he followed suit, stalking me like a great, dark, cat.

Or wolf.

My back made contact with the closet door and Abernathy planted his hands on either side of my head as he leaned closer. Slowly and with great precision, he breathed the air next to my neck, my hair.

My lips.

"And what are we doing, exactly?" I asked. Leave it to me to really sex up a moment.

"Testing," he said, his lips near enough that I felt his warm breath on the skin below my ear.

"For carbon monoxide?" I asked.

"For pheromones. If you wanted him, I would know."

Suddenly, my stomach felt heavy. My skin feverish. "You would know that?"

"Mm-hmm." His lips skimmed my neck, releasing a swarm of gooseflesh.

"Just from scent?"

He paused with his mouth just below my jaw. "Just from scent."

To my utter surprise and considerable delight, his hot, wet tongue, slid along the skin of my earlobe, conjuring an unexpected rush of moisture south of the equator. "Of course," he breathed across the skin he'd moistened with is tongue. "Taste and scent are closely linked."

"Is that so?" I held my breath as Mark's mouth moved from my ear to hover over mine.

He brushed my lips once. Twice.

On the third time, his hand moved from the door into my hair, his fingers digging deep into the unruly waves as he gently tugged.

In that moment. I would have joyfully given birth to an entire litter of puppies if he only kept doing what he was doing.

It was that image in particular, the puppies, that slapped me firmly back into reality.

"This would be significantly more arousing if there weren't a dead body in the closet," I said.

"Or maybe if I—what?" The meaning of my words caught up with him all at once and he snapped back as if I'd thrown a drink in his face.

"Dead body." I jerked my head backward toward the closet door. "Right in there."

He nudged me aside and nearly pulled the door off its hinges. The head rolled out of the closet and came to rest against my shoe. With the pointy patent leather toe, I inched the purple lip up to reveal the pearly point of a fang.

"You know," I said, "if there's one complaint I have, it's that there's just too much damned romance in my life."

"Poor bastard," Mark said. "Wasn't enough to get decapitated. Someone had damn near stab him through the ear."

I glanced down at the head and noted the dark blood oozing over one temple.

"Oops," I said, glancing down at the exposed metal spike of my stiletto heel. I'd meant to get that fixed at some point.

"Oops?" Mark's face took on the cold and stony demeanor it so often did when one of my many mishaps threw his planets out of alignment. "What oops?"

"I...um." Damned if there was any good way to say this. "I sort of kicked it."

"Jesus Christ, Hanna!" Mark hit the open closet door with the flat of his palm. "What the hell is wrong with you? We have vampires sniffing around here and you're playing soccer with undead body parts?"

"You would have preferred bowling?" I folded my arms across my chest and raised an eyebrow at him.

Abernathy's look could have seared the glaze off a doughnut.

"Look, I'm sorry!" I said. "The damn head jumped off a shelf at me and Morrison showed up and it's not exactly like I had time to knit a cozy to slip over it!"

"Shhh!" Abernathy motioned for me to be quiet and kicked the head back into the closet as a patron ambled down the hall toward us in search of the restrooms.

"See!" I hissed as soon as the potty door was closed. "You did it too! I don't want to hear another—"

"Okay, okay! Fine! We both kicked it." He pulled the closet door open to get a better look at the body folded neatly into thirds on the second shelf up.

"Look!" I pointed at the head's waxy brow. "You put a huge dent in his forehead! I only made a tiny mark!"

"Would you shut up about the head," Abernathy said, gripping my shoulders. "We have to get this thing out of here!"

"I'm just saying," I said. "It could have happened to anyone."

We heard the toilet flush and without a word, Mark shoved me into the closet and closed the door behind us.

"What are you doing?" I began. "The door—"

A large hand clapped over my mouth as footfalls passed down the hall. Little splashes of shadow slid across the wedge of light at door's base and the echoes quieted.

"Mmmph!" I protested against steely Mark's fingers.

He held me like that, my back against the warmth of his chest, his heart beating faintly between my shoulder blades. I felt his body relax when the hallway again fell silent.

"If I move my hand," he asked. "Do you promise to be quiet?"

I nodded into his cupped hand.

"Those were the vampires," he said. "One look at your face and they would have known what was in this closet."

"Hey," I said. "Not once, but *twice* today I have discovered decapitated vampires and still managed a normal expression in Morrison's presence."

"First of all, normal is not a word I would ever use to describe your expression and second, it's not your face Morrison is usually looking at."

"Please," I said. "The only thing he's probably looking at right now is the back of his own eyelids. And anyway, what I was trying to say before someone so rudely clamped his paw over my mouth—"

"Half the gallery could hear you." Mark's harsh whisper was cool on my clammy cheeks.

"All of the gallery is going to hear is me in a hot minute. You locked us in the closet with a decapitated vampire."

"We're not locked in," he said. "I installed this door knob myself."

I exhaled a long-suffering sigh as I heard the knob being clicked side to side in rapid succession but refusing to turn.

"What the...why won't this—"

"Because it's backwards," I said. "Always has been."

"I think I would have noticed if the door to my own supply closet was backwards," he said. The handle rattled more forcefully.

"Right," I said. "Because you come in here *so* often to get file folders, tape, pens, envelopes, cleaning supplies..."

"Fuck!" He growled, gave the knob one last try. "It *is* on backward."

"You think?" I reached out to poke him but connected with something wet and cold. "Oh dear God. I touched it! I touched the neckhole. Oh God! I have neck meat on my hand!"

"Quit flailing around and let me get it," Mark said, capturing my wrist in the dark.

"Not so hard!" I said. "It hurts!"

"Do you want me to get it or don't you!"

At that precise moment, the door flew open to reveal one Joseph Abernathy.

The excitement in his eyes quickly dampened to disappointment when he saw me with my hand frozen in Mark's grasp, the stump of a neck protruding between us, and the head wedged between our feet.

"Oh," he said. "I was hoping to find you engaged in far more entertaining pursuits."

Pushing past him, I raced down the hall to the bathroom, holding my hand away from my body like a dirty diaper all the way to the sink. I washed my hands five times in water hot enough to scald my skin and steam the mirror.

Joseph and Mark stood in identical speculative postures in front of the closet when I returned.

"This would be the third vampire those chaps were referring to," Joseph said. "And someone is definitely working with a theme here."

"Who is it?" I asked.

"Humphrey Bogart," Joseph said.

"No!" My heart sank in my chest remembering the many nights my grandmother and I had spent on her couch, popcorn bowl between us and silvery light from the TV flickering across our faces as we screened the noir-iest of noir flicks. "Not Bogey!"

"I'm afraid so," Joseph said.

I knelt in front of the crumpled body, gazing down into the cool, silent face.

"I loved *Casablanca*," I said. "And *To Have or To Have Not* really was a masterpiece. Don't even get me started on Bacall. She had *presence*, you know? I can totally see why you loved her. I mean, *I* loved her. Who wouldn't love her?"

"Hanna," Mark said, dropping a warm, heavy hand on my shoulder.

"Hmm?"

"Please stop talking to the head."

There are moments in a girl's life that cause her to pause and reflect to the circumstances that lead her to a pivotal moment.

Hearing this sentence spoken to me, out loud, by Mark Abernathy, was one of mine.

Gone were the days when I thought having three cats would be the thing people judged me for.

"Right," I said, struggling to my feet. I looked from Abernathy to his father, straightened my skirt, and squared my shoulders. "I think I'm just going to go check how things are going in the gallery. Because that's—that's a thing I should do. Right now."

"I think that's a good idea," Mark agreed.

When I returned ten minutes later, the head and body were gone, along with Joseph Abernathy. I had the unsettling feeling their expediency in disposing of the body in my absence might be insurance against my inviting the head out for cocktails after the gallery show. Or schlepping it home in my purse.

To be honest, neither of those options was totally unfounded.

"So what now?" I asked Mark.

"We finish the gallery show," he said.

"But shouldn't we try to find out who's behind this?" I asked, trailing him down the hallway and back toward the thinning crowd.

"How would you propose we do that at this very moment?" Abernathy asked, pausing to look directly into my eyes.

"Look for clues?" I suggested.

"There aren't any," he replied.

"How can you be so sure?" I jogged to catch up with his efficient, long-legged gait.

"I suspect it's less of a *who* and more of a *what*."

"What makes you think that?" An oily feeling congealed in my belly.

"Easy," he said, a twisted smile not quite at home on his handsome features. "Whatever it is, it doesn't make mistakes."

CHAPTER 9

Mistakes.

I've made a few. One of them was currently passed out on my doormat in a puddle of his own vomit.

I nudged Morrison with the toe of my shoe much the same way I had the head of Humphrey Bogart only hours earlier. Out of consideration, I used the other foot. He groaned and slung an arm over his face to shield his eyes from the old chandelier I'd flipped on in the house's common hallway. Seconds later, his sonorous snore marked a seamless passage back into an alcohol-induced coma.

"Hey." I prodded him a second time. "Sleeping beauty. Wake-up."

No signs of life permeated the haze of scotch and stomach acid lingering about him like a malodorous fog.

"Morrison." I said more forcefully. "Wake the fuck up."

Morrison jerked his head up and squinted at me, puzzlement clouding his features, hair stuck up in barf-crusted swirls on one side. "What am I doing here?" he asked.

"Other than decorating my welcome mat with your stomach contents? Beats the hell out of me."

We both looked down at the dark pool staining the braided rug. It had been relatively new, purchased after its predecessor had been home to a dead cat, and before that, a rotting raccoon, both left as gifts by a would-be werewolf suitor with a cowboy complex and penis problems.

Morrison lifted a hand to rub his eyes and managed to drag it through the slick coating of his own regurgitation. "Shit," he said, wiping his hand on his soiled shirt.

"Come on. Let's get you up." I bent down and grabbed him by the elbow, but he shrugged me off.

"I'm fine!" he said. "I can get up by myself." He shoved himself to his feet and lurched headlong toward the wood banister. I caught him by the back of his shirt and yanked him away, sending him staggering to the left, where he nearly put his head through the old plaster wall.

"Yeah, you're fine all right."

He took a few wobbling steps toward the stairs and straightened his shirt. "I'm going now."

"Going where?" I asked. "Your car isn't even out there."

"Home," he said.

"You live eight miles away." I shifted impatiently on my aching feet, long past regretting my choice in shoewear for the evening. "How are you going to get there?"

"I'll walk."

I held my breath as he attempted the first step, scraped it with the heel of his shoe, and went sliding down to the landing on his ass. He lay splayed out like a starfish, looking up at the vaulted ceiling.

With a beleaguered sigh, I set down my purse and coat and descended to him. I managed to get him to his feet, where he remained for about a nanosecond before collapsing backward on the stairs.

"Okay," I said. "Looks like we're going to have to do this the hard way." Lacing my hands under his armpits, I sat him up and proceeded to drag him backward up the stairs in a kind of modified crab walk.

When we reached the top, I propped him up against the newel post. "Stay," I ordered.

"I'll do what I want," he muttered to himself while I unlocked the door. "I'm a man."

"You're an exceedingly *drunk* man," I said.

With the door opened, I shooed my cats out of the way as I helped him stagger into my apartment. He made a break for the couch, but I spun him in the opposite direction toward the bathroom. "No you don't," I said. "Not before we get you cleaned up."

I plopped him down on the closed toilet lid and he sagged against faded floral wallpaper that might be as old as some of my unwelcome fanged visitors.

The cats followed us into the bathroom, weaving figure eights around my legs as I leaned in to get the shower started.

"I'll feed you as soon as I take care of our guest." The gleaming copper pipes that had been installed to turn the claw-foot tub into a working shower released a friendly groan as they filled with water.

Gilbert, the oldest and largest of my feline children, flicked his tail impatiently.

"I know," I said, testing the water's temperature. "But it's not like I planned on him passing out on the doorstep. I couldn't just let him break his neck falling down the stairs."

The expression of disdain on Gilbert's face made it apparent that he considered this a perfectly acceptable resolution to our current circumstances.

"You're not the one who'd have to answer to the cops," I said. "And with everything else going on, that's the *last* thing we need."

"What's *everything*?" Morrison asked. Even this far gone, the dogged thread of his cop's logic remained intact.

"Nothing" I said. "Aside from the occasional suspended cop showing up shit-faced to my gallery show then walking all the way to my apartment for the pleasure of baptizing my new doormat, life's peachy."

"Liar." He listed forward on the toilet, grabbing onto my leg to keep himself upright.

"Here," I said, handing over a spare toothbrush anointed with a liberal smear of paste. "Brush."

Morrison moved through the process robotically, muscle memory taking over.

"Time to spit," I said.

At my urging, he leaned over the sink and ejected a perfect splat of toothpaste. I admired the casual grace with which he completed this task. Even sober, I managed to splatter it down my chin half the time.

"Alrighty," I said. "Shirt off."

Morrison looked down at his buttons like they were an advanced calculus problem. Fingers I knew to be precise to the point of pain fumbled clumsily at the stained and wrinkled fabric.

"For God's sake." I left the bathroom to retrieve a pair of yellow dishwashing gloves—which I fully intended to burn later—and proceeded to undo the buttons and help him out of the sleeves. "Arms up."

Like a compliant child, he raised his arms so I could slide the undershirt over his head. I pulled it up his arms and had to suppress the urge to coo *now where's the bastard! Where did he go?* when it briefly obscured his head.

"Your turn," he suggested when he was at last free of the fabric.

"That'll be a no," I informed him.

He gave me a boyish pout.

"Shoes." I snapped my fingers and pointed down at his battered brown oxfords.

He successfully kicked them off and held still while I bent and peeled away his socks. With fingers hooked through his belt loops, I wrestled him to his feet and made short work of unbuckling his belt and pants.

"You're good at this." From the wondering way he looked down at my busy hands, I might have been sculpting the *David*.

Where Morrison was concerned, the comparison was especially apt. Before he'd become a booze-swilling gallery fly with terrible taste in women, he'd been a good cop with a secret painting penchant and superior culinary skills.

"Years of practice, my friend." Stripping his unsoiled belt out of its loops, I draped it over the nearby towel rack.

"I love you." The words were stated so simply and clearly that, for a moment, I thought someone else might have appeared in the room.

My hands froze over Morrison's zipper as blood thundered to my ears in a sudden rush.

"Did you know that, Miss Know-it-all?" He poked a finger at the center of my forehead.

"Sure," I said. "And I love cheese. Ain't love grand?" I yanked his zipper open and shucked his pants down his legs, trying not to look at one large, insistent reason *why* I had made this particular mistake.

"But it's even worse than that," Morrison continued to my great horror and consternation. "I don't just love you, I'm *in love* with you."

"You're drunk. It'll pass." Down came his black boxer briefs and Morrison stood fully naked before me. The sharp lines of his body had eroded since last I'd seen them, but even now Morrison was a specimen worth a second glance. Broad-shouldered, narrow-hipped, lean and hungry for all six feet.

"*Now*," he agreed. "But I wasn't drunk when you ran into the back of my car. Not very, anyway."

"That was when we first met," I said. It had happened on my

way to my first interview with Mark, in fact. Morrison had let me off with a stern finger and a boyish grin. It had been the first good thing that had happened to me in an epic series of clusterfucks and shit sandwiches.

"You smelled like rain," he said. "You were wearing black pants that showed off your ass and a sweater the color of the sea. Didn't hurt that it clung to your tits. God," he sighed, a wistful expression sweeping over his face. "I can still see them."

"That's because you have your hands on them," I pointed out.

He looked down and appeared genuinely surprised that his palms had come to rest on the space covered by my bra. He gave the ladies a squeeze.

"James Morrison!" Channeling my best and least sexy teacher/librarian/mom voice, I slapped his hands away.

"They were already there." He shrugged.

"In the tub," I ordered.

He leaned against me as he swung one leg in, then the other, and sat down in the shower's spray. His head came to rest on his knees as the steaming water beat down on his neck and back. Best to let him marinate until the steam pushed the fog out of his head.

I seated myself on the closed toilet lid and listened to him ramble through my damask shower curtain.

"You were the most beautiful woman I had ever seen. My world was gray. All gray. Then suddenly, there you were against that backdrop, your hair like a corona of fire. Little freckles across your cheeks. Your lip quivered. Actually quivered when you started crying. I wanted to bite it almost as bad as I wanted to see it smile. I got to do both, lucky bastard that I am."

Pain in my chest reminded me to breathe.

"I told you to go," he continued. "You were so relieved. Hugged me so hard I thought my ribs would break. Like there was something good enough in me to deserve it. I wanted to ask you your name, to know anything about you. Instead, I watched you drive away. It took everything I had not to follow you." His laugh was dark this time, smoked with bitterness.

"Imagine my surprise when I ran into you again, in *his* office. Half of me wanted to shoot him on sight. The other half was *grateful* he murdered his ex-girlfriend, if it was the reason I got to see you again."

Helena isn't dead! I wanted to scream. *She's about as not dead as you can get! She's pregnant and happy and rosy with love and life! And also a werewolf.*

It was this last bit that always made saying the rest impossible. But I knew better than to disagree with Morrison's assessment of Mark. We'd done this dance until our feet were blistered and minds numb with repetition. I'd let him swing it solo this round. Thankfully, he meandered on to a different topic.

"I had a dream about you the other night," he said.

"Oh?" I wanted him to stop.

"I was in a vineyard," he began. "Walking hip deep in groves of purple-red grapes.

An engine roared, and I saw an Aston Martin weaving up the back road to the villa. There was this flash of red hair tangling with the wind and I knew it was you, coming home to me. And you were mine."

"Sounds nice," I whispered, unaware of the tears pressing at the back of my throat until I heard them in my voice.

"We could do that, you know. I've been saving for years," he said. "Investing. So I could buy a rundown villa in Tuscany and restore it. Paint, and grow grapes."

Painting was a hobby he'd kept closely guarded for reasons I understood the second I saw his work. It belonged to the part of him that spoke like a poet and worshipped my body like he himself had sculpted it. The part of him that still mourned the loss of a child.

"James—" I said with as much gentleness as I could manage.

"I know," he said, heartbreaking heaviness in his voice. "I know. You can't."

Apologies felt like they would do more to insult than they would to soothe. I rose from the toilet and scooted the shower curtain away, perching on the edge of the tub. He was still folded in on himself, face between his knees.

"Sit back."

Quiescent for once, he obeyed.

I squeezed a dollop of shampoo in my palm and worked it through his wet hair, paying particular attention to the side that had been afflicted with the gastric ointment.

My fingertips explored his scalp at their own pace. The chaotic mix of longing, regret, and affection seemed to escape from my fingertips into his skin. I was part mother, part lover, both halves equally aware of the man who sat completely defenseless with his head in my hands. I'd seen him impassioned, enraged, ecstatic, and envious. Never before had I seen him afraid. He'd always worn his agenda like a second skin beneath his clothes, and now he'd shed them both.

"Rinse," I said.

He leaned forward and hung his head in the shower's spray. "No conditioner," he mumbled.

"Right," I agreed. "You're a man, after all. Men don't even use shampoo, do they? I thought y'all just beat your head on a rock to dislodge any dirt."

"Cinderblocks," he replied. "They're more abrasive."

"Well, someone's coming around, isn't he?" I pushed the wet hair off his forehead and slicked it away from his face. He caught my hand at the wrist and pulled it to his face.

"Another thing I love about you," he said, brushing his lips across my wrist, then planting a kiss in my palm. "Your hands. So delicate." He kissed the pad of each finger.

I marshalled my willpower and pulled my hand away. "You're getting me all wet."

"That's the idea." He managed a smirk. His finer motor functions were returning.

"With *water*," I said.

We looked at my chest precisely the same moment. My thin blue cocktail shift, now wet, did little to hide the anatomy beneath.

I clapped my hands over my chest and scooted away from Morrison, who was still staring with lust-darkened eyes.

"Did you buy a gun like I told you to?' he asked.

I was stunned and speechless by this rapid shift of topics. "No."

"Okay then." He swung an arm around my waist and pulled me into the shower, onto his lap.

"James!" I screeched. "What are you doing?"

"Getting you wet," he announced.

He dug his fingers into the ticklish spot where my legs met my hips until I was squirming, laughing, in imminent danger of wetting myself in an entirely different way. "Stop!" I begged.

When he relented at last, I was face down on top of him, soaked to the skin, wavy wet hair clinging to my neck, dress plastered to my thighs. He clutched a handful of cloth at the small of my back.

"You don't laugh enough," he said.

"Been short on reasons," I answered.

His heart beat beneath my chin. He rested his ear on the crown of my head. The water's rush had quieted the world. There was only the warmth beating down on my back, the skin against my skin through the thin fabric of my dress. He put a finger under my chin, urging it upward until our eyes met. The planet of sadness lodged in my chest seemed to be rising, gliding up my throat, hemorrhaging through my gaze. Salty tears mixed with the water dripping down my cheeks.

"There are those freckles," he said, a small, sad, smile breaking on his face.

The tears came harder then.

For me. For him. For the pain he felt and I couldn't fix. For the sudden and sure knowledge that I didn't, couldn't, love him the way he loved me.

With one hand on the side of the tub, and the other pressed against the wall, I peeled myself away from him and shut off the shower. Wrapping myself in a towel, clothes and all, I tossed another at him.

The cats stared at me from the kitchen counter as I padded through, leaving a trail of water from my sodden dress.

"What?" I said. "It's not like you do the laundry."

In the combined living and bedroom of my studio apartment, I dragged the wet dress up my hips and managed to get it stuck on my shoulders where it clung to me like a second skin.

"Shit," I grunted inside my cocoon of cold, wet fabric.

"Allow me." Morrison's hands skimmed my ribs, sliding under the dress, prying it up my shoulders and over my head.

"Thanks." Clad in only bra and panties, I crossed the living room and hung the dress over the radiator to dry. Morrison leaned against the wall, naked save for the towel wrapped around his hips.

"You could turn around," I suggested, digging in my closet for dry skivvies and a nightshirt.

"Could," he said. "Won't."

"You didn't feel like making a night of it with *Jess*?" I asked from my station in the closet.

"She took off. Left with those pretty boys I saw Abernathy talking with."

Hope they like extra-crispy.

"How do you know?" I asked.

"Kirkpatrick," he replied. "Told me she left with them when he saw me walking around. Which reminds me. Who is that woman who was hanging all over him? She looks so damn familiar."

My throat went all dry and scratchy. *That woman* was the one whose murder Morrison had been investigating when he'd come to Mark's office for the first time. Her throat had healed well enough—a handy side effect of her transformation into a werewolf. She'd also put on about twenty pounds, a handy side effect of falling in love and getting knocked up with Kirkpatrick's ginger werewolf spawn. That, and the expression of perpetual bitchiness that hardened her features had melted into something like domestic contentment. She looked just different enough to ensure deniability.

"Oh, Kirkpatrick's new lady friend," I answered. My casual shrug would have been far more convincing had I not been topless and freezing to death.

"No shit?" he asked.

"That's what I hear."

"She could do better," he said.

"Like you?" I asked. I considered the neatly folded stack of nightgowns on the shelf and selected the faded green knee-length oversized t-shirt adorned with little gray mice and cheese wedges. Let's see Morrison find *this* sexy.

"If I were going to knock someone up," he said, folding his arms across his chest, "it wouldn't be her."

"I'm sure Jess would make a stellar mother." I bent at the waist and used my discarded towel to squeeze moisture from the ends of my tangled auburn mane.

Fingers slid over my hips and I was pulled back against Morrison's chest. Apparently, the mice were falling down on the job. I'd have to invest in something in a floor length flannel.

"How about it?" he asked.

"How about you quit being a letch?" Peeling his fingers away from my hips, I shoved my wet towel at him. "Hang this up, would you?"

Once he was otherwise engaged, I wrestled a blanket down from the top shelf and tossed it onto the couch.

"You know you'd like it," he said.

I grabbed my phone, set the alarm and deposited it on the nightstand. "Just because I'd like it doesn't mean it's not a terrible idea," I said.

"It's always been a terrible idea. That's never stopped you before."

"Maybe I'm learning." I threw the deadbolt on the front door, slid under the covers, and clicked off the lamp.

"Room for one more?" Morrison's asked.

"Couch," I grunted.

He sighed, defeated. I was relieved to hear the soft sounds of blankets rustling in the dark as he settled himself.

"Stay," I whispered.

CHAPTER 10

The following morning, Morrison caught a ride with me back to the gallery to get his car. I pulled my Mustang into a parking lot several blocks away so we could strategize before I brought him within Abernathy's supernatural sniffing orbit.

"Okay, here's the plan," I said. "We're going to circle the block. I'm going to drive very slowly past your car. You're going to get out of mine and into yours and drive north as fast as you can. I'll give you a ten-minute head start before I set foot in the gallery."

Morrison slouched in the passenger seat looking like something I'd dug out from between the couch cushions. Wearing a dogged expression and the same clothes he had the night before —minus the few vomit stains I'd been able to wash out in the sink.

Just call me Martha effing Stewart.

"And why am I going to do this?" Morrison asked.

"Because despite your recent hiccup, you value your life and don't want your nose shoved through the back of your skull." I flashed him a quick, this is really no big deal smile.

"This would happen to me why?"

"Gee, I don't know," I asked mockingly. "Couldn't have anything to do with you crashing at my place the same night you and Mark got into an epic pissing match."

"How would he know I crashed at your place?" Absent the booze, his sharp-eyed hazel gaze fastened on my face.

Because he'll be able to smell you on me before I'm finished parking. "He's good like that," I said.

Morrison scratched the dark neck stubble that seemed to have doubled in length overnight. "So what, he's going to hunt me down?"

"Not if I can help it," I said.

"And if you can't?"

"Drive fast." I reached over and squeezed his knee reassuringly.

"I'm not afraid of him." Morrison's jaw was set in an echo of the determination that carried him through a record number of closed investigations. It would have been refreshing to see in any other context.

"I didn't say you were. But no good can come of you two beating the snot out of each other."

Or Mark eating you.

"I think the hope of anything *good* stepped out of this situation a long time ago." Morrison slouched down in his seat, staring out the window at the old brick buildings in the early morning mountain light.

"All the more reason to let it go."

"Or to end it." The flat finality in his voice drew gooseflesh to my neck. *Men.* Always so certain they had the world and everyone in it accurately pegged.

I decided a different tactic was in order. "What if I asked you nicely to get gone for a couple days?"

"*How* nicely?"

"Please?" I asked, in my sweetest, most placating voice.

"You're going to have do better than that." A sly grin stripped away a small measure of his sour expression.

"*Pretty* please?"

Morrison shook his head. "B minus at best."

On an impulse, I glanced around to confirm the streets were empty before unbuckling my seat belt, reaching down, and flipping up my shirt and bra both. "The ladies and I humbly request that you not show your face anywhere in the vicinity of the gallery until I let you know it's safe. Deal?"

Morrison's eyes had the drugged, determined look I recognized when he was turned on. "Three days," he said. "Any more than that is going to cost you."

"Deal." Tugging my shirt and bra into place, I re-buckled my seatbelt and pulled out into traffic.

"I meant what I said last night." His voice had a strange, hollow quality.

"Which part?" I asked.

"All of it," he said, turning to look at me. Threats and promises crystalized in his icy stare.

Before I knew what was happening, he launched across the car and planted a fast, hard, tooth bumping kiss on my lips.

I shoved him away by the shoulders, about to verbally scorch his hide, but he was already gone.

As I watched him make his way down the block, it occurred to me I'd managed to trade one mistake for two. I'd underestimated Morrison's abilities and overestimated my resolve. The time I'd bought might prove to be too costly when the final bill came due. There was nothing for it.

"All right." I grimaced at myself in the rear-view mirror, resigned to my fate. "Let's get this over with."

I cranked the engine over and drove the final few blocks to the gallery. Parking around the corner, I hoped the wind would drive away at least some of Morrison's signature scent.

No such luck.

I had scarcely eased the gallery door closed behind me when the door to Mark's office exploded off the hinges and slid down the stairs from the loft like an unmanned sled.

Well, shit.

Rather than follow it down, Mark—still in mostly human form—opted to leap over the railing and make the fifteen-foot jump directly to the gallery floor. The old wood gave a groan of protest as it absorbed his full weight. His nostrils flared as he circled me—six and a half feet of pissed off man clad in a hand-tailored shirt the color of the storm clouds and pants that fit him like the sartorial testament of original sin.

"A simple *good morning* would have been okay," I said in a greatly misguided attempt to lighten the mood.

Speaking had been a mistake. Mark's eyes zeroed in on my mouth, and narrowed. Yellow sparks danced in their honeyed depths. He bent his face to my neck, dragging his nose and lips along the sensitive flesh beneath my chin. Air rushed through the impossibly narrow margin between his nostrils and my neck as he filled the great expanse of his lungs. It seemed to ignite every single cell as it skipped across my skin.

He was *scenting* me.

In an uncharacteristically bold movement, I placed both my hands on either side of his face and did my best to hold him fast.

"Mark," I said, speaking to the rapidly waning human part of his nature. "Look at me."

His eyes seemed to flutter to a dozen spots at once, reading additional details from my hair, my face, my clothing.

"Mark, listen to me. Nothing happened."

The rough pads of his fingers landed on my lips, caging my words.

"You kissed him." It was part whisper, part growl, barely human.

"Incorrect," I said. "He kissed me. And only then because I had asked if he'd stay away if I asked nicely and he was all 'how nicely?' and I was like 'please,' and he was all 'no dice,' and then I was like 'pretty please,' and he said 'B minus at best' and I pulled the car over and everything after that is kind of a blur..." My head swam with lack of oxygen as I finished my breathless sentence. Best, I thought, to leave out the part about the flashing.

"Car? What was he doing in your car?" A vein pulsed beneath the skin of his temple.

Not good. Very not good.

"I, uh. He needed a ride. I was just—"

"From where?"

"Pardon?" I lifted a hand to my ear.

"A ride. From where?" The steely edge in Abernathy's voice sent my intestines crawling southward.

Lie! Lie our ass off! shrieked the little voice in my head.

"My apartment." I winced even as the words left my mouth. Since when had I been unable to fib to Abernathy? Fibbing to Abernathy was practically part of my job description.

No I'm sure the framer didn't hear you growling in the background.

I never would have known you were out traipsing through the woods all night.

A meat basket is definitely the best way to smooth things over with that canvas rep.

"What the fuck was he doing at your apartment?" Mark's chest rose and fell riotously with the effort of maintaining normal human breathing patterns.

"Nothing. I swear to God." I held my arm up, palm facing forward like someone taking the witness stand. "He just slept on the couch and that was it."

"He slept *over*?" Abernathy's hands curled into fists at his sides.

"No. Yes. Look, he was laying in his own vomit on my

doorstep. He couldn't even walk. I couldn't let him leave like that."

"You let him sleep on your couch while he was covered in vomit?"

"Not exactly," I admitted, trying to find anywhere to look except in Abernathy's direction.

"What do you mean *not exactly*?" He stepped closer to me, dipping his head so I had no choice but to look directly into his eerie orange-red gaze.

"I let him use the shower." By this point, my lungs had all but collapsed, completely and utterly refusing to admit much-needed oxygen into my bloodstream.

"He was too drunk to walk but he managed to shower?"

How was it that with each answer I provided, Abernathy's questions became progressively more frightening? And where was everyone anyway? Hadn't they heard the small sonic boom of Abernathy pulling a Spiderman leap from the landing?

"Kind of?" I said. "I mean, I helped him get in but—"

"You helped him? You *helped* him?" Rage simmered blood to the surface of Abernathy's skin, his color deepening from bronze to a color I would call *impending coronary purple,* were it to end up in a box of crayons.

"Yes, and that's all. It's not like I showered *with* him. Not on purpose, anyway. You can't really call it showering *with* someone if you have your clothes on the whole time, can you?"

"You had—you were—with him—" Abernathy's eyes had begun to wander again, twitching crazily everywhere at once. A resounding crack ricocheted through the gallery as his spine doubled over. His hands buried in his hair as he collapsed to his knees, an eardrum-rending roar tearing from his throat.

His body heaved and bent as every cell was hijacked by the animal that swam in his bloodstream and howled in his heart. Expensive clothes rent like a fabric cocoon from which he emerged at once whole and complete in a burst of animal grace.

Abernathy, the wolf.

A wolf larger than any found in the world's dark forests, deep-chested and powerfully limbed, padded toward me on silent paws. All traces of human understanding had evaporated from the pitiless brightness of his golden eyes. The velvet of his chestnut brown muzzle drew back from teeth like perfect daggers in a predatory snarl. The low growl registered as tightness in my stomach before my ears caught the bass notes as sound.

One foot behind the other, I retreated slowly, never breaking eye contact. Fear scattered my thoughts like marbles. Scream. Run. Beg. Fight. Ideas that seemed as remote as they were unhelpful.

Abernathy's dark haunches twitched, the muscles tensing with preparation to spring.

This, at last, prompted action on my part. Instinct took over and I slid into a crouch to protect vital organs, covering my head with my arms and squeezing my eyes shut tight. My brain summoned the ghosts of sensations to join me in the present: the tearing of skin, the crushing of bone. I'd learned them and lived.

What came instead was a spattering sound and an unexpected surge of warmth on my upraised forearm. Then came the scent.

I cracked on eye open and was rewarded with the underside of Mark's hind leg hovering over my head.

Abernathy was *marking* me.

"No!" I shrieked, recovering my senses and scampering away from him. "Bad wolf! Very bad!"

A wounded look widened his canine eyes as I pulled off my cardigan before it could soak through to my shirt. His nostrils flared, catching a scent released by the abrupt shift in my clothing.

His eyes narrowed, black lips drawing back from his teeth

once again as he sniffed the air.

Morrison.

If Abernathy got out of the gallery, Morrison was a dead man.

Without warning, Abernathy took off toward the gallery door at a gallop.

"Shit!" I darted into his path and blocked the door, throwing my arms wide against the frame.

"Say, Hanna. You got any—baby Jesus on a grilled cheese sandwich!" Steve froze in the doorway leading from the artists' studios. His mouth formed a little "o" as he saw Abernathy.

I spoke to him through the side of my mouth without taking my eyes off Mark. "Get. The. Shop. Door."

Mark looked at Steve.

Steve looked at Mark.

They launched into motion at the same moment. Steve's leopard print bathrobe flew out behind him like a cape as his skinny white legs peddled furiously to get a head start. He was vastly aided by rubber-soled green Chuck Taylors and Mark's inability to get similar purchase on the wood floor with his skittering black claws.

"Shaaaayla!" Steve yelled as he tore down the hall. "Get behind the desk!"

"What the—shit! Holy fucking shit!" I heard Shayla gasp as Mark's tail disappeared into the oddities shop.

As quickly as I could, I wrestled a credenza in front of the gallery door and jogged down the hall to provide reinforcement.

A crash and the sound of breaking glass resounded through the gallery. Steve had barred the front door to the oddities shop by tipping over a bookshelf in a similar configuration to my own improvised solution.

Foiled from flight, Mark had apparently turned his attention to pure, wanton destruction. He sprang to the top of a cabinet, sending Shayla's carefully arranged display of wooden heads and wigs flying every direction. From here he leapt to a row of bookshelves, his weight sending them careening like a row of dominoes. He was free of them before they had finished falling and flying toward a glass display of antique medical equipment.

"No!" Shayla moaned. "Not the lithotripters!"

Abernathy was heedless in his quest. The shop was reduced to sparkling rubble and splinters within a matter of moments.

Steve, Shayla, and I all ducked behind the expanse of wooden counter while Mark seized the neck of an old dress-maker's dummy and shook it like a rat.

"He. Is. *Huge*," Shayla marveled.

Oh honey. If you only knew.

"This is your first time seeing him all wolfy, isn't it?" Steve asked.

"Yup," she said, seemingly unable to tear her eyes away from him.

"You've seen other werewolves, though?" I asked.

"Just Steve," she said. "And only on special occasions."

I scrubbed the mental image out of my head while Mark turned his attention to tearing a set of 18th century erotic novels from the shelves in the corner. Bits of paper swirled like snow as he tore at the pages, growling.

"What did you *do*?" Shayla's impossible aquamarine eyes fixed on my face in glassy wonder.

"What do you mean what did *I* do? I didn't do anything," I said.

"She slept with Morrison again," Steve said.

"Hey," I said, giving Steve a gentle shove. "I did *not* sleep with Morrison. And why is everyone always assuming that I—"

"*Smells* like you slept with Morrison." Steve said, raising a brow at me.

"Fine, okay. He slept at my house. But I didn't sleep *with* him," I explained, attempting to sound less defensive than I felt.

Steve leaned over and gave me a sniff. "He was in your bed. And he was naked."

Mark paused in his assault and his ears shifted in Steve's direction like triangular satellites. He began to pant and drool, then took off back toward the gallery with a howl of rage.

"God dammit, Steve! You are not helping!" I slugged him in the shoulder as hard as I could, feeling the bony length of his bicep beneath my knuckles.

"Ow!" he yelped. "You really *are* getting stronger."

The abrupt scraping sound of wood on wood drove us all to our feet. "Shit! The credenza!"

We scrambled down the hall just in time to see a rolled up newspaper land a resounding *thwack* to Mark's snout. He yelped and shook his head as if to cast off the irritating sensation.

The distinctive cockney bray that followed produced a sudden burst of joy within my chest.

"Now 'ows that to behave? You shouwd be ashamed of yourself! Runnin' around 'ere, barkin' at peopwe like you're some kinda daft pup! And look at 'ese clothes! I spent days makin' that bloody shirt and you shredded it like a whore's knickers! I oughta box your ears!"

Clad head to toe in an expertly tailored suit of vibrant teal, Allan Ede of Ede and Ravenscroft Tailors, London, looked rather like a disapproving peacock. He stood, hands on his hips, glaring down at Mark through his black-framed Gucci glasses, his perfectly plucked dark brows drawn into a stern line.

"Allan," I said. "Thank God. I thought we were going to have to call animal control."

"Why Hanna, my girw! Lovely to see you again." His broad smile revealed two front teeth a shade longer than the rest, making him look more like the Easter Bunny than a 1000 year-old werewolf. "Give us a squedge," he said, holding his arms open.

His expression stopped me before I could cross half the distance.

"Cor blimey!" He clapped a hand over his nose and looked down to Mark, who was chuffing at his feet. "Did you *mark* her?"

How odd a sheepish expression looked on the face of a wolf.

Allan turned his gaze to me. "Right. What did you do, then?"

"Me? Really? Why does everyone immediately assume this is *my* fault?"

"Mostly cause you smeww like a naked chap who ain't him," Allan said, gesturing to Mark with his polished Italian loafer. "Looks like he gave you an 'ell of a snog besides," he added, blinking at my face.

A blush stung my abraded lips.

"For Christ's sake! He was drunk, and he couldn't even walk. And then he was making all these threats and he gave me a *B minus*!" I became vaguely aware that I was making not a lick of sense, and doing it pretty emphatically.

Sickening crunching sounds came from Mark's vicinity.

Allan, Steve, and Shayla all found various spots on the walls and ceiling to become interested in as Mark's fur began to recede, revealing patches of naked flesh.

I grabbed the shredded wad of his clothing and pressed it into his emerging hands. Mark pushed slowly into a standing position, stark naked save for the bundle covering his naughty bits and the sheen of sweat clinging to pale, clammy skin. His soaking hair stuck to his neck and cheeks in dark clumps.

Steve slapped a hand over Shayla's bulging eyes.

"Office," Mark groaned.

Allan and I each took an arm and helped him up the stairs. There, in his lair, we eased him down onto the leather sofa, where he collapsed into a heap.

"I fink Hanna can take it from here." Allan winked at me. "I'll just get acquain'ed wif the bride and groom and 'ave someone see to 'at mess downstairs."

"Is that why you're here?" I asked. "The wedding?"

"Course it is," Allan said. "Joseph gave us a jingle an said we 'ad a weddin' to plan. I 'opped the next flight."

I cast a look down at Mark, whose color was returning. His broad chest rose and fell in something like a normal rhythm.

"We'll be okay," I assured Allan.

When the door was safely closed behind him, I knelt down beside the couch where Mark's head rested on the rocky pillow of his curled bicep.

His eyelids fluttered open. "I can still smell him on you," he growled/half croaked.

"Really? Even through your…contribution?"

His face softened slightly. "Even through that."

Unfamiliar fire kindled in my belly. The words that came next had neither precedence nor logic to argue their cause. "Well, what are you going to do about it?"

CHAPTER 11

My first sense was of urgent, stomach-flipping motion. Though I couldn't be sure in which direction I was moving or how I was being propelled, the world around me blurred until it abruptly snapped back into focus.

When it did, I was beneath Abernathy on the leather couch, my hands pinned above my head, his mouth mere millimeters from mine.

He gazed down at me, naked hunger and bottomless need burning in his eyes. Yet, he was waiting. Seeking permission. Seeking assent.

A million questions crowded my mind. Why do you want me? What do I want? What will this change? What will I do?

In that moment, the only answer I needed was the body anchoring mine to this couch, to the earth, to life itself.

Tentatively, by degrees too small to measure, I pressed my lips toward his. When they met, a sweet, dizzying wave of crippling desire rolled through me from head to foot. The pure, chemical loveliness of this man. The taste of his lips, his tongue as it stroked my lower lip then dared further, tasting me, drinking from me as I drank from him, hungry as a baby bird.

Abernathy moaned, a ribcage rattling sound from deep in his throat that only threw gasoline on the banked coals at my center.

Then it wasn't just our mouths fusing, but every cell of our bodies. Our chests, our bellies, our hips, our thighs. Every available surface seeking out its match. In that moment, if I could have crawled inside his very skin, I would have done it.

But like, in a totally non-creepy way.

And did I want him. I wanted him like air, like breath, like food, like life. In that moment, I had never wanted anything more.

"I want *you*." Only when his lips disappeared from mine did I realize I had said this out loud.

His breath stopped. His pupils dilated. "I told you not to say that to me."

In fact, he had. In London, he'd told me in no uncertain terms that the next time I said those words to him, I deserved what I got.

"No." Something seemed to shift in him as he decided. "You don't."

"I do," I said. "You think I don't know how fucked up that is? You think I don't understand the many ways it would fuck up my life? *Has* fucked up my life? I've got heads rolling out of every storage space I touch, for Christ's sake! It's no mystery the kind of shit-storm you come with. And no, I'm not saying I'm ready for all the consequences that decision would bring. But I want you. I want you in my bed. I want you in my body. I want you—"

"Stop." The ragged plea was followed by a hand planted across my lips.

I parted them and slid my tongue across his palm. His eyelids fell closed as his nostrils flared.

His hand skimmed over my breasts, down my stomach,

dipping below the waistband of my jeans until I felt the heat of his fingers through my rapidly dampening panties.

"*Fuck*," he panted.

"Now that's more like it!"

At the sound of Joseph's voice, Mark and I leapt apart like teenagers caught in our parent's basement:

"I would have knocked." Joseph grinned broadly. "But it seems your door has been relocated."

"Get out of my office," Mark growled. "Now."

"Of course I wouldn't have interrupted at all, but you are urgently needed in the gallery," Joseph said.

"It can wait," Mark said, looking like he might relocate Joseph like he'd relocated the door.

"There's another body in one of the cabinets in the shop. Allan found it."

Mark's naked shoulders sagged. "I'll be down in a minute."

Joseph nodded and left us to put ourselves together.

I stole a greedy glance as Mark rose from the sofa and walked bare-assed to one of his cupboards. The contours of his body cast in the desk lamp's glow left me with the urge to throw rocks at Michelangelo's *David*.

Mark eased the cupboard open and tugged on the brass coat hook. The shelves pushed forward and out of the closet to reveal another door behind. A slight nudge of Mark's finger on a knothole and a rod bearing neatly pressed shirts, slacks, and ties rolled forward. Several pairs of polished shoes winked from the hidden cubby below. Undershirts and skivvies were bundled into parcels on a shelf above the shirts and pants.

"You've got to be kidding me," I said. "Do you have like special werewolf carpenters that install secret clothes stashes for you, or what?"

"Special werewolf carpenters," Mark snorted, stepping into a pair of boxers. "Your vivid imagination never ceases to amaze, Hanna."

"I'm serious," I said. "Where the hell do you get this stuff?"

"So am I," he replied. "Everyone knows that elves are the only carpenters worth having. And secret clothes stashes are standard issue."

Mark tossed a white undershirt and a pair of slacks at me. "Might want to put those on," he advised. "Until I can accompany you home to shower."

"You're not going to believe this," I said. "But I've been showering *and* dressing myself for years. I don't think I'll need any help."

Mark finished tucking a freshly pressed shirt into his pants. "I wasn't offering to help. Most of my security resources are here at the gallery, and there is no way in hell I'm letting you go unprotected. Speaking of which—" He paused to snug a silk tie against his corded neck. "Steve was on duty last night. I think he and I need to have a chat about the policy for *visitors*."

"That's funny," I said. "It sounded like you were planning on determining who I can see in my own apartment."

He cleared his throat. "When it comes to anyone who puts you at risk, that's exactly what I'm planning."

"I think I'm capable of deciding for myself who puts me at risk."

"Your actions this morning would indicate otherwise," he said.

"Odd," I said. "But I seem to remember arriving to work on time and in once piece, where I was nearly attacked and peed on by a werewolf that nearly destroyed his own gallery during a temper tantrum."

The muscles in Mark's jaw bunched until it look like he had a walnut squirreled away in his cheek.

"Mark Andrew Abernaffy!" Allan's voice called from downstairs. "Get down here 'afore I have to come up and drag you down by your taiw! You can get your end away wif Hanna when you ain't got a bloody dead vampire shackin' up in your cabinet!"

"We'll finish this later." Mark's voice was tempered with the unnatural quiet I had come to know and fear. He pointed at the leather sofa and fixed me with a warning glare. "*Stay*," he said.

I smiled, but said nothing. In my defense, Mark had been around me enough to know this was the equivalent of a double barrel bird flip complete with spitting through forked fingers.

As soon as I could hear Allan and Joseph's voices threading with Mark's in the gallery below, I slid down the stairs and out the front door.

❧

"DON'T ASK," I TOLD GILBERT, WHO HAD FOLLOWED ME FROM THE door to the bathroom where I shed my clothes in an unceremonious heap. He paused near the bathtub to sniff delicately at the pile, then looked at me with undisguised disdain. I fought the urge to apologize, and made a mental note to ask Steve about cat mind control powers.

It would explain a lot.

I emerged half an hour later in a cloud of steam and donned fresh clothes. Opting to wrestle my wet mane into a braid, I spent time on make-up instead. When Mark had not yet materialized after my full spackle and paint routine, I aimed the Mustang toward Jitters Java instead of the gallery. After what I'd faced this morning, something loaded with caffeine, sugar, and indecent amounts of heavy cream might be my only hope for bringing this shit-storm of a day around.

"Hey Dan," I called.

Dan, one of Jitter's regulars, glanced up from his conversation and gave me his somber smile. With his wire-rimmed spectacles, brown slacks, side-parted hair, and sweater the color of peanut brittle, Dan looked like a thirty year-old grad student who just couldn't get to a retirement community quick enough. Most days he could be found engaged in a game of chess with an octogenarian companion at one of the coffee shop's many two-top tables. Today, his audience was a man with a middle-aged spread, suspenders and a fedora. They leaned in conspiratorially over one of Dan's many tattered notebooks.

"Hanna." He nodded.

"How's the thesis?" I asked.

I'd been coming to Jitters for about four years now, and Dan had been working on his epistle on *Dhobar-Chu,* Nessie's smaller, sexier, fiery Irish cousin, for at least twice that long. Of course, the rules were different when one was "reading at Northumberland," or any other suitably European-sounding university. Most tenured professors of this persuasion seemed to regard my kind of exuberant insistence on finishing a degree in two years as the major cause for the downfall of western civilization. There was no rushing these things, they seemed to sigh from the dust of a thousand tomes.

"Still waiting on some archives material from Marsh's. The senior librarian is proving to be both reclusive and intractable."

I gave him my most understanding of dusty academic nods. "Not everyone understands the work."

"This is true," he agreed.

"Well, good luck," I said.

"Many thanks." He turned his attention back to his notes and his neighbor.

"Hanna! I haven't seen you in a wee—uh oh. Wet hair. What's up?" The bouncy little barista eyed me from behind the hissing copper monster she coaxed into producing magic elixirs.

"Darcy," I said, "you don't want to know."

She leaned across the counter and surveyed the carnage with quick precision of a field surgeon. "Quad shot venti S'more Mocha, extra whipped cream," she said, pronouncing her prescription with a nod of certainty.

“Marry me?” I asked.

She fixed me with a megawatt grin. “Honey, if I ever decide to ride the magic carpet, you’ll be my first.”

“Deal.” I perused the display of designer mugs while she flitted around behind the counter like a healer from another time. Then I was looking at Dan’s table, my eyes drawn to his notes by a word that landed in my subconscious like a bag of concrete.

Vampires.

“They’re everywhere,” Dan whispered across the table to a pair of rapt, watery blue eyes. “It’s the *Spring Lambing*.”

I inched closer, shuffling along a display of paperweights.

“But that’s not even the half of it,” Dan continued in hushed tones. “The werewolves, they *know*. And they let it happen. Every ten years, all over the world.”

Dan was staring up at me now. Any pretense of eavesdropping had been blown about the time I planted my elbows on his table and sandwiched my head in my upturned palms.

“Danno,” I said. “Tell me everything.”

CHAPTER 12

"Dan told me everything."

Mark sniffed the air, nostrils twitching. "Quad shot venti S'more Mocha, extra whipped cream?" He set his pen aside, folding his hands on top the papers on his broad oak desk. "How many of those have you had?"

"Why does that matter?" The pain exploded in my forehead as I sucked down another icy straw-full. "Four?"

"*Fuck.*" He massaged his temples with fingers I knew to have expert knowledge of human musculature. "I'm not having this conversation with you when you're on the sauce."

"Is it true?"

"There's true, and then there's *true,*" he said.

"You just repeated the same word twice with a slightly different emphasis. That doesn't work on me anymore. But the sex thing still has some mileage. You want to make a suggestive comment or something?"

Mark raised a dark eyebrow at me and leaned back in his chair. "That's the whipped cream talking, isn't it?"

"Probably," I admitted. "Sucks having your bluff called, doesn't it?"

He pushed himself away from me with a disgusted sigh.

"So?" I asked. "Is it true?"

"You need to take her." Joseph Abernathy had appeared from the clear blue ether, leaning in Mark's doorway.

Mark cast a gritty look at his father. "Great idea. Let's just bring a sixteen ounce ribeye to a dog fight while we're at it."

"Aww!" I said, oddly touched. "You think I'm a ribeye?"

"How is she supposed to decide if she doesn't know what being the heir really means. You can't keep her from that world forever." Joseph shrugged away from the doorframe and paced toward the desk.

"Right. How am I supposed to decide if—wait...are you saying I'm a ribeye because I have a lot of marbling?" I plopped myself down in my usual spot on the couch that I had almost agreed to have a litter of Abernathy's puppy on earlier that day.

"I'm not trying to keep her away from that world," Abernathy said. "I'm trying to keep that world away from her."

"Because sixteen ounces is a *huge* steak," I added. "And it would be really easy for me to assume you're speaking proportionally here."

"How long do you think you can do that?" Joseph asked. "The last few decades have cost a king's ransom in blood and treasure, and that with some pretty near misses."

"So are we talking a dry-aged ribeye here? Because now that I think of it, there are some pretty troubling implications there too."

"*You* try protecting this woman sometime." Abernathy gestured toward the couch with an impatient jerk of his chin. "When she's not hopping in the car with murderers, she's offering to sharpen their knives."

"Mock if you will," I said, folding my legs beneath me. "Good cutlery is as much a part of a proper eating experience as the food on the plate."

"Even if you're the entree?" Mark asked.

I slurped down the last gulp of condensed sugary slush at the bottom of my recyclable plastic cup and tried to smile, only to realize that I couldn't feel my face. "What were we talking about?"

Mark and Joseph looked at me, then each other. Something crackled between them like a static tightrope.

"You're coming to the state dinner," Mark announced, his eyes remaining fixed on his father, even as he addressed me.

"State dinner? For what?" I asked.

Mark turned to face me then, perhaps wanting to see how his next words would land. "For the Spring Lambing."

My sugar and caffeine haze evaporated as quickly as it had come. "The Spring Lambing is real?"

Joseph nodded, saving Mark the task of answering.

"This is beyond fucked up. You know that, right?" A throb began to pulse in my temple. I pushed the heel of my palm against it and closed my eyes.

"Go to the dinner," Joseph said. "Then make your judgment."

"What happens at this state dinner, exactly?" I asked.

Joseph looked at Mark, who waved a hand at his father as if to say *proceed.*

"Governing parties from both sides gather to review the terms of the Spring Lambing. When everyone is in agreement, the event begins."

"Governing parties?"

"Select werewolves and vampires of influence," Joseph explained.

A wave of relief passed over me. "Welp, that counts me out, I suppose."

"I'm afraid not," Joseph said.

"As a werewolf heir, you qualify." Mark delivered this revelation with all the enthusiasm of cinderblock.

"Don't sound so thrilled." Offended, I sagged back against the couch.

Mark looked his father. "If I'm taking her, you're coming with me."

"Of course I'll be there for the summit. But I won't be able to make it to the dinner." Joseph's handsome face was an artful rendering of regret. "I'm afraid I have a conflicting engagement."

"Cancel it." Storm clouds passed over Abernathy's face.

"Not possible." Joseph seated himself on the opposite end of the couch.

"I can meet with the council, or I can babysit Hanna." Abernathy pinned his father with an irritated glare. "Which will it be?"

"Excuse me?" I sat forward on the couch. "*Babysit* me?"

"Half the attendees at this dinner would kill you as soon as look at you, and this before you knock them down or and hump them," Abernathy said.

"I did *not* hump anyone. And, for the record, I only knocked over a guy *pretending* to be Vincent Van Gogh. A guy who tried to kill you, in fact. So pretty much, I did you a favor. In advance." I coughed into the silence. "Okay," I admitted. "Perhaps I could use a *little* guidance on these interactions."

"If by *guidance* you mean a mean a straight jacket and a gag, I'm inclined to agree. But it's a moot point." Abernathy ran a hand through his hair. "I can't take you."

"What? No! I *have* to go!"

"Can't," he said. "Too dangerous to take you on my own."

"Come on!" I rose from the couch and approached Abernathy's desk. "You're like *the* acting alpha werewolf. The big boss. The main man. You got this."

"Part of what keeps me and everyone around me safe is knowing my limits." Mark's face had taken on the stony resolution I knew brooked no argument. His mind was made up.

I turned pleading eyes on Joseph. "*Please* come to the dinner."

"Hanna—" he began.

"Please!" I turned my face to him, complete with big, watery pleading eyes.

"As much as I would like to accompany you, I am utterly committed elsewhere," Joseph said, thumbing the perfectly pressed crease in his trousers.

"Right. What's 'er name den?"

I swiveled to find Allan standing in the doorway, arms folded across a paisley shirt loud enough to deafen the blind.

"Whose name?" Joseph asked.

"Oh stuff it, Joe. It's not like I ain't knowed you for eight centuries. Your *commitments* mostwy come wif tits like cantaloupes."

"It's not one of those commitments." Joseph seemed genuinely disappointed at this admission.

"And I'm the bleeding' pope. Not 'at I blame you. These bloody state dinners are duller than a nun's knicker drawer."

A little lightbulb clicked on in my head. "You mean you've been to one?"

"Course I've been to 'em. I'm older 'an fuckin' dirt."

"So *you* can come with us." I clapped my hands together triumphantly.

"Oh no." He held up his small, sensitively shaped hands as if to stop an oncoming truck. "I ain't been to one in decades and I ain't about to start. 'Sides, I just bloody flew here from England. I'm not about to hop a flight to Scotland tomorrow."

"Scotland?" I looked from Mark, to Joseph, then back to Allan. "Who said anything about Scotland?"

"That's where the dinner is, of course," Allan said. "It's our turn to host. Castwe Abernaffy, if I ain't mistaken."

"Let's pretend someone in this room is capable of communicating all the relevant information in an order that makes sense." I turned to Allan. "Go."

Allan cast an exasperated look at Mark and Joseph. "Honestly, it's a good fing you two are so good looking because you're bloody useless. A'right. Once every ten years, 'ere's a Spring Lambing wherein de vampires get free reign for twenty-one days. A'fore de sucking, 'ere's a summit where de royalty from boff sides get to together to go over de rules. We alternate locations every ten years. Wast time, it were at Ahkentaten's pad on account of he's de vampire king. This time, it's at Castwe Abernaffy in Scotland on account of Mark's de king of de werewolves."

Joseph cleared his throat.

"Sorry mate," Allan added. "The *acting* king."

I looked to Mark, who stared at the ceiling like it held far more interesting conversations. "You're the *king*? What the hell? You've never told me this *why*?"

"It wasn't essential for your survival," he said flatly.

"So if my survival is your only motive, what was your hand doing in my pants earlier?"

"Crikey!" Allan said. "'ow come I always miss de good stuff?"

Irritation creased Mark's brow. "Perhaps if you weren't constantly fucking a broke-dick detective—"

"For the last time, I did *not* fuck Morrison! He was passed out on my doorstep and I—"

"Children," Joseph said. "You two can finish this conversation in private. The matter at hand is the state dinner. I, for one, think Hanna should attend."

"I would love to, Joseph. But Mark won't take me unless someone goes with us." I shot Allan my most hopeful look.

"Prowwy for de best love. A right bunch of gits dose vampires. Speciawwy Nero. Bleedin' psychopath he is."

I felt my eyes widen to the size of duck eggs. Mark dropped his face into his palms.

"The *Emperor Nero* is going to be there?"

Allan sent a contrite look in Mark's direction. "Sorry, mate. I forgot 'ow she gets. Yes 'es going to be there. Probably bring 'at creep old witch what's been followin' 'him around for years."

And then I was clasping Allan's smooth hands in mine. "Please come. I promise I'll be good. I won't hump anyone. Not even a little bit. In fact, I won't even talk. I'll be this quiet, gliding presence at your elbow. Silent. Ethereal."

The three men regarded each other. Laughter exploded in triplicate, filling Mark's office like a flash of light.

"I could be ethereal."

Allan was bent at the waist now, slapping his thigh. Joseph had collapsed onto the leather couch. Mark slouched back in his chair, shaking his head.

"You know what? You guys can suck a bag of dicks. I don't want to go to your stupid werewolf party anyway." I turned on my heel and walked toward the door, but was hauled back by Allan's hand on my waistband.

"A'right, a'right, I'll come."

"Really?" I bounced forward and wrapped him in a hug. "Thank you!"

"Ready for lesson number one?" Allan asked, his voice sounding strangely hoarse.

"Absolutely," I said. "Teach me all the things!"

"Let go of me neck, love. Neither vampires nor werewolves is all dat keen on spontaneous physical contact that doesn't involve eatin'."

"Right," I said, realizing that, in my zeal, I had nearly crushed his larynx with my alarmingly bony Shoulder of Death. "Of course. I totally knew that."

Allan blinked at me from behind his chic Gucci frames while rubbing at the red spot on his throat. "Right. What you goin' to wear, then?"

"I hadn't even thought of that!" My stomach became a nervous bird. Whether it was excitement of the prospect of dress shopping or the caffeine from the small battalion of lattes, I couldn't say. "What does one even wear to a cross species gathering?"

"Black tie only," Joseph said. "It's at least one common ground where the dead and damned can comfortably mingle."

I chewed on my lower lip. "The last formal dress I owned was a wedding gown, and its final resting place is the county landfill. Do I have enough time to shop?"

"Shop?" Joseph looked at me like I'd just suggested that I remove his testicles with a rusty spoon shank. "Oh no, my dear girl. You can't show up in something off the rack to an event like this. You'd be eaten alive."

"Metaphorically?" I asked hopefully.

Joseph's enigmatic smile told me way more than I wanted to know.

"Where the hell am I going to get a custom gown on such short notice?"

Joseph and Mark both turned to look at Allan, who had been slowly inching backward toward the door.

"Come on!" Allan threw his hands up in a dramatic diva gesture only he could pull off. "I'm the bloody babysitter, and now the seamstress too? What am I? Fuckin' Cinderewwa? You want I should go smelt some iron to build a jet for us to ride in while I'm at it?"

Joseph rose from the couch and laid a chummy arm across Allan's shoulders. "You know there's no one better."

"Course there isn't! I'm the bleedin' messiah of fabric. But in twelve hours? And wifout an assistant?"

"Don't tell me you're losing your touch, old friend." Joseph gave Allan's arm a squeeze.

"I don't know what's sadder," Allan sighed. "That you're stiww using 'ose crap lines on me, or 'at they stiww bloody work."

"That's the spirit!" Joseph clapped Allan on the back hard enough to make him cough out a mint.

Allan took a few steps back and eyed me like one of the gallery's spectators, thumb and forefinger pinching his dimpled chin. His gaze traveled the length of my neck, past my chest, and snagged on my hips for a moment before sliding down my legs. "Right," he said. "Sleeveless corset bodice, fuww skirt. Satin, not silk."

"Nothing too low cut," was Mark's first and only offering in this conversation.

"And why not?" I asked.

"The guests at the state dinner will either want to eat you, fuck you, or murder you. Some of them will want to do all three, and in an order that wouldn't please you."

"Oh, lighten up," Allan said. "Been at least twen'y years since someone snuffed it at one of 'ese dinners."

"Why am I not wildly comforted by this statistic?" I asked.

Allan laced his arm through mine and urged me toward the door. "Don't worry, love. You're more likely to be killed from boredom dan disemboweling."

Just what I had been hoping to hear.

CHAPTER 13

The gray dawn broke over Mark's face through the private jet's small porthole window. Shadows lingered in some of my favorite places: the underside of his stubbled jaw, the crease where his shapely lips met, the expanse of smooth skin where his silky, dark-chocolate colored hair fell across his forehead. Dark lashes rested against his cheekbones. His broad chest rose and fell beneath his tailored button-up shirt in time with the slow breaths of deep sleep. Considering his impossible beauty as he slept made all that had transpired between us seem like something out of a Surrealist painting. Events that might have occurred in a parallel universe.

Those lips had kissed me. His teeth had been bared at me, and for me. I knew what the body beneath those clothes looked like naked, covered in the sweat of passion. And blood.

I'd been watching him for the better part of an hour, courtesy of seats that faced each other, yet another aspect of this journey I'd have to get used to.

That, and being called *My Lady*. Hearing Mark addressed as *Your Highness* by the flight crew had been one thing. To have them fall at my feet and wash my stiletto boots with their tears was something else entirely.

An heir, they'd said. *Alive. A miracle!*

Me? A miracle? *A mess* seemed far more accurate.

Mark's long fingers began to twitch, peddling in the air. His eyelids fluttered. His shoes scuffled along the jet's deep blue carpet.

My mouth broadened into a smile. *Wolf dreams.*

"My Lady, we'll be touching down in Edinburgh in a half hour." An attendant with a crisp white shirt and navy skirt leaned into view.

"Valerie," I said, glancing at her nametag, "please, call me Hanna."

Panic creased her pretty features. "Oh, Your Highness, I couldn't possibly—"

"You really can, I promise."

Her young, pink cheeks lifted into a smile. "Lady Hanna, can I bring you anything? A hot towel? Coffee? Tea?"

"Oh my gawd. I'd kiww for a cuppa, love." Across the aisle, Allan pushed his glasses up on his head and rubbed at his eyes. "And troof be towd, I'd give you me firstborn for a hot towel."

Valerie straightened and tucked a few stray hairs back into her chignon. "Lord Ede, that won't be necessary."

"Good. Cause I ain't got a firstborn and ain't likely to sire any pups any time soon."

"Back in a moment." Valerie bustled up the aisle with the steadiness of a woman used to remaining steadfastly upright even in the worst of turbulence.

Would that I could do the same.

"Did you get some sleep?" I asked, stretching my legs as best I could while still buckled into my seat.

"Not enough," Allan answered, yawning widely. "How you howdin' up?"

I arched my back and reached for the jet's ceiling releasing a totally unsexy series of pops and cracks. "Not too bad."

"Wiww you look 'ese two?" Allan asked, glancing at Joseph and Mark in their matching reclining satyr sprawls. "Sleep like the dead, they do. And the snoring!"

"I know, right? Joseph too?" I asked.

"I'd rather sleep next to a jet engine turbine," Allan said, shaking his head.

"Mark too!" I said. "When we were coming back from London—"

"What about London?" Mark asked suddenly, completely, startlingly awake.

"Lovely city. Lots of history. Can't wait go back." I beamed my biggest *totally wasn't talking about your snore* smile at him, glad I had washed my face with a travel wipe and reapplied my make-up while he slept. "Hey! We'll be landing soon."

Valerie returned with a tray bearing two steaming cups, setting one in front of me, and the other in front of Allan. Tendrils of life-restoring bergamot-scented steam caressed my nose.

Joseph's hand shot out and seized Valerie' arm. His eyes lazily blinking open, he visually meandered from her hair to her shoes. "Well, good morning," he said.

"Good morning, my lord," Valerie replied in a register slightly huskier than she'd employed for Allan and I.

"Glad I slept through the sunrise," Joseph said, grinning up at her.

"Why is that?" Valerie asked.

"The better to see you with, my dear."

Valerie giggled and made her way back to the front of the plane.

"Was that strictly necessary?" Mark asked his father, irritation plain on his face.

"There's necessary, and then there's *necessary*." Joseph revealed a wide shark-like grin.

At least Mark came by some of his more irritating habits honestly. My ears popped and I sent a prayer of gratitude toward the heavens as the jet began a gradual trajectory toward the earth. Leaning toward the window, I looked down on a patchwork quilt of fields embroidered by seams of dark trees. Squares painted moss, emerald, olive, chartreuse, and pistachio pushed up against each other like paint cards, competing to be selected as the official color of earth's yearly rebirth.

"Home sweet home," Joseph sighed.

Mark glanced out his own window, his thoughts inscrutable as he looked at the land below. "Once upon a time."

❧

CASTLE ABERNATHY GREW FROM THE ROCKS AT THE RIVER'S EDGE like it had erupted from the earth itself. The rough-hewn shapes of the battlements' edges scratched the gray sky beyond gnarled trees, too old and stubborn to yield to the first blush of spring.

If I had expected drafty stone halls and worn Persian rugs, I was sorely mistaken. The castle's interior was as modern as its exterior was antiquated. Expansive wood floors spanned the broad stretches of space. The walls had been insulated, stuccoed, and painted. The ceiling's lofty climes revealed wooden beams and trusses that brought the room's height down to approachable proportions. Tapestry after tapestry was tucked away in the nooks aligning the great hall.

Our luggage sat in the entrance like a pile of building blocks, stacked there by the driver with more pressing concerns than our arrival.

"Everyone grab your gear," Mark ordered. "There should be rooms prepared upstairs."

"Where are all the servants?" Joseph surveyed the area surrounding the twin staircases spiraling into the castle's heart like great arteries.

"*Staff*," Mark corrected. "I only keep as many as needed to maintain basic functionality."

"Bloody 'ell, Mark. If I knew I'd be schlepping me bags about like a porter, I might 'ave left a few fings behind." Allan approached the jumbled stack and dug out his matching Burberry bags with their distinctive horseferry check.

I slung my duffle bag over my shoulder and dragged my grandma's powder blue suitcase out of the pile. It had been manufactured in the days before people understood the necessity of attaching wheels to luggage, and boasted a brass toothed zipper that was as likely to bite a hole in your clothes as it was to hold the suitcase closed. It had begrudgingly let itself be dragged up hostel stairs and down cobblestone sidewalks, and through puddles of asphalt scented rain. Never in the world would I have guessed that one day, it would end up in the foyer of the estate belonging to my centuries old werewolf boss/occasional make-out buddy.

I grunted as I hauled its taciturn bulk. "Did this thing gain weight on the plane?"

Taking this as a cue, Mark relieved me of both my burdens and strode toward the stairs. "This way," he said. In my mind's eye, the ghost of a small, dark haired boy haunted his practiced movements, a reflection of a much younger Mark who might have raced around these halls.

"Usual rooms, 'en?" Allan asked, red-faced and panting at the top of the stairs.

"Should be." Mark, looking annoyingly fresh and well-rested after such a long journey, turned to the right, leading our bedraggled parade down a grand hallway punctuated with tapestries, paintings, and even a suit of armor. He paused when we reached a set of large wooden doors of burnished walnut.

"This one is yours, Hanna."

Joseph stopped short behind us. "You're giving her *this* room?"

"Do you object?" There was more aggression in the question than Mark's stony expression revealed.

"No," Joseph said. "It's just...*interesting*, don't you think?"

"I *think* it will be easy for Hanna to find." Abernathy set my suitcase down by the door, extracting a large, intricately carved key from his pocket.

Something inscrutable hid behind Joseph's smile. "If you say so."

Only when Allan and Joseph were out of earshot did Mark slide the key into the lock and turn it, releasing a brassy click from deep inside the wood. Mark pushed the door open and held it so I could enter first.

My mouth hung open in pure, dazzled shock.

Slick wood floor gave way to carpet thick enough to cushion every echo, submerging the room into a breathless kind of peace. An enormous four-poster canopy bed formed the room's focal point, the lush wood-paneled walls a reflection of the tapestries and priceless masterworks we'd encountered in the hall.

As if drawn by a magnet, I floated over to the bed letting my fingers explore the intricate carvings. A story unfurled itself beneath my fingertips. Mermaids and sailors, faeries and knights, angels, demons, flowers, tree branches, all offering themselves up to my curious touch.

My hands fell to a green satin bedspread and brushed the tassels of an army of bed pillows. "This is lovely," I said.

"You haven't even seen the best part." Mark crossed the room and tugged a gilded rope attached to the wall opposite the bed. Forest green curtains parted, a giant panoramic window.

The landscape unfolded beyond them like a living painting. The carpet of green ended abruptly at insistent rocks. Beyond them, the ocean shifted in endless brushstrokes of green, gray, blue, and white.

Padding across the sumptuous carpet, I joined Abernathy, where side by side, we surveyed the countryside of his birth.

"Thank you," I said.

"For what?" he asked.

"For bringing me here. For giving me this room."

Amusement lifted his lips into a smile. "As if I had a choice."

"You could have said no," I pointed out.

"I did, as I recall." I saw his smile in my peripheral vision.

"Well, yes. But I wouldn't be here if you *really* meant it. You could have made me stay, and you didn't."

"I try to give you what you want, when at all possible."

What I wanted at that particular moment was to have Abernathy naked and sweaty in that giant, sumptuous bed.

Mark cleared his throat in the adorably official manner that usually preceded a serious announcement. "There's something I need to talk to you about."

"Oh, don't worry. I already promised Allan. No jumping. No hugging. No stealing food from other people's plates and/or hiding it in my purse," I said, ticking each forbidden action off my outstretched fingers. "And under no circumstances am I to ask famous artists or writers if they want to make out."

I flatter myself to think the slightly bemused expression on Abernathy's face was fondness. The miraculously wrinkle-free fabric of his button-up shirt tightened over his chest as he took a deep breath. "Perhaps we ought to sit down for this discussion."

Uh-oh.

Together, we surveyed the seating options. A brocaded chaise longue before the SUV-sized fireplace. Two intricately carved but severely straight-backed chairs on either side an end table that probably cost more than my entire college education.

And…the bed.

I lifted an eyebrow at him in a silent challenge.

Abernathy tucked his hands in the pockets of his criminally

well-cut trousers. "I'm perfectly capable of controlling myself in the face of temptation."

That made one of us.

"After you," I invited.

This had less to do with deference and more to do with the rear view of the aforementioned trousers.

We crossed the sumptuous Persian rug with its tangle of forbidden forest colors. Languishing rose petals. Dead leaves. Weathered grapes.

Abernathy managed to seat himself on the waist high mattress without even having to do a cheek-lift. I, pragmatic creature that I am, availed myself of the small wooden set of stairs at the bed's base. Opting for safety separation, I crawled up to the headboard. It would give me a good six feet of separation should Abernathy leap at me.

Or vice versa.

Snagging one of the many throw pillows, I hugged it to my chest and hunched over, elbows resting on my thighs. "So, what's up?"

"While you're here at Castle Abernathy, you're going to experiences some—" he paused, clearly seeking a word that wouldn't freak me the fuck out "—changes."

"Changes," I repeated. "What kind of changes?"

The buttery afternoon light filtering in through the window behind him limned his hair with a corona of gold as he sat there, considering.

"There are places in the world with a will of their own and a long memory. Castle Abernathy is one of those places. For close to a thousand years my ancestors have lived in these halls, and as a result, those halls bear their signature. Their life force, if you will."

"K," I said. "I think I'm following you. But I don't quite get how that would change anything for *me*."

He shifted to face me, angling his knee toward the center of the bed. "Speaking in energetic terms, like attracts like. And, you yourself have, in an unexpressed fashion, the kind of energy Castle Abernathy is attracted to."

"You're saying that the castle itself is attracted to me?"

"Maybe not *you* as much as it the transformative energy inside you. As a result, that energy will express itself in ways you might not be used to."

"Like my leg hair will go crazy, or I'll have sudden urges to hump legs and bay at the moon?"

Though, to be truthful, two out of three of those things already happened on the regular.

"Maybe I'm not explaining this in the right way." Abernathy scratched the darkening stubble above his crisp white collar. "Okay. Let's think of it this way. What's the difference between an acorn and an oak tree?"

"Do we have to do riddles?" I sagged back against the pillows. "I'm having a very *Alice in Wonderland* moment right now."

"I really want you to think about this," he said, fixing me with that dark, panty-dropping gaze.

I blew air through my pursed lips, feeling entirely too exhausted to commit myself to riddles. "Time? And the right conditions."

"Exactly," he said. "The acorn *wants* to become an oak. That is its purpose. It's a compact container for an entire life that wants to come into being. The thing that makes you an heir is the same."

"You're saying this...this thing that makes me an heir *wants* to me to change?"

"I'm saying that every single cell in your body is like that acorn. Now, what would happen if you dropped an acorn in a field that had nourished a whole forest of oaks?"

"As cute as this little enigmatic quiz is, I'm jet-lagged and in massive need of a nap. How about you just tell me what's going to happen?"

Abernathy stood, walking toward the wide picture windows. "Whatever powers you've been beginning to develop while you're around me will be amplified."

"Like it was when Allan's blood was in my system?" After my post-Wilde transfusion, not only was I capable of tossing humans around like so much meat confetti, I had pretty much gone flying at Abernathy crotch-first about every other nanosecond.

"Worse," he said.

Acidic panic spread in my stomach. *Worse* was not a word I loved in any context. "Worse how?" I asked, my mouth metallic from adrenaline.

"This time it's not a foreign body influencing you. It's the you that you would be if you chose to complete your transformation. All your hopes, all your dreams, all your *desires*. Translated to their purest forms and fed by infinite power with which to acquire them."

"Everything I want, *and* the power to obtain it? But that would make me a...a monster."

"Welcome to my world." Mark gave me a small, sad smile. "Which brings me back to why I brought this up in the first place."

"And that would be?" I picked at the silky tassel on the corner of one of the pillows.

Abernathy caught me with the full force of that whiskey in the sunlight gaze. "You might want to work on not thinking so loud."

"*Thinking* so loud?" Talking, I could understand. I wandered about with a filter like swiss cheese, my mouth a direct conduit to the freakshow circus of my brain. But my *thoughts*? If those were broadcast wholesale, I'd be in deep sheep dip.

"Sheep dip?" Abernathy asked, a wry grin twisting his lips.

"Wait," I said. "You could hear that?" Just how much of what went on my head did he have access to?

"All of it, at the moment," he answered.

I clapped my hands over my ears, as if that could somehow stop information from leaking out of my head.

"Normally, it's like a radio station I can tune out," Abernathy explained. "And I do. But here, it's like a direct feed."

Well, fuck. How many times had I thought about riding him like a birthday pony since we'd arrived?

"About twelve. I especially like the scenario involving the grand piano and an ice bucket."

"Okay, I officially don't like this."

"Listen," he said. "It's not a completely constant thing. And I'm going to do my best *not* to listen. Just try to help me out, if you can." He pushed himself off the end of the bed and moved toward the door. "I'm going to go check on everyone. Try to get some rest."

Rest.

Right. Like *that* was going to happen.

I sat in stunned silence, ideas buzzing around my head like blue-bottle flies. What would I, Hannalore Harvey, be like as a werewolf?

I thought of the pure, thrilling ecstasy I'd felt every time I'd given in to bone-deep longing for Abernathy. I thought of the hungers, both physical and emotional. The colors, the sounds, the savage poetry and beauty of the world experienced through Abernathy's painfully acute senses. I thought of the terrible sounds his body made when he'd transformed right in front of me in the gallery. The destruction he'd wrought both because of me and on my behalf.

Could I do that?

Could I *be* that?

Too twitchy to sleep, I found my way into the bathroom, which, oddly enough, was larger than my entire studio apartment. Wall to wall marble, mirrors, and a shower boasting approximately 87 heads and jets. When I figured out how to adjust it to a setting that neither fire-hosed my eyeballs nor my nether-regions (though I made note of the latter for future reference), I stripped, scrubbed, wrapped myself in a fluffy towel, and padded back into my room.

Not wanting to slip back into my wilted travel clothes, I wrestled my surly vintage suitcase over to an equally vintage trunk. There, I popped open the brass catch that never failed to snap my knuckle and opened the lid.

There, looking up from the candy-colored mound of panties, was a face.

Not just a face. A head.

A woman's this time. Heavy lids sank halfway down filmy brown eyes. Straight, dark brows slanted across the pale forehead beneath a wild corona of brown curls. It was the lips beneath a long, thin nose that gave her away. Angular and precise like they'd been carved from living porcelain by a surgeon's scalpel.

I didn't need Joseph to identify this face. I'd seen it in countless 19th century paintings and grayscale film stills. From the paintings of Alfred Stevens, leading man in my master's thesis about dangerous women in art.

Sarah Bernhardt.

Blood had leaked from her severed neck and stained several pairs of my white socks a bright crimson. Only at the edges had the color begun to darken to brown.

My heart felt heavy in my chest. My face numb and my lips tingling.

How was this my life?

On wobbly legs, I walked over to the nightstand next to my bed and picked up my phone. Not wanting the mind-reading Mark to be involved and not knowing where Allan or Joseph were quartered, I tapped a quick and exceedingly strange text.

There's a head in my suitcase.

Mere moments later Joseph and Allan came tumbling through the door like dominoes.

Allan, who had traded his customary vest and button-up shirt for a smoking jacket, silk pajama bottoms, and gold monogrammed slippers, gazed down into the suitcase, his eyes puffy with sleep. "Weww, you got to 'and it to them vampires. She looks bloody fabulous."

And she did. Even severed from the rest of her body, her iconic beauty remained as pure and timeless as a marble monument. She held us all in her thrall, even dead.

Re-dead? Un-undead?

Fucking vampires.

"What I don't understand is how she got here," I said. "I mean, I feel like TSA would have been at least mildly concerned should they have discovered this in my luggage."

"When have you not had it with you?" Joseph asked, bending to take a closer look at the case's contents.

"We stopped at the pub in Edinburgh for lunch," I said. "Also I did take a quick shower to rinse off the travel funk."

"This happened in the last half hour," Joseph said, his voice grave.

"And 'ow do you figure?" Allan's tone held as much wonder as genuine curiosity.

Joseph plucked something out of the suitcase and tossed it to Allan, who received it with a mix of concentration and disgust.

"The blood has only just started to dry around the edges." Joseph carefully poked through the contents of my suitcase and I felt a rush of relief that I had opted not to bring my magic rabbit at the last second.

"And when did you turn into Perry fuckin' Mason?" Allan held up a black and white scrap of fabric and inspected it against the waning light from the windows overlooking the moors. The sun had crawled toward the green hills, leaving splashes of purple and orange to battle for the expanse of sky. "Wai' a tick." He squinted at the fabric. "Are those giraffes?"

My heart sank in my chest with the inexplicable sadness that only the loss of a treasured everyday object could bring. "Not my favorite panties!"

"'ere's de head of a vampire in your suitcase, and you're fussin' over a pair of knickers?" Allan asked, a perfectly groomed eyebrow raised in curiosity.

"I *loved* that pair," I explained. "They were like a hug I could wear under my pants."

Using a slim finger, Allan sling-shotted the soiled panties back toward the suitcase. "I'm right sorry 'bout your knickers, love. But I'm afraid we've got oursewves a bigger problem."

"Like the fact that those have been discontinued and I will never be able to find another pair?" I asked.

"Like the fact that someone put this head in your suitcase sometime after we arrived at the castle."

Ice water seeped down my spine at the thought of someone stealing into my room while I showered. Head in hand, listening to me warbling Patsy Cline through the door amongst that spattering water.

"I'll ask Mark 'ooh's on the property," Allan said.

"Speaking of which." Joseph clipped my suitcase closed. "I'd better take care of the luggage before any other guests arrive."

"Bring back what you can," I called after him.

"I'll go with 'im," Allan offered, shuffling toward the door. "I know a fing or two about getting blood out of fabric."

When they were gone, I reluctantly slid back into my used tank top and panties, and flopped facedown on the gigantic boat of a bed.

Under the watchful gaze of a thousand unblinking, lacquered eyes, I surrendered to a black-brained sleep.

I AWOKE IN PURE, MORTAL TERROR.

Unable to breathe. Unable to move. Unable to scream.

It was neither day, nor night, but some hellish unidentifiable interval in between. Not light enough to see, not dark enough not to.

Something cold brushed the soles of my feet and began a slow, sinister journey upward. Gripping my ankles, stalking slowly up my calves, slithering up the insides of my thighs and over my hips.

Mute, suffocating, panicking, I couldn't so much as twitch as it licked its way up my stomach and settled itself on my chest. Faceless, formless, ancient.

Looking at me.

I felt its regard on my face like the tingling of a numb limb, knowing instinctively when it moved to my hair, my eyes, my mouth.

My throat.

A touch as light as the tip of a feather began at the indentation at the base of my throat and slowly slid upward, ending beneath my chin. There, it grew to the sort of gentle pressure a lover might apply to turn your mouth to theirs.

The chill sank downward, circling my neck like a scarf.

Then, tightening.

Beneath that inexplicable, deadening grip, my heart beat hard enough for me to feel it against my ribs, my oxygen-starved brain beginning to shrink my vision to a single darkening point.

Hot tears leaked from the corners of my eyes and ran down my temples. Pooling in my ears.

The scream I couldn't release vocally tore loose within my mind. I imagined it echoing off the rough stone walls like a singular, violent choral note as I sank deeper into the circling black.

Just as I began to go under, the doors to my room flew wide, and all at once, I was free.

The pressure vanished and I felt the strange hot surge of blood rushing into my head. I lay tangled in the sweat-soaked sheets, the canopy of the four-poster bed with its embroidered stars exactly as it had been when I'd fallen asleep.

Abernathy rushed in, wild-eyed and wild haired.

"Hanna?" he said, rushing over to the bed. "What happened? Are you all right?"

Clearly, my mental gymnastics had roused him from an equally deep sleep.

I sat up, panting as I clutched the silky sheets to my chest, trying to find words for what I had just experienced. "I don't know," I said. "I woke up, and this, this...thing was on top of me."

"What did it look like?" Abernathy seated himself on the edge of the bed next to me, the depression in the mattress rolling me slightly toward him.

"It didn't look like anything," I said. "It didn't have a face, or a...a body."

Even in the half-light, I could see Abernathy's face take on a too-familiar skeptical expression. "It didn't have a body?"

"No. But it was on top of me and it was crushing me and I couldn't breathe."

"Sleep paralysis," Abernathy said, relief lightening his expression. "It's where your brain wakes up before your body—"

"I know what sleep paralysis is," I broke in. "That's not what this was."

"Then what was it?" Abernathy folded his arms across his chest. The movement released a warm current of air that smelled like his warm, sleepy skin. I knew the exact texture of the well-worn fabric, what it would feel like if I pressed my cheek to his chest.

I took a deep breath, steadying myself for what I knew would make me sound utterly crazy. "It was a ghost."

CHAPTER 14

"A ghost?" Mark repeated this word with all the cynicism I had expected, adding a dose of disbelief for good measure.

"A ghost." I sat up straighter in bed, trying to appear as credible as one can be when pants-less and braless and wrapped in four trillion thread count Egyptian cotton sheets.

He shook his head. "No such thing."

"Are you saying there are werewolves and vampires and Nereids and unicorns, but there are no ghosts?" I ran a frustrated hand through the tangled red rat's nest of my hair.

"There might be ghosts," he said. "But there are no ghosts in Castle Abernathy."

"How can you be so sure?"

Abernathy shrugged. "Because in all the years I've lived here, I've never seen one."

I made a rude sound with my mouth. "Um, I hate to be the one to inform you, but by definition, *not* being seen is kind of one of the chief characteristics of ghosts as a rule. They don't show themselves to just anyone."

"But you just said that you didn't see anything either." I could literally feel him arching an eyebrow at me.

"I didn't see it, no. I felt it." I brought a hand to my chest in the precise spot where the pressure had been at its worst as my voice broke. The panic rushed back full force, and to my great surprise and horror, I began to cry.

Once the dam broke, I was helpless to stop it. Boundless and bottomless, the grief-quake rolled through me, dragging those horrible, dramatic, double-pumped inhales for every watery exhale. I cried for every single thing I had covered with casual jokes and wisecracks.

"S-something was in here with me," I insisted, wiping my salty face with a handful of sheet.

"All right." Abernathy scooted close to me on the bed, placing a warm hand between my shoulders and moving it up and down my knobby spine. "It's all right."

"N-nothing is all right!" I sobbed, the tears cartoon-squirting sideways from my eyes. "Vampires invading my ap-partment, someone sneaking a gross decapitated head in my luggage, and now we're in Scotland and there's a ghost who wants me d-dead!"

Abernathy cleared his throat, a clear barometer of his discomfort with my unexpected hysterics. "It's not like plenty of other beings don't want you dead, Hanna. There's no reason to get so upset over this one."

Now I wasn't just sobbing, I was wailing. Howling my grief at a decibel local banshees would likely find objectionable.

"What I meant to say is, maybe the ghost doesn't want you dead," Mark said with such forced, un-Abernathylike optimism that a smile almost broke through my anguish. "Maybe it just wants to communicate with you."

"By s-suffocating me?" I hiccoughed and a small, clear bubble of snot blew out of my right nostril. This only made me cry even harder, which, honestly, I didn't even know was possible at this point.

"Come here." Abernathy found my hand beneath the sweaty, tangled sheets and gave it a tug. "I know what you need."

"If you're t-talking about your p-penis—" another gasping double inhale "—I'm going to b-be very upset."

"It's not my penis," Abernathy promised. "But if it would help…"

I snorted, and instantly had to sniff back a hard-on shriveling sinus-load of snot.

Wearing only my tank top and panties, I allowed Mark to lead me toward the bathroom. He snapped on the light, the chandelier above rinsing every polished surface in mellow gold.

Catching a glimpse of myself in the mirror, I crossed my arms over my wilted tank top and tried to angle my backside away from all reflective surfaces.

The copper handles squeaked under Mark's grip, sending water sloshing into the Jacuzzi-sized tub that, just like the bed, had its own set of marble stairs. Testing the temperature with one hand, he leaned in to stop the drain.

I looked at Mark, then at the tub, then at my nearly nude carcass.

"As kind as it is of you to want to help," I said, "I really think I can handle this bathing thing all by myself."

Wordlessly, he crossed to the ornate gilded vanity and pulled out one of the drawers, returning with a silken pouch. Tugging the drawstring, he upended it, releasing a waterfall of powder into the tub.

"Arsenic?" I asked even as the luscious scent of lavender perfumed the air.

"Get in," Abernathy ordered. He leaned backward, his hips making contact with the giant vanity as his eyes darkened from amber to toffee (but like, the good kind of toffee. Where they let the sugar brown before adding the butter and cream).

"After you." I caught the flash of my own nervous smile in the glass of the separate shower door.

Mark reached down to unbuckle his pants, calling my bluff.

"Kidding!" I said. "Totally kidding."

"You're already thinking about me naked." His grin bordered on predatory. Which made sense, given that he was a werewolf and all. "What's the harm?"

That's totally unfair," I said. "Because even if I hadn't been thinking about you naked, you saying that I was thinking about you naked would make me think about you naked."

Abernathy rolled his eyes, a move I would swear under oath he hadn't even known about until I came into his employ. "Just get in the tub, Hanna."

I sighed, rubbing a foot against the opposite calf by way of ignoring a much deeper itch. "Can you at least turn around?"

"You do remember that I've seen everything you have?" Mark's mouth tilted upward in a smirk.

"I remember," I said. "But that doesn't necessarily mean I want you to see it now. Many poor food decisions have been made since London."

Obediently, Abernathy turned his broad back to me. I quickly piled my messy red mane into a sloppy bun, pulled my sagging tank top over my head, and stepped out of my panties. The plush bathmat tickled my ankles as I lifted one foot into the tub, then the other. Fragrant water lapped at my calves, then my thighs as I sank into it. Thankfully, the salts Mark had added to it turned the water the exact shade and opaqueness of 2% milk.

"Decent," I announced, hugging my knees.

"Debatable," Mark said, reaching into the beribboned basket on the counter and selecting a sea sponge. Slowly, purposefully, he crossed the room and perched on the tub's edge, rolling up the sleeves of his shirt—yes, Virginia, there is a Santa Claus—before dunking the sponge into the bathwater. After unwrapping a cake of Fiori d'Italia soap, he scuffed it over the sponge's porous surface before bringing it to my exposed back.

Working in slow circles, he gently scrubbed, pausing only to squeeze warm water over the areas he'd just washed. A fresh surge of goosebumps followed every pleasantly scratchy stroke. Muscles that had been tight since the moment of my birth began to go buttery and loose.

"Can I ask you something?" Chin on my knees, arms wrapped around my shins, I felt as calm and sleepy as a cat. Not one of my cats, you understand, with their multitude of emotional challenges, but a well-adjusted cat. If there is such a thing.

"You always do."

"Why did Joseph say that thing about you giving me this room?"

The sponge paused directly between my shoulder blades.

"My father says all kinds of things of dubious reference." In this room with all its hard surfaces, Mark's voice had the resonance of priest in a cathedral.

"True," I allowed. "But I was looking at your face when he said it and you got that look that you usually get when you're hiding something."

"Look?" The sponge resumed its leisurely passage down my spine. "I don't have a look."

"You *so* have a look." I stretched my legs out in front of me, toes splayed against silky marble to allow him better access to the aching muscles of my lower back.

"What kind of look?" he asked, sounding somewhat peeved.

"It's a cross between *I haven't pooped in weeks* and *something just touched my scrotum.*"

"Your descriptive prowess is, as ever, astounding."

"Thank you," I said, not entirely sure he'd meant it as a compliment.

"Did you know that soap was originally made from lye?"

"That's the other thing." I glanced at him over my shoulder. "You are absolutely abysmal at trying to change the subject. You're trying to make me forget that I had a question."

"Nonsense." The sponge slid from my lower back around my hip until it met my stomach. "I have more effective ways of accomplishing that."

I took the sponge from him and set it on the edge of the tub. "I had a question."

"What else is new?" Abernathy sat back against the marble backsplash.

Tired of the verbal ping pong, I elected to go straight to the biscuit. "Whose room is this?"

Mark's face took on the grayish cast and impenetrability of the stone composing the cast walls.

"When we arrived," I continued, "Joseph said, 'You're giving her *this* room?' What did he mean? Whose was it?"

Mark picked up the sponge and resumed his scrubbing. "No one of particular significance."

I heaved a disgusted sigh. "And here we'd made so much progress. It's been a while since you stonewalled me." The smooth, cool moonstone of an idea crystalized in my mind.

If Abernathy could hear my thoughts…

In the silence, I reached out through the cool, lavender-scented air and found nothing but shifting gray fog behind his eyes.

"Don't," he said aloud.

"Don't what?" I blinked at him, all lashes and innocence.

"You're about as psychically sneaky as you are in every other aspect of your life," Mark said.

I sought a way to communicate my frustration and quickly discovered that *indignant* is hard to telegraph when you're naked. "What's that supposed to mean?"

"Elephants stampede through the Serengeti with more subtlety than you just attempted to read my mind." Mark reloaded the sponge with soap and concentrated on my neck and shoulders. My trapezius muscles were roughly the texture of the marble from a lifetime of hunching.

"You're doing the thing again," I said.

"Which thing would that be?" The sponge crawled over my shoulder and tracked a path along my collar bone.

With great dexterity and considerable will, I managed to rotate myself around to face him while keeping my limbs covered with milky bathwater. "Whose room was this?"

The muscle in his jaw flexed, a sure sign his teeth were clenched. Whatever words, whatever facts and memories lay behind his lips, they would stay there. "A story for another time."

"What other time?" I asked.

"A time that's not this one," he said infuriatingly.

My irritation eased slightly when the sponge slid down between my breasts, making a lazy circle over my stomach before riding the ridge of my hip bone. Or the general area where my hip bone would be had I not a passionate devotion to triple crème brie.

"I did have...one other question." I sank backward as Abernathy dragged the sponge up my inner thigh.

"Yes?" Mark's voice had dropped into that smoky French roast register I loved best.

"This mating thing...when does it become official?"

The sponge made a leisurely voyage down my calf. "Official?"

"Yeah. What *exactly* has to happen before you're officially mated?"

Abernathy raised an eyebrow at me. "I believe we've discussed this before."

"You said that sex is what mates you for life, yes. What I'm wondering is at what *point* during the sex?"

"What *point*?" At that particular moment, Abernathy looked

like he would be happily and willingly walked out in front of a speeding 18-wheeler if it meant he didn't have to finish this conversation.

"Yeah," I said. "Is it like an upon entry situation? Like the second you slide it in, *pow*! You're mated?"

Abernathy's mouth opened. Closed. Opened again.

For a man who had nailed as much tail in the course of four centuries, he had a prudish streak a mile wide when it came to the nitty-gritty of sex mechanics.

"*Or*," I continued, "are we talking about the actual depositing of baby batter?"

"Baby batter?"

"You know," I said. "Man chowder. Nut butter. Snake spray. Oyster droppings. Gentleman's relish."

Now, Abernathy looked like he didn't want to leave the room, he wanted to leave his own body. Like if his brain could sprout little legs, open his skull like a soup can, and jog away, it absolutely would. With his soul right on its, small, sticky heels.

He cleared his throat, setting the sponge aside. "From what I understand, it is both the willing surrender of both bodies to each other, followed by the exchange of—" he paused, presumably searching for terms as dissimilar as possible to the ones I supplied "— biological matter that seals the bond."

"Any biological matter at all?" I asked. "Or does it have to be a certain quantity?"

"I'm not certain I understand what you're asking," he said, sounding for all the world like a man who wasn't sure he wanted to.

"What I mean is, if it's just the consensual entry *and* the biological matter, then technically you could be mated even if it's just the tip. You do know that pre-ejaculate matter can contain active sperm? Unless it's different for werewolves."

A wave of burgundy crawled up over Abernathy's collar and climbed his neck like the mercury in a thermometer. His ears were roughly the color of a beet. "To my knowledge, there is no difference with regard to that area."

"Really?" I asked. "Not even when you're in wolf form? Is it one of those kinds of *Into the Woods* situations where everything is the same, but …you know…furry? Oh! What about when both mates are in wolf form? Do they have wolf sex? Is that a thing?"

"I really don't see how this is relevant to anything—"

Water lapped at the sides of the tub as I repositioned myself to look Abernathy directly in the eye. "Because if I'm trying to decide if I want to be werewolf instead of human, I really need to understand the mechanics."

He met my gaze, his eyes full of an emotion I couldn't begin to name. "Is *that* the deciding factor, Hanna?"

My name rolled through his mouth like a late summer breeze. Hot, longing and full of nostalgia. I blame that more than anything else for the cascade of thoughts that spilled through my head before I could stop them.

The deciding factor is whether I'm still just an assignment. Whether protecting me is the only reason you'd be willing to mate with me.

The deciding factor is whether or not you love me.

Abernathy abruptly stood, turning his back to me as he wiped his hands on the towel slung over an antique quilt stand near the tub.

My bath water turned to ice. "Where are you going?"

"I need to check on things," he said, retrieving the antique watch he'd left of the gleaming countertop.

"This exact second?" My heart fell like a lead weight. Falling, falling through endless, indefinable space.

"Yes." He stalked into my bedroom without another word.

I grabbed a plush towel from the gilded hooks on the back of the door and hastily wrapped it around my naked body as I chased after him. "Now wait just a goddamn minute—"

But by the time I got to my room, he was already gone.

Goddamn wolfy fast-moving bastard.

I stood there, sad and dripping, wishing with a fervency that made me queasy that I could call my thoughts back.

Perhaps it had been the bathtub. The memory of how easily and effusively Morrison had shared his thoughts. His feelings.

Allan came bustling in through door Mark had left swung wide open. He paused, taking in the same towel I had been wearing when he showed up earlier. "You did pack clothes, di'int ya, love?"

"Yes," I said. "Unfortunately, they were all in the suit case now contaminated with decapitated vampire cooties."

Allan breezed over to the large, ornately carved armoire, turning the brass handle and peering in. "'ere we are," he said, walking back to me with a fluttering scrap of sea foam green fabric that turned out to be a silky robe.

I eyed it suspiciously. "What are the odds that this belonged to a woman who died tragically and whose restless, vengeful spirit will now torment me for stealing her clothes?"

"You've got to stop readin' them gothic romance novels, love. Had this stocked as soon as I knew you'd be comin'." Allan shucked the robe from its hanger and held it up while I slid into it, dropping my towel once I had the cool fabric fastened against me.

"Valid question," I said. "Given the afternoon I had."

Allan took me by the hand and led me to the brocaded chaise lounge by the crackling fireplace, where he seated himself across from me in its twin. There, I told him everything that had happened since he and Joseph had left with my vampire head suitcase in tow. Beginning with my ghost-interrupted nap and ending with my disastrous bath thoughts.

"Cor blimey, love. We've got to do somefink' bout that brain of yours before the state dinner. You're like to start a war, finkin' that loud."

"How?" It was both a question and a lament.

"Hanna, my love, you 'ave to protect your mind like a fortress."

I re-crossed my legs and smoothed the fire-warmed silk over my knees. "And how would I do that?"

"The fing about a fortress is, it's designed to keep people out," Allan said. "To keep protected what's inside it."

"That I understand." A shiver surged through me as I took a sudden chill from the air around us. Fine hairs rose from my skin, white against the gray stone. I pushed my toes across the ornate rug and angled them at the fire-warmed stone.

"Right. At de moment you're not a fortress, you're fully stocked larder with an open pantry door."

I nodded, appreciating his willingness to work in food metaphors. "I don't know how."

"It starts wif de intention. You can't keep le'in people take from you. Especially Mark."

"But Mark doesn't—"

"Oh yes he does." Reflected flames danced across the surface of Allan's glasses as he leaned closer to me. "You fink cause he's de king of de werewolves and a four hundred-year owd pain in de ass to boot that he's above takin' what he wants?"

"No, it's just,—"

"'ere's what," Allan said. "Next time he reaches into your mind, you're gonna fink the word giraffe."

"Giraffe?" I asked, blinking at him.

"Yes, love. Next time you sense him reachin' into your foughts, you're going'ta go on de offense. You fink the word *giraffe* as loud as you can."

"I don't know if I can," I said, remembering the overwhelming, all-consuming, world altering effect that Abernathy's presence always seemed to have on me.

"You can," Allan urged. " And you will. Believe me, I've known Mark since he were a pup. You need to give 'im firm boundaries."

The dreaded word. "This would probably be a good time to tell you." I exhaled. "I kind of have boundary issues."

Allan erupted into a gale of spontaneous laughter. "No, love," he said, catching his breath. "You have to have boundaries a'fore you can have boundary issues."

"You sound like my therapist." I collapsed forward, elbows on knees.

"Only I'm an 'ell of a lot cheaper and probably better lookin'." He dusted the shoulders of his smoking jacket and tucked his ascot further beneath the satin lapels.

"Also you've never slept with my ex-husband." A flame of irritation licked at my brain. "Which only recommends you."

"Weww we boff know what a right git he was," Allan said.

"You know him?" I asked.

"Don't need to." Allan favored me with an endearingly rabbitty grin. "But he let you go, di'in't he?"

Warmth twice as intense as the fireplace before us flared in my heart. "Kind of you to say," I said.

"Trust me, love. Someone needs to tell you de truth, and Mark don't seem to be de man for de job."

"Thank you," I said. "For pretty much everything."

Allan reached out and captured my hand, giving my fingers a reassuring squeeze.

"Don't mention it, love," he said, rising. "Now, I be'er make sure Joseph ain't chasin' around the scullery maids. Dinner's in 'alf an hour. Get yourself dressed and come down."

"Will do." I gave him a little salute, making a note to text Joseph to see if any of my clothes survived ASAP.

Then his voice was bouncing off the walls of my mind, more voluminous than a cathedral choir. *And remember what I said.*

GIRAFFE! I mentally belted.

Allan clapped his hands to his temples and rocked back against the doorframe. "Good God, girl! Blow out me fuckin' eardrums out why don't you?"

"I'm so, so sorry!" I said, getting up from the chaise. "I didn't know you could hear me too."

Allan dropped his hands from his ears. "No need to apologize." His mouth quirked up in an amused grin. "Mark's in for a bit of a surprise I'd say. I pity him when you figure out just how strong you are." He winked at me behind his black-framed glasses and closed the door behind him.

And what did he mean by that? In this world of creatures with unlimited power and sophistication, I felt like a stick figure. A cipher. A non-entity. What kind of strength could I possible bring to the party?

A brisk knock at the door almost had me running up the wall. I opened it a crack to find Joseph standing there, clutching my suitcase. "Looks like I got here just in time," he said.

Were I not already acquainted with his son's habits, I might have missed the quick flick of his dark eyes down to the robe and back to my face.

"Was any of it salvageable?" I asked, reaching for the suitcase.

"Most of it, actually. The suitcase itself wasn't stained, though I'm afraid your *nightgown* had to be sacrificed." At this, Joseph's handsome face wrinkled with mirth.

"Don't judge," I said. "I'm sure plenty of women have nightgowns with mice and cheese on them."

"I'm sure," he said, clearly humoring me.

"My pleasure. You're coming to dinner, I assume?"

"Wouldn't miss it." It may have been the truest thing I'd said all day. Not much could come between me and meals. Vampire heads and vengeful spirits included.

"See you then." His face was a mirror reflection of Mark's—everything opposite of the man I knew. Lines carved from smiling rather than worry. A brow lifted in levity rather than anchored by suspicion. Lips shaped by humor instead of solemnity.

I flung my suitcase on the bed and unclipped it, receiving a knuckle thwack for my efforts. I peeled the lid back slowly, noting that my clothes had been refolded. The fresh scent of fabric softener and the faint aroma of bleach wafted upward. Had it really been long enough for Joseph to launder my clothes?

The strangeness of this day, of the events within it, had been enough to relieve me of any kind of ability to accurately gauge time.

Pawing through the contents, I was delighted to find my little black cocktail dress thankfully free of wrinkles. And blood. I pulled it out of the suitcase along with a matching pair of black panties, bra and my make-up bag. The clothes were still warm as I hugged them to my chest on the way to the bathroom.

I wriggled into the underwear and slid the dress over my head, inspecting my reflection in the full-length mirror flanking the tub. The ornate, gilded frame surrounded my image like something that belonged on the blood-red walls of the Louvre's Baroque collection. Not bad, I decided. If a little pale.

What else was new?

But this hair, though. I'd made the grave mistake of sleeping on it wet from the shower and throwing it in a messy bun for my post-ghost bath. Now it fell from my head like shoulder-blade length manic fusilli. No choice but to curl the everloving shit out of it.

Seating myself at the vanity, I decided that sex kitten make-up was definitely called for. Black liquid eyeliner, blood red lips.

While I painted, I replayed every word of the verbal and mental conversation I'd had with Abernathy, right up to the point where he quit the room so fast it had been like his tail was on fire.

Can you blame him? Asked the little voice in my head.

Castle Abernathy, it seemed, made it so even *I* could hear my own thoughts more clearly. Which, to be honest, is about the shittiest gift I could possibly imagine. Before, I could bop them away like so many balloons. Now, it was like having a conversation with an actual person.

Me.

"For what?" I said aloud, settling in the damask upholstered chair in front of the luminous vanity.

For running. You thought the L-word.

A tightness gathered in my chest, at once familiar and unwelcome. I'd felt it before.

When Morrison told you he loved you.

"I don't want to talk about this," I said, trying to concentrate as I slapped my own face with a blending sponge

What do you suppose he's doing now? Mental Hanna (has there ever been a more appropriate descriptor?) asked. *While you're gone?*

"I don't care." The contents of my makeup case spilled across the vanity as I upended the bag. I caught the eyeliner as it rolled toward the counter's edge and set it upright. Seizing the big fluffy brush, I began to dust mineral powder across my face.

I'll bet he's fucking her again.

"Who?"

Tinkerbell. Goddamn, she was dumb, wasn't she? How much you wanna bet she moans like a porn star?

"Nothing," I answered. "I don't care. What he does is his business. He can fuck whoever he wants."

Then why are you so upset?

"I'm not upset!" Dragging the fluffy brush across a rosy disk of blush, I raised it to my cheekbone. Problem was, I didn't know where it should land. My cheeks were already pink. *Fuck.*

Right, Mental Hanna taunted. *Not upset.*

Slightly Less Mental Hanna: "Fuck you. I already told you I don't want to talk about this."

Then stop talking.

I moved onto eyeshadow, creating an artificial sunset over

my lashes. Matte black eyeliner streaked across the sky, followed by a heavy application of mascara. Tracing the outline of my lips with blood red lip liner, I slicked an equally viscerally-hued matte lipstick across them. Satisfied with the face looking back at me in the mirror, I flipped my head upside down and began to brush out the waves.

How come Morrison hasn't called, do you think?

"I don't think." Blood rushed to my face as I massaged my scalp as I'd once watched on a YouTube Sex Kitten Hair video tutorial.

Through the curtain of my hair, my glance strayed to my purse, still on the antique sideboard where I dropped it in my exhaustion. Flipping my hair over my head, I floated over to it and extracted my phone. One missed call, one voicemail, and two text messages. All from Steve, who had graciously volunteered to watch my cats on short notice.

Nothing from Morrison.

Feel that? Your heart just sank.

"Whose side are you on, anyway?" I asked.

I could ask you the same thing.

I ignored this and instead clicked on Steve's voicemail. Silence, then the sound of background noise. Had Steve butt-dialed me on accident? Then, a whispered voice. "Come on buddy, say hi."

A low, worried meow sounded in my ear, and my face split in a grin.

Steve's voice came on the line. "Gil just wanted to say hi." He paused. "What was that? Oh, right. He also says, bring him back a haggis. He's always been curious." And with this, he disconnected.

I shook my head. I talked to my cats too. But they actually *answered* Steve.

They answer you too. And you could hear them if you were a—

"No thanks," I said, turning my thoughts to Steve.

Steve, my brother. Steve who still believed he was an orphan. Did Abernathy expect to keep this secret indefinitely? How was that even possible? True, our father was dead, along with both sets of grandparents. But I had become accustomed to being the sole genetic link of a dying line, and now I knew I had a brother. Another human being in the world shared my blood, my bones, my DNA, and I had to pretend he was just a friend?

Irritation at Abernathy rose anew. Who the fuck did he think he was, anyway?

The man you're in love with? Well, one of them, anyway.

"I'm about tired of you." I slammed my phone back down on the lacquered wood.

And what are you going to do about it?

The bottle of Balvenie forty year-old scotch beckoned from the antique sideboard like a siren cast in amber glass against the lead-paned windows. The dark shapes of the moors around Castle Abernathy rose within the liquid like a miniature sunset captured in seductive sepia hues. The glass tumbler tipped rim side up on the creamy linen looked like a personalized invitation.

You don't even like scotch.

"I could. I've never tried it."

Are you really going to open a thousand-dollar bottle of liquor just to shut me up?

The cork squeaked as I extracted it from its glass embrace. I lifted the tumbler and poured it full. The glass floated up to my lips as if conjured by some spell. The smoky, honeyed liquid burned a path down my throat, building an artificial fire in my belly. I closed my eyes and waited.

Something tugged the muscles of my belly and hips toward the earth as warmth suffused toward my fingertips.

This won't solve anyth...

The words stretched into fine threads and dissolved like spun sugar on my tongue. I drained the rest of the glass. Silk, not blood, flowed through my veins. I felt reasonably certain not even Hemingway could draw away the power throbbing from my heart.

Blessed silence followed the taste of burnt wood on the back of my tongue. I swallowed not just the scotch, but every thought that lived in the shadows rendered on my palate by smoke and sin.

"Okay," I said to no one. "Let's do this."

CHAPTER 15

"For God's sake, suck it in!" Allan yanked at the silky black strings of the corset currently doing it's best to perform an impromptu dissection of my liver. It was the most intimate contact I'd had in two days, during which everyone but I had somewhere to be and something to do in preparation for the state dinner. Not that I was complaining. The solitary stretch of time had somewhat salved the emotional angst proceeding it.

"I *am* sucking it in!" I gripped the bedpost with both hands, drawing my belly button toward my spine with every ounce of my might as the ornately carved face of a mermaid bit into the meat of my palm.

"Stop talkin'. You have to breave to talk. Now. On de count of free, you're gonna blow like you're sucking off a bloody gladiator! Ready?"

I nodded, having very little idea of exactly how much pressure would be required to stimulate the aforementioned entity.

"One. Two. Free!"

Air shoved up my throat in one long gust, and with a triumphant shout from Allan, I was fastened. Inside the dress's black velvet cage, my lungs rebelled against a sharp inhale, causing a momentary panic as I scrambled to catch one of life's most elementary rhythms.

"I can't breathe," I announced.

"Meanwhiwe," he said, turning me around to face the full-length mirror. "Your tits look bleedin' brilliant!"

And to my great astonishment, he was right.

Above the corset's ribs, my cleavage was a creamy swell. The long lines of my neck and shoulders were unbroken by sleeve or collar. Allan's tugging had narrowed my waist to a gentle curve that fed into the gown's full skirt like the stem into the head of a flower. He had managed to give me in cloth a measure of the grace I lacked in person. I turned sideways, then back, transfixed by the satin's whisper around my legs.

"Go ahead," Allan invited. "Say it. I'm a bloody genius."

"You're a bloody genius."

"Good. Now let's do somefink about 'at hair."

I perched at the vanity in my palatial bathroom and offered Allan bobby pins as he hovered behind me. Heat from a handful of curling irons breathed onto the delicate skin of my wrist as I leaned forward and turned my face right to left, checking my make-up.

"Quit faffin' about," Allan said, releasing a long, red coil of hair, warm against my collarbone. "You look lovely."

"He hasn't spoken to me in two days." Even as I said it, a sharp, metallic tang punctured my heart.

Mark had seen to it that I would be sequestered in this one wing of the castle. Banned from the official meetings and assigned my own security detail, I had wandered the halls like a planet dragging satellites. At least my uninvited entourage had been kind enough to make themselves scarce when I discovered the library. There, in front of windows overlooking cliffs on the River Tay, I'd snuggled down into an overstuffed velvet armchair, stroking and sniffing my way through book after leather-bound book. Meals had materialized under silver-domed dishes. Steaming pots of strong tea and dainty plates of rich, buttery shortbreads became my afternoon companions.

Mark? Mark who?

I kicked off the stilettos beneath the itchy tulle of my skirt and ran my toes over the rough stone wall behind the polished wood. At least part of me could move.

"My gawd, do you 'ave a lot of 'air."

"That's what I hear."

"A'right," he said, releasing one last curl from the iron. "Hold your breaf!"

"As if I had a choice," I said, shifting within my corset cage.

Allan took up a can of hairspray and shrouded me in a cloud of aerosolized fixative. "'ere!" He tugged at a few of the dark copper curls, arranging them around my face and neck with an architect's scrutiny.

"Tailor *and* stylist," I said, admiring Allan's handiwork. He'd managed to coax my unruly mop into a romantically chaotic upsweep, half of it piled on my head, the rest falling down around my neck and shoulders. "Is there anything you can't do?"

"Women," Allan said. "Much to me mom's disappointment. I'd put a necklace on you, but I fink it'd be best not to draw any more attention to 'at area dan is strictly necessary."

"Right," I said, remembering. I hadn't met any of the other guests, half of whom would be vampires, or so I imagined.

I rose as stiffly as a statue. Allan grabbed my shoes from under the vanity and carried them out to my bedroom, where I slid back into them with his assistance.

Allan leaned back, hand beneath his chin as he evaluated the final product. "Mark Abernathy ain't going to know what hit him."

"I hope you're right," I said, knowing that the only thing I wanted to hit him with was a two-by-four.

IF JAMES BOND HAD EVER SEEN MARK ABERNATHY IN A TUXEDO, he would have turned in his gun and cock at MI6 and become an accountant.

As I floated down the stone stairs on Allan's arm, I scanned the crowded ballroom and found him in an instant. His silhouette burned a space in my memory no other body could fill.

Allan helpfully flicked a finger under my chin to shut my yawning yap seconds before Mark's amber eyes fastened onto mine. His nostrils flared, finding my scent even from this distance. Heads began turning in my direction, working across the crowd like a wash of dominoes.

"Shit," Allan muttered. "Dis is goin' ta be a fuckin' nightmare."

"I'm sorry," I whispered out of the side of my mouth.

Abernathy cleared his throat, and suddenly every gaze in the room jerked in any direction but mine.

All but one.

Mark's eyes stayed fixed to my face as Allan wove us through the crowd. Cold and heat washed over me in waves as we threaded past vampires and werewolves alike. I was too distracted to search the sea of bodies for famous faces, drawn by the unyielding intensity of Mark's attention.

"Well," Allan said, depositing me at Mark's side. "I fink I see Lady Godiva over dere. Better chat with her while she still 'as 'er knickers on." His turquoise velvet jacket was swallowed by the black tuxedoed crowd like a peacock sinking into a murder of ravens.

"Hanna." Mark's voice was as heavy as the monoliths arching overhead.

"Mark."

My fingers were caught up in an icy grasp from behind as cool lips pressed a kiss against my knuckles.

I spun around to find a man bent over my hand.

"Lady Hanna." My first thought was to wonder how he knew my name. The second, how the speaker could force entire words out of a mouth puckered tighter than a nun's ass. Tall, dour, and silver-haired, he looked more like a ruler dipped in black paint than a human being. His unfortunate choice in monotone clothing served only to highlight the fine dusting of snowfall at his shoulders and wrists from skin that was clean, but exceptionally dry.

He reminded me of someone. I struggled for a moment fighting to drag the image haunting my mind's depths to the surface.

A butler.

That's who he reminded me of. A starchy, glowering, stoop-shouldered servant perpetually disapproving of people with more power than he had.

Behind the black-clad bony arch of the "Butler's" back, a servant stood at attention. If you threw a marine and a biker into a blender with a dash of rock star and baked the resulting batter in a blast furnace, the guy hovering at the Butler's elbow was about what you'd get. He wore a tight black shirt stretched over an amateur body builder's physique, jeans, motorcycle boots, and a smirk that would frighten predators and charm prey. Not human. But not a vampire either.

"Aren't you going to introduce us?" The knuckle-kisser's pale, milky blue gaze slid from Mark to me.

Mark's eyes fastened on the spot on my hand the Butler had kissed. "Tiberious Klaudios Epaphroditos," he said, pronouncing the name like the Latin classification of a flesh-eating virus.

"Klaud," the man corrected, offering me his long, spidery fingers.

"Hanna," I said. "Lady isn't necessary." His cold flesh felt like a loose glove over spindly bones beneath my brief grip. I let go quickly, plagued by the vision of his skin sliding away in my hand.

Klaud followed my gaze over his shoulder and rewarded me with a smile that looked like it required the help of gears and pulleys. "This is my servant, Crixus."

The full lips that found my knuckles were as smooth as the voice was rough. And hot.

Literally.

Heat sank through my skin and found the veins below, where it sent a vibration up my arm, down my shoulder, through my chest, and then found its way south. Tightness gathered at the place where my femoral arteries fed the nerve-rich flesh between them. When the first spasm found me, my eyes flew wide. This couldn't be happening.

Crixus smiled, rising.

The sensation didn't relent. It redoubled. My shallow breath became a pant. Another spasm. And another.

I swayed on my heels as an orgasm expanded outward through my body like the ripples on a pond. The familiar rush of wet heat didn't follow, and I was grateful. Abernathy would have smelled it.

Why are you panting? Mark's voice was an earthquake in my skull.

Stupid cors—

Think louder! Mark's voice arrived in my mind.

Dude. I can hear you too?

It would seem so, came the terse reply.

I worked on slowing my breath. Pulling air into my lungs slowly, softly.

"The Emperor Nero wishes he could have been here this evening," Klaud said, interrupting our mental conversation with his verbal one. "He was most *eager* to meet you."

To my embarrassment, this handful of words still carried

enough power to sting a blush to my cheeks. *The Emperor Nero was eager to meet* me? *"Me?"* I asked. "Why?"

Klaud's pupils flared in time with the throbbing of my pulse within its corseted tourniquet. "It's been centuries since an heir was brought to Castle Abernathy. Why, the last time—"

"Is none of your concern," Mark interrupted. His look was colder than the heart that failed to beat in Klaud's chest.

Heir. I had barely begun to accept this word as applying to me. Bound by blood as the process seemed to be, it wasn't a stretch to include my mother and grandmother within the label. But there had to be other *heirs*. From other bloodlines. Were there any now? Was Mark protecting them the way he protected me?

"Who was the last heir you brought here?"

Mark seemed as irritated as Klaud was pleased by the question. "Hanna, this isn't the time or place to discuss this."

"Oh dear," Klaud's fingers came to rest below the colorless ribbon of his thin lips. "I assumed she knew."

"She doesn't know," I said, directing my narrowed gaze at Mark. "But she'd like to."

"Hanna," Mark warned. "Later."

"Yes," Klaud agreed. "We would hardly have time to do her story justice here, would we?"

Her. Three letters with the power to set my body ablaze.

"Anyway," Klaud continued, "I didn't come to discuss your past loves, Mark."

Loves? What the fuck is he talking about, Mark?

Not. Now. Hanna. Mark's voice rolled through my mind like thunder. "Then what did you come here to discuss?"

"I came to discuss the recent *disappearances*. It has come to the Lord Emperor Nero's attention that several of his colleagues have gone missing, as of late. Colleagues who happened to be visiting your fair city, Mark."

"Your kind doesn't *visit*, Klaud." Abernathy leaned in toward

Klaud, broad shoulders looming over the painfully thin man. "They were hunting. You and I both know that's a breach of the Spring Lambing terms."

"So is murder of a vampire by a werewolf." Klaud's voice was as rough and metallic as the edge of a rusty saw blade.

"You can't murder the dead," Abernathy said.

Klaud bore the distinctive look of a man—or whatever—who'd just had his Cheerios peed in. "Semantics won't stave off war, Abernathy. When the council learns of this, there will be blood. It's only a matter of time."

"The council would be equally alarmed at the string of recent, unexplained murders in my town," Abernathy said. "Humans tend to get a little worked up when the corpse is marred by two puncture holes at the jugular. Perhaps Nero would be well-served reminding his *colleagues* of this."

"You don't deny that you killed them, then?"

"My time is precious," Mark said. "Wasting it on hunting your kind would not serve me. But—" Mark leaned close to the Klaud's ear "—if any more of Nero's cronies decide to hunt in my city, you can be assured, the terms will be enforced as I see fit."

"Is that a threat?" The dusty caterpillar of one gray eyebrow crawled toward Klaud's receding hairline.

"It's a promise." Mark's hands contracted into fists at his sides.

"I will convey your sentiments to the Lord Emperor Nero." Klaud performed a starchy bow. "Lady Hanna, it was a pleasure."

I looked at his hand as it hovered in the space between us. Hesitantly, I met it with my own. When the cold lips again found my skin, a shudder worked its way up my spine. I suppressed a gag.

Klaud turned from us and looked to the crowd. "Crixus, come."

This word conjured a whirlpool of blood to my cheeks.

A smirk stole one corner of Crixus's mouth. "Lady Hanna." He nodded.

I closed my eyes and bent my head to him in reply. They disappeared into the crowd of milling bodies.

"Do you really think there will be a war?" I asked when they were gone.

"I'll do anything to avoid it." These were the first words Abernathy had spoken to me out loud in two days. "But there are no guarantees."

"What would that mean?" My question was swallowed by the sweet strains of stringed instruments arching through the grand hall. The jostling bodies condensed into pairs, orbiting each other like atoms.

He looked at me then. Really looked at me. My face. My lips. My hair. My dress. "Dance?"

Unable to manage actual words in the presence of the tuxedoed Abernathy, I only nodded.

His hand registered as a patch of warmth against my corset-clad waist as he steered me through the crowd. Reaching a relatively unpopulated spot, Mark pulled me to him and captured my hand. Inside his warm, heavy grip, my fingers felt like kindling for a fire not yet set ablaze.

"You didn't answer my question," I reminded him.

"The last time werewolves and vampires went to war, a third of Europe died. They called it the Dark Ages."

"Not the bubonic plague?"

"Vampires were killing at will. Disease was a much more comfortable explanation."

"No," I said. "That's not possible."

"Humans flourish within the same cycle that governs us all. When a territory is over-inhabited by predators, the numbers dwindle. When those predators are reduced, civilization flourishes."

"You mean to tell me the Renaissance happened because the werewolves defeated the vampires?"

"What the hell do you think Da Vinci was? Or Michelangelo? Or—"

Only recently had I understood. Artists were werewolves, and writers, vampires. "Okay, yes. I get it." *Kind of.*

"Renaissance. Think about the term, Hanna."

"Re-birth," I said.

"Werewolves are reborn. Born to another life. Vampires surrender life. That is the price of immortality. Death is part of life. And they won't have it."

My head spun in a haze of non-comprehension.

Bodies moved around us until the whole room became an impressionist painting. Gestures rendered by quick brush-strokes in my periphery. Mark pulled me in closer. The long, dark skirt of my gown whispered against his legs. "About the other day..."

His broad, muscular back stiffened beneath my hands. "I'd rather not talk about it."

"You'd rather not talk about *anything*. But I need to. I'm not trying to make anything more complicated for you."

"You haven't." Mark steered us away from another couple, using the opportunity to put some space between us.

A familiar, dull ache started up in my chest. I told myself the corset was to blame, though I knew better. What he'd said was 'You haven't.' What I'd heard was 'You couldn't.' *Not you. You'd have to mean something to me first.*

"Who was the last heir you brought here?" Better to move the conversation to a topic more painful for him than for me.

"I'd rather not talk about that either." His hand tightened over mine. The amateur psychologist in my head deciding this to be a subconscious signal of closing down.

"It's a perfectly reasonable question," I said, squeezing my hand right back.

"Reason is relative."

I resisted the very ungraceful and undancerly urge to kick him in the shin. Not that my dress would have allowed me anyway.

Trying to get information out of Mark reminded me of navigating a maze. Walls rose higher than my line of sight in many directions, and most paths terminated in sudden dead ends.

"Remind me why you brought me here again?" I tilted my chin up towards his, as much so he could hear me as to remind him of how easy it would be for him to kiss me. Should he want to. Ever again.

"Because you begged me." Abernathy punctuated these words with a quick, violent turn, spinning me with dizzying force.

"How am I supposed to make my decision when you keep sheltering me from the things I want to know about this world?" I asked when I had regained a measure of my equilibrium.

When Abernathy wouldn't meet my eyes, I reached up and placed a hand on his beautifully carved and cleanly-shaven jaw, angling his face to mine. For one simultaneously brief and endless moment, we were the only two people in the room, the castle, the country, the world.

His gaze had the power to do that to me. To render everything not in its direct path utterly obsolete. Meaningless.

"I will spare you as much ugliness as I can for as long as I can. If you choose to remain human, there are certain aspects of my world you would be better not knowing." He took my hand from his face and put it back on his shoulder. *Not* I noted, over his heart.

"How does my question fall into that category?"

"The answer is ugly." The half flirting, half teasing lightness on his face evaporated then, leaving something darker and more impenetrable.

Great.

"Speakin' of ugly." Allan materialized at my elbow and despite my boundless love for him, I could have cheerfully strangled him on the spot. "Pharaoh has requested your presence. Gawd, but I'm amazing," he said, stepping back to admire the gown. "'is thing is a work of bloody art."

"Now?" Mark dropped my hand, irritation clear on his features "We had our one-on-one earlier today." This was easily the most work-related thing I had ever heard Abernathy say.

"You had a one-on-one meeting with *the* Ahkenaten and you didn't let me take notes?" I asked, disappointment further crushing my already collapsing chest.

"Because you *taking notes* would have been more akin to you jumping in his lap and choking off his air-supply with a patented Hanna neck squeeze?" Abernathy and Allan traded a look that suggested they were both in agreement with this assessment.

"Ah-ha!" I said, holding up my finger for emphasis. "But vampires don't need air, do they?"

"Their bones also don't heal for years. If anyone could manage to pulverize the millennia old ruler of an immortal species, it would be you," Abernathy said.

I folded my arms across the velvety fabric of my corset. "Like *you've* never attack-hugged someone, Mr. Judgy McJudgypants."

"I'll be so bloody glad when you two shag and get it over with."

"That's not—" Mark began.

"I haven't—" I added.

"I know, I know," he said, holding up silk-gloved hands to quiet us both. "'ere's no tellin' what'll 'appen. Hanna 'asn't decided, and there are plenty of available female alphas slobberin' for the chance to jump on Mark's royal knob. You can deny it all later. Right now, sod off and talk to the Pharaoh."

"I'll be back," Mark promised before disappearing into the crowd.

"Nice to see you two are talkin' again." Allan tucked a few stray curls back into the nest of hair piled onto my head.

"Not about anything of substance," I said.

"Give him time, love." Allan gave my shoulders a reassuring squeeze.

Gasps and shrieks rose from a clump of bodies in the crowd. The word 'naked' floated up above the general din.

"Oh fuckin' 'ell," Allan sighed. "That'll be Lady Godiva. I towd de bartender not to serve her. One flute of champagne and 'er tits are out quicker'n than green grass frough a goose. Be right back."

No sooner had he departed than a cold hand closed over my wrist. I glanced over my shoulder to find Klaud fixing me with a rictus grin, the roots of his yellowed teeth were visible above his retreating gums. My fingers began to tingle, this simple contact with a vampire enough to change the patterns of my blood flow.

"Klaud," I acknowledged, I jerking my hand from his grasp.

"Forgive me, Lady Hanna." He bowed. "Our conversation earlier gave me pause. There's something I feel you need to know. Will you accompany me?"

The mere suggestion filled me with dread. I glanced around the room, but was unable to locate either Abernathy or Allan. "I don't think that would be a good idea."

"Forgive me, I just feel that it's only fair that you are given all the information about the previous heir." His voice had an unpleasantly dry quality that suggested if he coughed, a cloud of dust might just erupt from his thin, livery lips. "There are things I can tell you."

"Why should I believe you?" Curiosity gnawed my insides hollow as I searched his dampish, rheumy blue eyes.

"Werewolves are notoriously secretive." Klaud cast a baleful glance over the swaying, chattering crowd. "Not that my kind doesn't also have our…quirks."

"That's putting it rather mildly." My hand drifted up to my neck, where the faint scar from Oscar Wilde's vicious bite still ached with the memory.

Klaud gave me a mirthless smile. "An heir has considerable power within both worlds. I only think that, should you decided to take on that role, it should be with all the information available."

"Why do I feel like my ability to make this decision with full information is not your sole motive here?" I raised an eyebrow at him.

"Because it is not," he admitted. "Of course I have an interest in the Emperor retaining his current scope of power, and should you take your place, he stands to lose that."

"I thought that might be the case," I said, shifting to take pressure off my aching feet. Still, Klaud's having readily admitted this was a far cry from the verbal hand waving and frequent subterfuge I had become accustomed to in Abernathy's case.

"Purely hypothetically," I said, fully aware of my tendency to leap first and look much, much later, "if I was to accompany you, it wouldn't be alone. I have a security detail. They're watching us, even now."

"I should be disappointed in our host, were that not the case," Klaud said. He offered me his arm, then pulled it back. "Forgive me. I forget the affect our touch has on your kind, with such infrequent contact. Will you follow me?"

I nodded, grateful to escape the sickening, numb tingling. "I will."

His long, dark shape cut a path through the crowd to a secluded hallway of stained glass windows overlooking the moor. Their colors should have been dark at this time of night. Instead, moonlight set them aburst as if they were lit by silver flame. Klaud paused by velvet curtains rising to meet the hall's indecent height. Could they absorb thoughts as well as they absorbed conversation?

"What has your *valiant protector* told you on the subject of how heirs are born?" Klaud asked when the din of the crowd had died away.

I felt a sudden stab of panic that soon Klaud would be whipping an illustrated guide out of his pocket and beginning with something like *when a mommy werewolf and a daddy werewolf love each other very much...*

"I know that heirs are all born of the same genetic line, and that if that particular heir decides to remain human, the genetic material remains dormant until the next of the line is born."

"Correct," he said, looking entirely too smug by half. "But did he tell you that not all heirs in the same line carry equal potential and power?"

"No," I said, feeling irritation crawl up my spine on spiky insect legs. "He failed to mention that."

His laugh felt like a slap stinging across my cheek. "Why does this not surprise me?"

That made two of us.

"The world of werewolves is governed by cycles. Cycles of the moon. Cycles of the tide. Cycles of birth. Cycles of death."

This last word between us like an icicle. Cold. Jagged. Dangerous.

"True heirs," he continued, "*pure* heirs are born in cycles as well."

"I'm not sure I understand what you mean." My heart fluttered in the tight cage of my corset.

"The last *true* heir came to Castle Abernathy two hundred years ago." Klaud paused, blue eyes milky in the moonlight. "That is, until you."

The stone floor shifted beneath my feet. I reached out to steady myself against the wall. "What?"

Klaud scanned my face but failed to maintain eye contact, his gaze lodging squarely at my jugular. I tried not to enhance its pulsing by swallowing.

"Her name was Lily. She was to be Abernathy's mate. He brought her here for the formal ceremony. The night before the wedding, she was nearly strangled to death. Following that incident, she was somewhat less interested in becoming the alpha female of the ruling clan. She left the following morning."

The edges of my vision faded to a strange, smoky brown as I fought to drag air into my compressed lungs. Blood roared in my ears.

"Since she elected to remain human, all that she was, all that she might have been stayed dormant from generation to generation. Abernathy knew that, given time, the next true heir would be born. Which is why, I suspect, he remained near Cuxhaven, where Lily settled with her human family."

Goosebumps spilled from the crown of my head all the way to my feet. "She settled in Cuxhaven?"

"Oh yes, she did. And for generations, they lived in secrecy, until your grandmother discovered some of the letters *her* grandmother had written to Abernathy. I suppose Abernathy told you your grandmother sought his assistance?"

"He did." I said, deep melancholy spreading like hot tar through my middle.

"But not *how* she knew to seek his help?" Klaud's face bore an expression of indecent pleasure as he delivered this revelation.

"No." I let myself lean back against the wall, the rough-hewn stone, cool and surprisingly comforting between my naked shoulder blades.

"He was waiting. Or so, I imagine. Protecting your line against any interference would make infinite sense, if I were waiting for the love of my life to return."

"But I'm not her," I insisted. "She's not me. We're *not* the same." I could feel the hard knot building at the base of my throat. The tears stinging my eyes.

That same, slow smile crept across his face. It should have been warning enough. "No. Not the same. But, the resemblance is—well I'll let you be the judge." He reached toward his pocket and withdrew a phone. His long, pale fingers danced over the screen before he handed it to me.

It felt unnaturally cool upon my palm. Even in the photograph, the painting caused me to gasp, and shrink. Those eyes. The auburn hair. The pale skin.

It was me.

CHAPTER 16

"Where did you get this?" The photograph of the painting looked to have been taken hastily, but the stones beyond the painting's ornate, gilded frame belonged to Castle Abernathy. There could be no doubt of this.

"Under this very roof. In a section of the castle I suspect Mark has guarded against your entering. He has restricted your movements while you were here, yes? Under the pretense of some threat, I suppose. To think. You've been sleeping in *her* room. Remarkable how well he's kept it. It's been updated, I'm sure. But it *was* hers, all the same."

"This isn't possible." I was backing away from him now, his phone still clutched in my hand. Shivering and hugging myself as I retreated.

"I can certainly understand why you want to believe that," Klaud said, casually ambling toward me. "But lies wouldn't sting so, would they? What you do with this information is entirely up to you, my dear. Leave him. Forgive him. Whatever you choose. Do what you will, but do it with your eyes open."

His phone slid from my hand, broken pieces scattering against stone. The delicate sounds of breaking didn't register in any ears but mine, and perhaps that of Klaud who laughed in my wake.

I ran from him then. Knocking bodies out of my way, tripping up the stairs, skirt catching on my shoes, lungs pressing against the contracted cage of my ribs, my heart drumming a terrified rhythm around a single word, repeated over and over again.

No. No No. *No*.

Down the hall I flew, the heavy tapestries a blur of ornate stitching in my peripheral vision as I threw myself into my room, *her* room and heaved the heavy wooden door shut behind me. The brass key was cold in my hand as I cranked the lock. Its landing was muffled by the plush carpets covering every pathway in this room. *Her* room.

Were these colors chosen for her? *By* her? These fabrics? Had she sat in the antique chairs facing the fireplace? Curled up in the window seats with a book?

The assault came from all sides, leaving me spinning in the room's center, my only path of escape to fold further into myself until implosion felt like an inevitability. I fell to the bed, my body drawing itself into the smallest ball the yards of fabric cocooning me would allow.

She was everywhere.

I was nowhere. No one.

I pulled the pillows down over my head, grateful for the darkness and silence when the first sobs racked my body.

"I'M SO SORRY, HANNA. I'M SO SORRY." MARK'S VOICE PULLED ME to the surface, helped me kick free from the undertow of unpleasant dreams. The room was dark and cold, the fire having died long ago. The velvet drapes had been drawn, blocking out even moonlight.

His body warmed my bare back. The immense weight of a large hand wrapped my naked bicep in a singular spot of heat.

"I should have told you," he said. "I should have told you about her." The hand slid down my arm and found my hand, which he brought to his lips, and kissed.

His apology and its attendant admission was more painful than a denial would have been. "So it's true?"

"Yes. Her name was Lily, and I loved her."

Another wave of pain crushed my chest.

"I loved her," he said again. "But not like I love you."

And here, my breath ceased. Only when the pounding of my own oxygen-starved heart grew deafening in my ears did I take the next breath. "You love me?"

"Hanna, how could you not know that?"

Muffled voices filtered up from the great hall below. Was the party still going? How long had I slept?

"You've never said it before. Not even when—"

He pressed a finger against my lips. "Shhh. You know how I am. How hard it is for me to express my feelings."

"Of course *I* know how you are," I whispered. "But I didn't know that *you* knew."

His reply was anything but playful. "Of course I know. I want to tell you *everything*, Hanna. I do. But it will take time."

"Time is okay, Mark. Finding this shit out from Nero's creepy manservant is not." I pulled away from him, as much to recover my wits as to communicate my displeasure.

"Which one?" he asked.

"Klaud." I shuddered.

"Not Crixus?" Mark's lips brushed the back of my neck, eliciting a shudder of an entirely different kind.

The blush sizzling to my cheeks at the mention of that name had me grateful for the dark. "What about him?"

"Did you like it when he made you come?"

A little bubble of panic rose in my chest. "It was an accident," I insisted. "I didn't mean to. It just sort of *happened*."

"It's not your fault," Mark said, tracing my earlobe with his tongue. "He has that effect on women."

"What is he, anyway?" I asked, somewhat alarmed that Mark wasn't more upset about this.

"Many things. A demigod. A Roman gladiator. Most recently, the stakes in a blood oath sworn to Nero." His lips found mine in the darkness. The tongue that had been seductive and gentle moments earlier now invaded as fiercely as any Roman legion. He groaned into my mouth as he shoved a hand down my corset, pulling my breast free. He rubbed a rough thumb over the nipple, swallowing my moan.

He threw his leg over mine, capturing my ankle with his heel to slide my legs open. The gown rustled in the darkness as he pulled the fabric upward, Gathering it in his hand. Cool currents of air slid up my bare legs followed by his fingers. He found the waistband of my panties and slid under them.

"So soft," he growled against my lips, before biting one, and then the other. "So beautiful. Even better than I imagined."

I stopped short, planting a hand against his chest. "What did you say?"

He crushed his lips to mine in answer. An electrical current slid down my neck, through my heart, and followed every vein and blood vessel downward, where blood pooled and began to throb.

I fought against the sensation, even as fighting became yet more energy dedicated to the cause. "Stop," I panted. "You're...you're not Mark. You're...Crixus!"

The door to my room exploded open, the splintering boards making a crack like thunder cleaving the sky. If I had a cheese wedge for every time that happened lately...

Light pouring in from the hall revealed two silhouettes at once. Mark's broad body, filling the doorway.

And Crixus, leaning over me on the bed a split second before he vanished. Like the Chesire Cat, the last thing to disappear was the ghost of his impish grin.

In a flurry of activity, Mark surged toward the bed as I pushed my dress down my legs and tugged the corset back into place. Rage burned in his amber eyes, twin flames in the half light. They caught the light in a thousand different ways daily, but never before had I actually seen them *glow*.

"*Mark*," I said, hoping to snap whatever trance held him with the sound of my voice. "Mark, I thought it was *you*. He *sounded* like you. He *felt* like you!"

An arm snaked around my chest and I was flying backward into darkness. The hand clasped over my mouth trapped the scream in my throat. I thrashed within a world without sound, feeling air surge over my skin as my body hurtled through space. We crashed through a door and up a set of spiral stairs to a place I had never been before—Castle Abernathy's attic.

THROWN TO A MATTRESS, MY BODY SENT A CLOUD OF DUST UP toward the exposed wooden rafters. Ghosts of paintings, sculptures, old furniture lurked in the shadows created by the light of the full moon through the dust-caked windows. I squinted through silvery wash to find the glowing amber eyes of my captor. A mockery of the setting sun's glory set in a face I knew, and didn't know.

Mark, but not Mark.

Mark's face, Mark's body, but an animal's instinct.

The words came, but I didn't speak them. They would not be heeded.

Hands gripped my ankles and pulled me to my back. Teeth bared, he caught my hands and pinned them to the mattress above my head as he brought his full weight down on me.

Springs pressed into my back as the mattress groaned beneath us. Mark's face hovered above mine like the specter of every sinful dream I'd barred from the light of day. He held my gaze, even as his powerful thighs forced my knees apart. Both wrists fit easily in the grasp of his one, large hand, which he brought down against my stomach, freeing him to move lower.

With his wide shoulders between my legs, I could do naught as his face slid up my thigh. He found my panties beneath the flared skirt of my dress with a grunt of pleasure. Heat from his breath bloomed on my skin where he rubbed his nose and mouth against me through the silky fabric. Vibrations tingled through me as he hummed a mixture of approval and hunger.

He nudged my sensitive flesh, nipping at me, letting his tongue dampen the fabric where he amplified my scent by the addition of a secondary sense.

Terrific heaviness gathered beneath my bound hands, drawing in its wake a rush of moisture. A rough, low growl erupted from Mark and I was in motion again, shoved face down on the mattress. He jerked my hips upward, backward. My panties gave way with a brief sigh of protest as they were rent in two and tossed aside. I felt the crisp material of my skirt shoved up my back and the silken slide of Mark's hair as he shoved his head through my thighs. His neck turned at an owlish angle beneath me as hands dug into my hips to open me to him.

His tongue was rough. His lips were smooth.

Sandpaper and silk, working in concert to wrench the sanity from me in controlled undulations and feather light flicks.

I forgot to fight.

Delicious friction caught fire on my flesh. His tongue was unnatural in its control, unyielding in its punishment, unhurried in its exploration. A gasp tore from my throat as the cupped tip began a relentless circle around, but not on, the place that throbbed in time with my heart's erratic song of want.

Fingers trailed the curve of my hips, finding the flesh made slick by the combined efforts of tongue and time.

He split me with the length of his middle finger and fastened his mouth around me in one concerted stroke. My back arched away from the sudden, intense onslaught even as my cry of pleasure echoed through the darkening attic. He gripped my dress, holding me fast, even as he shoved his hand harder against me, driving his finger deeper, lifting me with the force of his thrust. I felt myself contract around him, a shockwave warning of the coming storm. His pace catapulted from hungry to savage, his palm abrading sensitive folds of flesh as hands that had killed on my behalf now sought to cripple me with pleasure.

Unable to move with its own undoing, my body shot the pleasure up my spine where it erupted outward in a ragged scream. Head thrown back, fingers tearing into the mattress, I felt a final searing rush between my thighs.

CHAPTER 17

"You are going to be the death of me." Mark stared toward the ceiling overhead, unblinking. His words were neither expression nor hyperbole.

"That's less than flattering." It was an effort to force levity into my voice. In our shared silence, I'd been drowning in unwelcome revelations. Crixus had apologized to me. Crixus had told me he loved me. *Not Mark*. What little comfort those words brought had been torn away with my panties. Stripped from me along with any hope for resolution. Two beings sharing the same space, and occasional pleasure, but nothing more. Worse than that. Combatants with opposing sets of neuroses. The living illustration for the intersection of weakness.

"What do you want from me, Hanna?"

I sat up on the mattress and tucked my knees under the shredded remains of my skirt. "Rhetorically speaking, or is this an actual invitation?"

Mark did not rise, remaining prone as he stared at the ceiling. "Actual invitation."

Love?

I swatted the word away as quickly as it had arrived.

Love was not something I was willing to ask for.

"I want the whole story. *My* whole story. Just when I think there's solid ground to build on, it crumbles, and I learn I have further to fall. I'm tired of falling. I'd rather it was just as bad as it can be. That would be somewhere to start, at least."

"It's not just *your* story, Hanna. It's *my* story. The story of people long dead and gone, and others still living in danger. You have no more claim to it than anyone else. You're not the only one I've made promises to."

"You mean *her*?" A childish tactic, I knew, and told more than I intended of hurt feelings and jealousy.

Mark sat up. After re-buttoning and buckling his clothes, he grabbed my wrist, hauling me to my feet. "Come on," he ordered.

"Where are we going?" Digging my heels in to slow the progress would do no good, so I let him tug me over to a corner of the vast attic where he flipped a switch, bathing those dusty environs in a rosy glow. Directly in front of us, a spiral stair climbed up to a loft, where shapes obscured by old sheets gathered like a congregation of ghosts. Dust muted all the objects like the fine sprinkling of snow.

Save for one spot.

"Look," Mark said, holding an open-palmed hand toward the one sheet puddled on the floor.

I walked past him toward a painting leaning up against the broad silhouette of an armoire or portmanteau.

Not *a* painting. *The* painting. I knelt before it, the hush of satin like the sigh of awe I couldn't properly give voice. As I looked at her face, a moment of déjà vu rushed into my head, rocking me back on my heels. The white neck, the green velvet bodice. The hood circling the auburn waves like a halo born of earth rather than heaven. "Kirpatrick," I whispered, awed. "Kirkpatrick painted this." I knew the careful hand, the unabashed celebration of textures rendered by a brushstroke so fine it erased the evidence of its own making. "This was the woman in Kirkpatrick's painting."

What I had read as judgment on our first meeting, had in fact, been surprise, in Kirkpatrick's limited bandwidth of facial expressions. And perhaps distaste for the pale imitation of the savior he remembered.

"Yes," Mark said. "She saved his life. That's how I met him. In saving yours, he finally repaid the debt."

My fingers floated out to trace the white curve of her face. The texture was glass-smooth under my fingertips, like a mirror reflecting the past rather than the present. "Is it true?" I asked. "Am I pretty much the genetic equivalent of microwaved Lily leftovers?"

Mark's sigh was heavy enough to create a flurry of dust motes in the blue light of pre-dawn. "Hanna, I will give you the story you want. When I can."

This wound was too old, too deep to avoid irritation. "Please," I said, staring at my own face on a centuries old canvas. "Please don't do this to me. Not again."

Mark deliberately avoided looking at my face as well as the ghost of it captured in the gilded frame. "If I could tell you more, I would."

Rage boiled in my belly. I turned back to the painting. For a brief moment, I felt the satisfying rip of stiffened canvas as I slashed her face to ribbons with the blade I didn't have.

Who are you trying to hurt?

"Think about this, Hanna. For one minute. Listen to me."

I half glanced over my shoulder. "What?"

"Look at the sheet. Pick it up."

I did as bidden. The pattern of wear followed the jutting swirled and flowered recesses of the frame I had traced with my fingers. A sneeze erupted from my nose as a cloud of dust swirled out from the sheet. "But I saw this painting on a wall." I said.

Mark smiled, pleased with my observation. "Correct."

"Which means someone came up here, got the painting, hung it, took a picture, and put it back? That doesn't make any sense."

"Indeed not," he said.

"There are no footprints!" The realization came to me all at once as I scanned the area, seeing the trail of my skirt and the distinctive marks of my own bare feet.

"Who do you suppose could come up here, retrieve a painting, hang it on the wall, take a picture, and depart without leaving a single footprint?"

"Not a vampire," I answered. "Or a werewolf. But a demigod..."

"They're fucking with you, Hanna. And you're letting them. I will tell you about her when I can. I'm not hiding some shrine of a secret love from you. Her painting has been here since Kirkpatrick gave it to me. The room you are staying in is the most secure in the castle. Yes, *she* stayed there. But so have many others."

"Did you love her?" The question came from a place neither polite or practical.

Mark looked like he'd taken an uppercut to the gut. He'd been on a roll. He hadn't expected this. At last, he looked not at me, but the painting. "Love isn't a useful—"

"Did you love her?" I asked again, meeting his eyes, and refusing to look away.

If I had ever thought myself the victim of a broken heart before, I had surely missed the mark. For what I saw in Abernathy's face at that exact moment buried an axe in my sternum. "Yes," he said.

"Do you love me?" I would have given every sunset, every leaf wet with rain, every treasured experience in this life or any other to take those words back the second they left my mouth.

Abernathy's jaw hardened, his eyes going cold and dark as tree bark. "I can't," he said.

A cold finality settled in my chest, shrinking my heart to a pebble lodged between my lungs. My nose stung, my eyes filling treacherously with tears. I bit the inside of cheek hard enough to taste copper on my tongue.

"You will always have my protection," he said. "Whether you want it or not."

"I know." It was not a presumption, but an understanding. "I'll stay on at the gallery through the wedding. There's plenty of planning needed between now and then. But after that, it's probably best that we—that I move on to something else."

Mark nodded, offering me his arm. "I'll take you back to your room."

I looked at it, craving its warmth, his touch, more than I craved air, but shook my head no. "I know my own way."

ON THE FLIGHT OVER TO SCOTLAND, IT HAD BEEN MARK'S sleeping face I'd studied. On the way home, I scrutinized the snoring Joseph, whose body held half the DNA responsible for the werewolf I loved.

And I did love him.

This was the only reasonable conclusion given the facts. And *the facts* pissed me off. Lying would have been so much simpler than the truth I acknowledged in the form of a list. Written, of course, in the notebook where I recorded my tasks with a pen whose voluptuous ink rivaled the thickness of a balsamic reduction.

Number one: my stomach felt as if I'd swallowed a brick when Allan told me Mark wouldn't be boarding the private jet home, owing to a yet another meeting with the Pharaoh, aka, Akhenaten.

Number two: I couldn't stop staring at Joseph's hands, so much like Mark's, and remembering how they'd felt shoving me down on the mattress. Looking at them, I couldn't squelch the feeling that they belonged to me. Belonged on my skin. The piece of a puzzle God himself had architected in a moment of divine humor, or hysteria.

Number three: I'd written down a list of everything Mark had said to me from the moment we'd arrived in Scotland until the moment he'd let me submit my resignation and return to my room alone. Next to each group of words, I'd scratched out possible interpretations, all of which read something like: *Nope. Totally doesn't love you*.

Number four: If I had a daisy—or any flower, for that matter —I would pluck the *fuck* out of those petals. *He loves me, he loves me not because he is a heartless, self-centered, stubborn, irascible bastard, he loves me...*

Heartbreak fucking *sucked*.

"You know his mother was Li'il Red Riding Hood, right?" Allan leaned over the arm rest as I stared at Joseph's face with unhealthy interest.

"I think Joseph mentioned something to that effect. At least, he said something about being the Big Bad Wolf."

Allan's smile revealed the edges of his elongated front teeth. "He had dat reputation a long time 'afore he met her."

"*Her* being Mark's mother?"

"S'right." He caught the elbow of a passing flight attendant. "Bring us a voddy and soda, will ya, love?"

"Of course, Lord Ede. And anything for you, Lady Hanna?"

I had a feeling this story would benefit from the application of liquid courage. "Extra dirty martini. Three olives."

The flight attendant—Paige, this time—nodded, and was gone.

"Right, where was I?" Allan rubbed the salt and pepper stubble on his pointy chin.

"Little Red Riding Hood?"

"Yes, of course. As it 'appens, the woodsman were actually a witch hunter. 'e'd sharpened his axe, determined to find Li'il Red Riding Hood, and toss her on the burning pyre once and for all. He was heading over to her house in de woods, bent on chopping her 'ead off, when dis wolf showed up, and run him off. After de wolf scared de woodcutter away, de rumors grew and de story got twisted."

"Mark's mother is a witch? I thought he was a pure bred."

"*Was* a witch. Bein' the son of a purebred werewolf is about as pure as anyone gets dese days. Well, except for you, that is. Which, I imagine, is why Kaferine wants you dead. She never could accept that her mother was a witch. Always 'ated not being from a *pure* line."

Paige returned with our drinks, settling them carefully down our respective lacquered wood tray tables.

"How did she die?" I asked when she'd returned to the galley. "Mark's mother?"

Allan glanced at Joseph's sleeping face before answering. "She was one of twenty-two what were burned that day. On Abernethy Hill. Mark was only fifteen when it 'appened."

He watched his mother burn.

I knew it at once and completely. He fought the men who arrived to take her. Maybe even killed some of them. When overpowered, he followed them. And stayed until it was done.

"She didn't deny it," Allan said. "Spat at her captors."

"Where was Joseph?"

Allan's shoulders sagged toward his chest. "In 'is time, Joseph were one of de strongest, one of de brightest. But rules is rules. We are forbidden from transforming in front human beings, and de mob dat took her were too many for him to fight off. For *all* of us to fight off."

The sorrow in Allan's eyes infected my chest like a viral colony. "I can't imagine what that must have been like."

"Mark left Castle Abernathy after that. I couldn't blame him. He wanted something beau'ifuw." His dark gaze found mine through the barrier of Gucci frames. "I suppose he found it."

"Are you on his payroll?" I asked with narrowed eyes.

"He'd be bloody lucky to be on mine!" Allan laughed a refreshing cackle. "Croesus comes to me when he needs a few quid."

"Understood," I said.

"D'you understand why I'm tellin' you this?" The warmth in his eyes begged from me compassion I might have refused a lesser man. "Mark is de way he is for a *reason*.

"I love Joseph like me own brother, but his love of Mark's mother was a disaster from the word go. At least, the daughter they had is likely responsible for the death of her own mother, if not more. Your predecessor included."

I repressed the urge to grab Allan by his red and purple striped bowtie because I was a grown ass woman capable of working on things as I'd promised.

But barely.

"You know about *her*?" I hissed. "*What* do you know about her? What did he tell you?"

"He didn't have to teww me anyfing," Allan said, squeezing his lime into the effervescent liquid before him. Hundreds of tiny essential oil droplets burst from the zest, catching the light in the cabin. "I bloody introduced 'em."

I took a healthy slug of my own drink, appreciating the searingly cold, briny liquid. "Tell me everything."

"I kept tabs on Mark as 'e roamed all over Europe, makin' money and becomin' a big name in the art world. When fings started to go souf with Joseph, I called him home to take over de empire. He was onwy about two 'undred and firty, and a right mopey bastard. I fought introducing him to a nice girl might do de trick. Of course, she was also a pure blood heir, which would have made him de most powerful werewolf in all de world, if they mated. Seemed like a good idea at de time." He shrugged.

I pictured a young (in werewolf years, anyway) Mark called home to bear the weight of an entire empire. Stoic and cantankerous as he tended to be, companionship would have been my first recommendation as well. "But they didn't mate. Klaud said she died unmated."

Allan turned his eyes toward the window. The sky slid across the twin rectangles of his glasses. "Yes, she did. And I'm afraid that part of the story in't somefink I can teww you."

"Not you too." I slid down in my cushy leather seat, sulking as I sipped at my drink.

"You know I'd teww you if I could, my love." Allan took a goodly gulp of his own. "So, how about this weddin' we're plannin' eh?"

"Oh my God. The *wedding*!" With the trip to Scotland and all that had transpired there, Steve and Shayla's wedding had all but disappeared from my mind. I clicked onto my phone's home screen to check the date. "It's the day after tomorrow!"

"That's right," he agreed. "The wedding guests will be arriving already, I suspect."

"What do you need help with?"

"I measured everyone afore we left, so the clothing is aww arranged. I fink Joseph had a decorator coming to gussy up de gallery, and he called de caterer you recommended. I fink we ought to be pretty well set."

"I am such an asshole," I said, feeling even lower than I previously thought possible. "I feel like I haven't done shit to help with this."

"You've had pwenty on your plate, I'm sure," Allan said.

"Not for much longer." I pulled the skewered olives out of my glass and slid one off with my teeth. "I resigned."

"I know," Allan said, swirling the contents of his glass. "Mark told me. What'll you do now?"

I'd asked myself the same question at least a hundred times since the moment I'd resigned and always came back to the same answer. "Get my PhD. I've always wanted to."

"I've a good many friends in de academic world, should you need a recommendation." Allan's normally buoyant face looked leaden, even as he said this.

My heart leapt at the thought of admission to the storied halls of somewhere like Cambridge or Oxford, but I swallowed the excitement. "That's very generous of you Allan, but if I'm going to do this, it will be on my own steam."

"On your own *human* steam, you mean." He skewered me with an assessing gaze.

"It's what I am." I shrugged.

Allan took a sip of his drink. "It's half of what you are. And the lesser half, if you ask me."

I hesitated on the words '*I didn't*', but was glad I didn't speak them after what came next.

"Have you ever stopped, even for a moment, and asked yourself why de 'ell you love art the way you do?"

"Lots of people love art," I said. "Museums wouldn't even exist otherwise."

"There's loving, and there's *loving*. You love it for the same reason your *grandmother* loved it. She was drawn to it. She made it. She didn't fight dat side of her nature."

"Technically, she didn't even know what that side of her nature was before she found those letters from Lily," I said.

"You'll want to be careful of anyfing Klaud tells you," Allan warned. "Vampires are good at giving you just enough of de truth to let you fill in de rest wif assumptions."

A little pang of guilt tugged at my heart. Not that I *ever* jumped to hasty conclusions...

"Anyway, it's true 'at Mark had been keepin' en eye on de

heirs he was aware of, but it wasn't until he learned his sister had been hunting dem that he stepped in."

"It's not that I don't appreciate the protection he provided to my family," I said, sitting forward in my seat. "It's just that I'm super-weirded out about this idea of my being some kind of quasi-reincaration of an uber-powerful heir who I happen to look just like."

"If it's any consolation," Allan said, signaling to Paige for a refill, "I bet it started generations earlier than your gran. You, love, are the completion of a cycle centuries owd."

"But I don't want to be a completion?" I asked, shooting the remainder of my martini. "What if I just want to eat cheese and be happy?"

"And who says you can't do dose fings *and* be a werewolf?" Allan pushed his glass aside to make room for the impending refill. "All I'm saying is, don't ignore this part of yourself, Hanna. Not 'tiww you've heard what it has to say."

I laughed, equal parts nervous and dismissive. "And how am I supposed to do that?"

"Easy," he said. "Listen. Don't argue wif it. Don't mute it. Don't *numb* it."

"I'm not saying you need to become a teetotaler, I'm saying you need to listen to what de werewolf part of you wants before you decide to silence it forever."

"I guess that makes sense," I said.

"Of course it bloody does." Allan slid down in his seat and pulled a blanket in the Abernathy tartan up to his chin. "Sleep if you can. 'ese next few days are gonna be 'ell."

If I had known just how right he would be, I might have listened.

CHAPTER 18

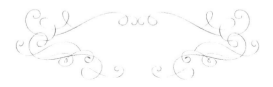

"Is that...black light paint?" My taxi driver leaned across the empty passenger seat, staring at the front of the house containing my apartment. A strobe light pulsed behind one of my windows. The other lay in shards on the front lawn. "*Welcum home Henna*?" he read.

"Hanna," I corrected, handing him a wad of cash.

"Right. Well, thanks. Have fun." He winked at me.

"I'm not sure if that's humanly possible." I dragged my suitcase out of the back seat and hauled it behind me up the winding sidewalk. At the point where I usually began to search for my keys, the front door burst open, ejaculating a handful of topless women into the night. Their squeals shattered the darkness as their horny pursuer gave chase.

And he was horny. Literally. Two small horns poked up through his mop of curly hair, precisely like those on the Renaissance statues of Moses prey to a mistranslation of the Bible.

On the other hand, the only cloven hooves Moses had to deal with belonged to sacrificial animals. Not so for the thing chasing six jiggling tits across my shared lawn. It had a man's torso, sure as day. But the area below his umbilicus ended abruptly at waistline of his fur pants.

Yes. *Fur. Pants*. Only, they weren't pants. Pants would have covered the erection stabbing into the night. Fucking satyrs.

A satyr. On my lawn. And half naked women. Even now, House of Pain's "Jump Around" floated out my window. My *broken* window.

Inside the stairwell, the glow of black lights turned smoke into a pale blue miasma floating out of my *open* door. In the mist, more topless women rode the banister. I had to step over what appeared to be three separate homeless people passed out on the stairs to get to my apartment. And that's where shit *really* got weird.

My couches had been stacked in a corner to accommodate the mass of writhing bodies. More black light paint splattered the walls, cutting through the hazy air like an electric oracle's message. *Fuck me stooped*, said the wall behind my bed. The message above the couch was more enigmatic. *Wallis has a big crock*. Another unfortunate misspelling I hoped.

Had Steve not texted me earlier to let me know he'd taken the cats for a sleepover, panic would have forced my hand sooner. When an empty beer can bounced off my forehead, major motor functions kicked in, and I hit the light.

Bodies sought the darkened corners like cockroaches.

"What the fuck is going on here?" I demanded, finally finding words.

The humans in the room, mostly topless, some completely nude, were predominantly female. The men varied widely. More satyrs. Werewolves.

And...leprechauns? At least I *hoped* they were leprechauns. Despite their disparate sizes, the bodies in my living room had one thing in common.

They were pointing toward the kitchen.

"I am going to move out of the doorway," I announced. "And

I would recommend that you all consider this an invitation to exit without bodily harm." I pulled my suitcase up by the door and turned into the kitchen.

A parade of hurried footsteps behind my back provided little comfort against the sight in the kitchen.

The horse's muscular white body glowed ultraviolet in the black light. It reared back onto its hind legs, forelegs pawing at the air in slow motion like a commercial honoring the Wild West's former glory. A silvered mane, tossed from the majestic neck, rippled like a violent rainbow. The sound of hooves crashing against the wooden floor echoed through my apartment like the apocalypse.

"Chug! Chug! Chug!" came the shouted order from the kitchen's perimeter.

Only then did I notice the woman on the horse's back.

Chug she did. From one of my crystal champagne glasses, which she turned over upon a golden horn with a victorious shout.

A golden horn. Sprouting from the forehead of the horse she was riding. In my kitchen.

No, not *horse. Unicorn.* There was a *unicorn* in my kitchen.

I slapped the overhead light switch at the precise moment the words found their way out of my mouth. "There's a unicorn in my kitchen!"

The sleek white head turned toward me, its dark lips parting to deliver some mystical edict. "You don't fucking say?"

I rushed forward, clapping my hands over his elegant, velvety muzzle. "Those are *bad* words. *Swear* words. You're a unicorn. You shouldn't say those things." I moved my hands upward, stroking his nose.

"*Harder,*" he neighed.

"What did you just say?"

The beautiful beast regarded his audience, his expression

both discerning and wise. "I said...*show me your tits*!" A cheer rose from the crowd.

My arm swung of its own accord, the flat of my palm landing squarely across the proverbial horse's mouth.

A collective gasp silenced the kitchen and a sudden horror seized me. "I just slapped a unicorn!"

"Do it again."

I looked at his face, and saw genuine pleasure there. Additional revelations followed at a snail's pace. "You're a pervert. You're a perverted unicorn!"

"Joe said you were *fast*." A golden hoof stroked my thigh.

I slapped it away. "Stop that! You're a unicorn. You're supposed to be all magical and shit."

"You got it all wrong, lady. I'm not *a* fucking unicorn. I am *the* fucking unicorn. Name's Wallis, and it is a *pleasure* making your acquaintance." When his long tongue snaked out of his lips and stroked his horsey teeth, I felt the first stirrings of rage.

"Wallis, is it? What, *the fuck* are you doing in my apartment?"

"Easy, honey," the unicorn said, casting a comforting glance at his posse. "Joe said we could crash here, okay?"

"No, not okay. And who the hell is Joe?"

"If you don't know, then I'm sorry for you." Several feminine laughs tinkled like bells. "Joe Abernathy. The man. The wolf. The legend."

Bang bang bang.

All heads, mine included, whipped toward my front door. Someone must have shut it on their way out. We held our collective breath.

Bang bang bang.

"Shhh!" I hissed. "That's probably the landlord!"

Only it wasn't. It was someone much, *much* worse.

"Hanna?" Morrison's instantly recognizable voice demanded. "What the hell is going on here?"

"Someone want to join the party?" Wallis asked, arching an eyebrow.

"No, you idiot," I stage-whispered. "That's a police detective!"

"It's the fuzz!" the unicorn shouted.

Bodies tripped over each other as they scattered, some diving from the windows to risk minor injury at the lawn's mercy rather than face justice.

I scanned my kitchen, searching for a place to hide. Then I looked at the unicorn. Hide me? Fuck that. Hide *him!* "Get in the shower!" I ordered, swatting his flank.

He looked at me from foot to head and nodded in approval. "Get clean before you get dirty. I like the way you roll."

"Are you out of your goddamn mind? The police are at the door, and I have fucking *unicorn* in my kitchen! Shut your fucking mouth and get in the fucking shower!"

Bang bang bang. "Hanna! Open up!"

I reached into the drawer and pulled out my grandmother's well-loved rolling pin. "So help me God, if you don't get in the shower, I am going to beat your magical head in."

"All right, all right," he said, trotting toward the bathroom. "You don't have to be like that."

At the last minute, I grabbed a crumpled party hat off the counter and swapped it with the champagne glass on his golden horn. "Just in case."

It took him a few tries to get all four hooves over the tall sides of my claw foot tub. I yanked the shower surround closed behind him. "Not a peep," I warned him.

Looking over the kitchen, I was overcome by a tsunami of futility. Every available surface was littered with glasses, bottles of booze in various states of consumption, trash, and *dear God,* was that a *used* condom? I stepped over a pair of legs jutting out from under my kitchen table and made my way into the living room, where the situation was about the same.

I flopped a throw pillow over yet another topless woman, this one passed out on my couch, unplugged the stereo and strobe lights, and opened the door to Morrison.

His appearance had improved considerably since the last time I'd seen him. Last time he'd been on my doorstep, he'd been the one passed out in a pool of his own vomit. Now, he was a stark contrast to the pantsless man Morrison nudged with his shoe.

We looked at each other and then looked down.

"Want to tell me what's going on here? I heard a public disturbance call for your address go out over the scanner. You are damn lucky I'm the first one to respond."

"So you're off suspension?" I said, tossing my hair in what I hoped was a flirtatious manner. "That's great!"

His cop face had returned, pressed and polished, along with his button-up shirt and tie. "Don't even *think* about trying to change the subject, Hannalore Harvey."

Shit. Conversations using my full name tended not to end well for me. I glanced at the wreckage beyond him in the hall, trying to decide which way to play this. A pair of sequined G-string panties dangled from the newel post at the top of the stairs. "Oh, you know. Just one of those little get-togethers that got a little out of hand."

"Hanna, I had to step over two homeless people to get to your door. And one of them thinks he's a dog."

Shit. Still, 'thinks he's a dog' was acres better than 'transformed into a wolf.' Even better, he hadn't said anything about satyrs.

"They just had a little too much to drink is all. I thought maybe they should sleep it off, you know?"

"This is a known drug dealer," he said, giving 'ole No Pants another nudge with his shoe.

"Oh?" I tried to look interested but unconcerned.

"Yes." He looked past me into the apartment. "And the

woman passed out in your bed got picked up for prostitution for the eighth time a couple days ago."

"Huh," I said. "So crazy."

"I have a hard time believing you know these people," Morrison said.

Me too. "They're friends of a friend. Of a friend."

"Friends of friends of friends notwithstanding, I need to take a look around."

"Nah, you don't want to come in here. Just more of the same. I'll have it cleaned up by morn—"

"Your landlord is pressing charges for vandalism. She also asked the dispatcher about starting the eviction process. If you have any of hope of keeping this place, you had better let me see the damage."

I let all the air out of my lungs in a giant whoosh and stepped aside. "Be my guest."

Glass crunched under his shoes as he stepped on the remnants of a broken bottle. "What...the fuck...happened here?"

"A welcome home party?" I picked after him in the debris, trying to avoid limbs.

"Home from where?"

"Scotland," I said. "Business trip."

"So that's where *he's* been."

I rolled my eyes at Morrison's back. There was only one *he* in Morrison's world. "Yes, *he* was there with me, as were many other artists and collectors." *Who also happened to be vampires and werewolves.*

"He came back with you, then?" The question failed to sound as casual as he'd tried to make it.

"No, he had to stay behind for a meeting." *With the millennia old ruler of the vampire kingdom, Akhenaten.* Details.

"Handy how he never seems to be around when shit goes sideways for you."

Actually, I found it decidedly un-handy. "Who said anything went sideways? I like a party as much as the next girl."

"There's a little person in your refrigerator," Morrison informed me.

"I totally know that," I said. Truly, I hadn't even glanced in that direction. The door hung ajar, the light having long since burned out. The fridge's entire contents had been emptied, and in their place was a tiny man, folded like a contortionist, snoring.

"Why the hell is he dressed like a leprechaun?"

"He was part of the...entertainment?" Embarrassing how easy the lies came these days.

Morrison shuffled through clinking bottles to the center of my kitchen and waited for me to join him. "Hanna, there is thousands of dollars worth of damage to this home. Your landlord has a solid case for eviction."

My heart sank into my shoes. "I was afraid of that."

"The way I see it—"

A high-pitched giggle erupted from under the bathroom door.

"What was that?" Morrison asked.

"What was what?" I blinked at him.

"It sounded like a baby laughing."

I gave him my best exasperated expression. "Yep, you got me. There's a baby in my bathroom."

He shook his head and began again. "Anyway, as I was saying. Unless you—"

The laugh came again, louder this time, and longer.

"You have to have heard it that time," Morrison said.

"Old pipes," I shrugged. "This place makes weird noises all the time. There was a week, a *solid* six days I was convinced there was a badger living in my cabinet."

"And it was the pipes?"

"No. It was a raccoon, but you get the point. You were saying?"

Eyes narrowed, he continued. "Here's the deal, Hanna. The eviction process takes longer than most people think, but this place isn't—"

And that's when the laugh of all baby laughs rattled the bathroom door on its hinges.

"That's it." Morrison lunged toward the door, but I threw myself in the way to block him.

"It's just someone else passed out in there, sleeping it off. Probably if we go in there we'll see a bunch of vomit, and we'll both get nauseous, and then we'll throw up, and then there will be *thrice* as much vomit on the floor, which is just more work for me, and is there really any reason why you'd want to do that to me after everything we've been through?"

"Did you just use the word *thrice*?" A familiar, heart-softening, panty-melting grin slanted across Morrison's mouth.

I gave him my most charming, *there's totally not a unicorn in there* smile. "Yes. Yes I did."

"Hanna, don't make me move you."

My fingers tightened on the doorframe. "That would be a use of excessive force. I am being completely non-threatening right now."

"I have probable cause to believe there is an infant at risk in your bathroom. You're obstructing an officer."

"You haven't presented me with any documentation that—"

"Oh for fuck's sake," Morrison grumbled, grabbing me by the hips and swinging me easily out of his path.

Damn. I had been so much more commanding in the version of events transpiring in my head. "James! Don't—"

"*Jesus fucking Christ!*" Morrison staggered backward out of the bathroom, his face ashen. "Hanna! There's a horse! A horse in your bath tub!"

I wondered if his mane was only rainbow-colored by black

light. And this was to say nothing of the horn. Thank God Wallis had kept the party hat on.

"And he's wearing a fucking party hat!"

"Yeah, I know," I said summoning my best beleaguered sigh. "Someone brought him as a gag. I guess you can rent party horses these days. Isn't that the damnedest thing?" God, but I was getting good at this shit.

"Who the fuck rents a horse?"

"My guess? The little guy in the fridge. He looks like the type, am I right?"

Morrison's mouth opened, closed, and opened again before he finally found words. "That doesn't explain that creepy baby laugh."

A thought that had occurred to me as well. Knowing it had something to do with Wallis brought little comfort. "Told you. These pipes are crazy."

Morrison regarded me through a narrowed gaze. "Okay, here's the rub. There is way more going on here than you're telling me, but I'm exhausted, and from the look of it, so are you. I'm calling for back up to come and pick up everyone that's left in the apartment. In the meantime, you're going to put that suitcase back in your car. You're coming home with me."

"Oh no I'm not. This is my apartment, and I'm staying right here." I folded my arms and planted my feet stubbornly on the floor.

"You *do* know you're standing in a puddle of piss," Morrison said, glancing down at my feet.

I gritted my teeth against the urge to take off like a bottle rocket, refusing to look down. "Of course I know. You think I just stand around in piss without knowing it? When I'm standing in piss, I fucking stand in it, it's what I do."

"And horse apples," Morrison added.

"What?"

"You're standing in a puddle of piss and a pile of horse shit."

At which point, I jumped away screaming like a little girl. Searching the kitchen for something to wipe my shoe on, I settled on the legs still sticking out from under my table. "That is so not okay," I said, dragging my boot down the length of his jeans. Or *its* jeans because who the fuck knew, anymore?

Morrison leaned toward the pile I had just catapulted myself from. "What the hell are they feeding that thing? This shit is like...rainbow-colored."

My eyes widened. Of course it would be. After all, it wasn't a horse that left it, but a unicorn. "Who knows what the poor thing ate while wandering around the kitchen, you know?"

"Like I said." Morrison looked at me, and through me at the same time. "There's plenty you're not telling me. But this place is uninhabitable and it's three o'clock in the morning. I'm calling for back-up, and you're coming with me. Got it?"

Having exhausted all other possibilities after a quick mental review, I had already decided to agree. "Okay, fine. Let me just grab a few things."

As soon as Morrison migrated toward the living room with his cell phone attached to his ear, I shot into the bathroom.

Wallis was exactly where I'd left him. Only when *I* looked at him, I saw golden hooves and a rainbow colored mane. "What the *fuck* was all that about? God, are you lucky he thought you were a horse!"

"Luck has nothing to do with it," he said. "Only other paranormals can see this goodness. And seeing as you're a werewolf—"

"Heir," I corrected. "A werewolf *heir*."

"Ohhh. So you mean you and Mark haven't done the deed yet? Cause if it were up to me, I'd bend you over—"

I grabbed a handful of his rainbow-colored mane and jerked it. "Listen you four-legged shit-stain, there is a detective in my living room calling for back-up, and probably agents from the ASPCA. You had better find a way to get out of here without being seen. In fact, the more *people* you can get out of here before the cops come, the better."

"Easy, girl. Wallis will take care of it." And then he winked at me.

"And you know what else? If there's anything worse than a perverted unicorn, it's a perverted unicorn that refers to himself in the third person."

"Wallis has decided not to take that personally," he whispered, swatting my ass with his tail.

"Hanna!" Morrison called from the living room. "Let's go!"

"Just a second! I'm feeding the u—horse a...waffle! He looked hungry."

"Rather eat your muffin," Wallis mumbled.

"And I'd rather punch you right in your horseface." I grabbed a can of shaving gel from the sink and stomped out of the bathroom, slamming the door behind me.

Morrison had cleared a path for me in the living room and had my suitcase in his hand and my carry-on bag slung over his shoulder. "Steve have your cats?" he asked.

"Yep. Took them for a sleepover."

"Good," he said. "I've always liked that guy. You'll follow me?"

I gave him a half-hearted salute. "Yes, sir."

The smile he sent back to me in reply slid right off propriety and into suggestion. "Maybe I'll think of a few more interesting requests, if you're feeling so compliant."

A shiver started at the back of my neck and raced to my knees, leaving a burning trail right through my center.

This was going to be a long night.

CHAPTER 19

"You've made some improvements." I wandered around the formerly bare living room of Morrison's townhouse, noting the addition of a credenza topped by a huge flat screen TV, two overstuffed buttery leather couches, and matching end tables.

I mean…the man had end tables topped with *two matching lamps*.

The last time I'd been here, we'd taken a late night supper sitting across from each other at a coffee table, the only other piece of furniture in the room aside from two Wal-Mart bookshelves. The bookshelves had both evolved and multiplied, now taking up the entire wall.

I forced myself not to look at the titles, having had enough trouble not pole-vaulting onto his cock last time I was here based on his book collection alone.

This was to say nothing of the artwork lining the walls, these having been painted by Morrison himself.

"I had some free time on my hands," he said.

Free time, being code for *being suspended for beating Abernathy to a pulp during an interrogation.*

"The couches look really comfortable. I don't mind sleeping down here if you have a blanket I could use." I would have brought mine with me, had it not been stuck under a pile of prostitutes.

"Come upstairs," Morrison said, looking over his shoulder.

"James, I don't think—"

"That's where the guest room is," he added.

"Oh. Right." At some point, I really should stop assuming everyone wanted to sleep with me. Just because I'd been propositioned by a unicorn didn't necessarily mean every male on earth wanted a go.

I followed Morrison up the stairs, smiling to myself as he schlepped my oversized bags without complaint. He paused at the first room and flicked on the light.

This was *his* room. I knew it even before the warm glow washed over the king-sized bed. His scent filled my chest, my head, my heart. Not just any scent. His *sleeping* scent. The heavenly distillation of his skin, his cologne, his deodorant, concentrated by hours of applied body heat. The same scent he'd left on my pillows, my sheets after he'd warmed them for a night.

A little ache radiated out from the center of my chest when I saw the pile of books slanted across the nightstand on the side closest to the bathroom.

Just like mine.

The other nightstand was bare.

"Hanna?" He'd continued walking, and was now standing in the doorway of another room, the light already on.

"Oh, sorry." I shuffled down the hallway to meet him in the doorway of the guest room and had to stifle a gasp.

A four-poster wrought iron canopy bed. Filmy, diaphanous swags of fabric slithered between the ornate rods and fell, shimmering to the carpet. The plush velvet damask bedding and matching throw pillows looked like they'd been seduced from a courtesan's boudoir. Somehow the configuration sailed past *feminine* and landed squarely in *erotic*. This was a bed you tied someone to. A bed built for begging mercy, and being given something far better.

I had always wanted one of these.

"I always wanted one of these," Morrison said, hauling my suitcase onto the vintage steamer trunk at the foot of the bed. "Guest room seemed like a good place for one."

I walked past him to click the lamp perched on the nightstand. The glow revealed a stack of books that might have been at home on a coffee table. Large, ponderous tomes about Da Vinci, Rembrandt, and Van Gogh.

Van Gogh.

Even if his brother had stabbed me a few times, I couldn't find it in my heart to hold it against Vincent, my first and longest art historical love. I smiled, thinking of the impossibility of my situation. Vincent Van Gogh's brother had tried to kill me. And here, a book about him adorned the guest room where I was staying.

Given a thousand years, Morrison could not have guessed the reason for my grin.

"What?" he asked.

"Nothing," I said.

"That's not a *nothing* smile." His observational acuity had ever been finer than a razor's edge, and so it remained. The source of equal parts pleasure and problem for me.

"This room is more me than *me.* Does that make sense?"

"No. And yes. We share some territory." He reached out and caught up a length of the silky fabric. It sighed as it yielded to his fingers, much as I would, and had. And wanted to.

The ache in my heart found my breasts. Something pulled my magnetic center south.

You're coming into heat. This is so, so not the place to be when your every cell is begging to be fucked.

"You should go," I said.

"Where?"

"Anywhere."

"Why?"

Surprise etched every muscle in his face when I leapt at him. Though not yet a werewolf, I moved faster than he expected. A familiar sensation of falling, the world blurring around us, then ceasing to spin on its axis when our bodies made contact. One moment of perfect stillness held us before I descended, pinning him to the bed beneath me. Like the predator I might yet be, I devoured him—my prey, my prize. I lost and found myself in the taste of him, essential as water, his tongue surging against mine like the tide.

The hands he'd pressed against my chest in surprise melted, sliding around my back to pull me closer.

My fingers threaded through the thick dark sugar of his hair. I bit then licked his lips, his hard jaw, the smooth skin of his neck.

His groan moved heavy desire through my veins where it gathered in my stomach. I ground my hips against his, knowing what I'd find there already.

As ever, James Morrison did not disappoint. "Such a big boy," I whispered, nibbling the spot below his ear that I knew could drive him to frenzy. "I could ride you until your back broke." Greedy, I pushed my hand against his pants, feeling him, hard beneath my palm.

"*Jesus*," he panted. "I don't know what's gotten into you, but I'd like to."

What's gotten into you? Why don't you tell him? Tell him you're a – "No!" I tore myself away from him, rolling off the bed, putting as much distance between us as possible.

Guilt clubbed me over the head as I took in his wounded, bewildered expression. How could I do this? This man loved me, and I was going to use him like my own personal scratching post? Sharpening my claws against the willing flesh around his good heart. I struggled to regain my breath as well as my composure. "I'm so sorry, James. I shouldn't have done that."

"You're right," he agreed, pushing himself to his elbows. "Get your ass over here and finish what you started."

"See, I'd really love to, but I think that would be a bad idea." *Don't look at his pants. Do. Not. Look at his pants.*

"I'm having trouble validating your assertion. You're horny as hell, I have this erection, there's this big bed right here, and we've done this enough to know it will end well for *both* of us."

I had to admit, the man was making a whole fuck-ton of sense. "Yeah, but that's just, *physical*. And we both know it's not that simple."

Morrison followed my gaze to his aforementioned erection. "It could be."

"But it isn't." I loaded my look with every ounce of pleading I could muster. *Please understand.*

"Why not?"

No such luck. "Because. Because of...what you said."

He looked at me like my tits had suddenly migrated from my chest to my forehead. "What did I say?"

Shit.

"Forget it," I said.

A knowing smile slid across his lips. "You think it would be insulting to use me for my body because I love you, and you don't love me."

My eyes must have gone as wide as duck eggs, judging from the amusement on Morrison's face. "I didn't—"

"I'm touched, Hanna. Really I am. But I'm also a man. *Please.* I ask you, I *beg* you, use me for my body."

I blinked at him, unbelieving. "You would really be okay with that?"

He shrugged. "Don't shit yourself, cupcake. I want everything you have. *All* of you. But I'll take what I can get. If that's your ass, for a night, so be it."

"That's horrible!" I protested. "That makes it *worse,* not better!"

"Any man who told you different would be lying." He rolled over onto his side and patted the space on the comforter before him.

"What if it was less than my ass? Would you take that?"

Morrison's boyish laugh was more contagious than Cholera. "I sleep with a pair of your panties under my pillow. I think we're past any illusions of pride at this point."

Arousal stormed my senses anew. "My panties? When did you—"

His smile was less enigmatic than Abernathy's by half. "You have your secrets. I have mine."

"Do me a favor?" I asked.

"Depends." He pushed himself to a seated position on the edge of the bed. "Does this favor involve oral sex and multiple orgasms?"

My knees threatened to give. "Could you *please* stop being so fucking charming? You're making this really hard for me."

"Only fair, considering how *hard* you've made things for me." We both glanced at his erection, still insistent upon participating fully in this conversation.

Moisture flooded my mouth. "Get out of here and go lock your door. Now."

"Nope." He rolled off the bed and slung an arm around my neck. "Come on," he said, tugging me through the door toward his bedroom. "Let's go to bed."

"*No,* James. I told you. I can't. Even if you're okay with it."

"You're not going to," he said.

"What?"

"We are going to *sleep* together," he announced. "That's all."

"Sleep?" Visions of me pole vaulting onto the half-naked, sleeping Morrison sprang through my head. "James. I don't think you understand. I'm going to attack you again. It *will* happen."

"People try a lot of things in my line of work, Hanna. And none of them succeed without my say."

"I'm...stronger than you remember," I warned him.

"Okay," he said, sliding past me into the hallway. "Come at me."

"Excuse me?"

"Come at me." He gave my shoulder a playful shove and squared off against me.

I looked behind my back to the guest room. "I already did. Remember?"

"Now try it while I'm *resisting*." His broad shoulders flexed as he hunkered down, preparing for an attack. "Come get some."

"I am *not* doing this. This is ridiculous. I'm going to bed." I turned to walk into the guest room and was caught by a forearm around the waist. Morrison tripped me over his outstretched leg, and I fell to the carpet, pinned beneath him.

"Single leg takedown," he announced. "Didn't know you were shacking up with the Croton High state wrestling champion, did you?"

No, and it certainly wasn't helping me not want to climb him like a tree. "Congratulations sixteen years ago. Now let me up."

"You're dangerous, remember? You're going to attack me. Let's see what you got." He brought his full weight down on my hips, keeping my arms pinned above my head. The second he shifted, I jerked my hips upward, tossing him off to the side.

A quick roll, and I scrambled out from under him, only to be tackled again from behind. My elbows stung as Morrison pulled my legs out from under me dragged me backward on the carpet. His body came down on my back, and in a swift succession of arm and leg locks, I was face down on the floor, trussed up like a Thanksgiving turkey. Only that wasn't a meat thermometer pressing against my ass.

"That all you got?" His lips were warm against the already feverish skin of my neck.

It wasn't all I had. Not by half. But any further demonstration would raise more questions than it would answer. "You win," I sighed.

"The lady yields?"

"For the moment…"

He rolled off and pulled me up by hands, but dove toward my hips at the last minute and slung me over his shoulder.

"Put me down!" I tried for *indignant* but came much closer to *delighted*.

"Not until you say the magic word," he teased.

"Please?" I guessed.

"What the hell kind of magic word is that?" He reached up and spanked my ass. "Try again."

"Stop!" I laughed.

"Nope. Try again." He started to spin in a circle.

The hallway blurred around me as I grabbed handfuls of his shirt. "James! I'm going to yark!"

He stopped, but the world kept spinning. "Say *yes*."

"Yes *what*?" I asked, unable to stifle a giggle. When was the last time I'd felt this giddy? The last time I'd laughed so much?

"*Yes*, James. I would love to have a platonic sleepover with you tonight," he said.

"Do I have to?"

"No. But just so you know, I have excellent stamina. I could spin you for hours." He took a few steps to demonstrate.

"Okay! Okay," I relented. "*Yes* James, I would love to have a platonic sleepover with you tonight."

"Good," he said, walking into the bedroom with me still draped over his shoulder. "Because I am going to cuddle you so fucking hard."

CHAPTER 20

I awoke to the sensation of lips pressed to my forehead. My body rolled into Morrison as he lowered himself down on the edge of the bed. "Morning," he said.

"Morning," I mumbled into his pillow.

"I'm heading out. There's coffee and doughnuts downstairs."

I cranked my head off the pillow. "This would be a very cruel thing to lie about."

"I don't lie," he reminded me.

"Good. Cause I'm going to eat the shit out of those doughnuts."

"Make them pay. Gotta go to work." He planted another kiss on my cheek, leaving in his wake the scent of shaving lotion and clean skin.

"Thanks," was my lame reply. I rolled myself out of bed and padded to the window, watching until I saw Morrison's iconic Gold Crown Victoria exit the complex at speeds to the north of legal. Another dead body, perhaps?

He'd hinted last night that Georgetown had been experiencing a surge in unexplained deaths. Some looked like murders. Others looked like medical anomalies: cardiac arrest in previously young, healthy adults; organ failure due to lack of blood volume.

Not blood *loss*. Blood *disappearance*.

Fortunately, Nero's associates seemed capable of concealing the evidence of their contact. And this was only half of the story.

They would have had twice as many bodies on their hands, were Joseph not adept at disposing of them.

War. The implications of this word pressed down upon my shoulders, driving an ache into my neck and head, turning the tendons in my body tighter than a bow string.

A world populated by more creatures than I had ever reckoned, humans the youngest and most volatile of the species I knew. Beings as elemental as the foundation of the earth poised to destroy each other, and many more innocents in the process. The fate of the entire planet hung in the balance, and I, the lynchpin in this intricate Rube Goldberg machine, could only think about doughnuts.

Only one way to stop thinking about them.

I flipped open my suitcase, thankfully sans any new heads, and extracted my pig slippers. In naught but an oversized t-shirt and panties, I shuffled downstairs.

Navigating Morrison's kitchen proved eerily easy. Coffee cups were exactly where I would have stored them, in the slim cabinet over the coffee maker. Half and half was tucked neatly in the refrigerator door, beneath the butter and eggs. Sugar could be found in the cabinet nearest the stove, where spices could be selected and quickly added to pots simmering on the range.

Some people snooped medicine cabinets. I'd found a man's spice collection could tell a person loads more.

Morrison's, of course, read like the pantry of a professional chef, which description was not far off the mark.

Bottles of aged balsamic vinegar as thick as chocolate syrup, slim jars of caramelized shallots, white truffle oil, exotic sea salts in pink, white, and black, tins of Herbs de Provence, Tellicherry black peppercorns, and saffron.

Even I had never shelled out the cash for real saffron. What I had looked more like confetti soaked in red food coloring than the stamens of rare crocuses.

"Creepy," I mumbled, lifting to my lips the oversized Salvador Dali mug I'd selected from Morrison's eclectic collection. This, at least, he had not yet had time to upgrade. The silverware, too still looked like a bin you might find in the kitchen section of Goodwill.

Creepy? Or kismet? Inquired the little voice in my head, who, luckily, had receded significantly in power outside of Castle Abernathy's grounds.

"Those are not mutually exclusive," I answered aloud, taking a sip of my coffee. Smooth, roasty smoke slid like velvet over my tongue. "Fucking A. He cuddles, he buys doughnuts, his coffee is better than my grandma's. Sorry!" I added, sliding a glance heavenward. "You know how much I love your coffee."

But grandma would have forgiven me. She'd had a thing for cops, too.

"I know he's no *Walker Texas Ranger*, but I think you'd like him," I said. Grandma had never been too shy about letting *nice young men* know when they could butter her toast, or mow her lawn, or an innumerable assortment of other innuendoes.

My pig slippers slid over to Morrison's new dining table, where two doughnut boxes were stacked upon each other.

I opened the first box, still warm at the sides, and the aroma of melted sugar filled my senses like a siren's song. In the whole box of glazed doughnuts, only three were missing from the bottom row. Morrison would have popped it open while he drove, too hungry and eager to wait.

A smile tugged one corner of my mouth upward as I shifted the first box to the side and opened the second.

All my favorites, present and accounted for. Maple glazed. Cinnamon buns. Lemon filled. Chocolate cake. From this box, nothing was missing. I picked up the maple-glazed and destroyed half a doughnut in one bite.

"We could have used you in the Parthian War."

As it turns out, half a doughnut heaved at the head of an opponent offers little defense, even when combined with an eardrum shattering shriek.

Crixus brushed a flake of glaze off his forehead and ate the remainder of my weapon in another bite. "Gods, these are good."

Gods. Plural.

He reached into the box and picked out a raspberry jelly filled doughnut, which he deflated with one, swift suck. "Have you ever had a fucking honey cookie?" he asked my open-mouthed panic-stricken mask of a face. "Honey, stone ground wheat flour, and sesame seeds mixed into a paste that could double as cement and baked until it surrenders. Tell me I didn't get fucked over in the dessert department." Half the doughnut disappeared between his shapely lips.

"*You*! You shouldn't be here. How did you get in here?"

"I'm a demigod," he said, by way of explanation.

"Yeah. I heard. How did you get in here?"

"Materialized." Another half doughnut disappeared as quickly as the first had.

"You came through the wall?" I tried to assign irritation to my words, and anger.

"Hanna, if I *came*, you'd know." He picked up one of the maple glazed doughnuts and relieved it of icing with a dexterous flick of his tongue. "You always talk to yourself out loud?"

I forced myself to focus on anger instead of arousal, though I had them both in unequal measure. "*Exactly* how long have you been here?"

"Long enough to be disappointed at the lack of nocturnal happenings around this place." Sapphire eyes winked below dark brows. His skin was too smooth for such hard features, his small ears too beautifully shaped and boyish. Today, those ears bore small silver hoop earrings that lent him a piratey sort of mischief. The shifting mounds of muscle in his arms bunched as he squished the doughnut into a ball and shoved it into his mouth whole. Even his *jaw* was buff, flexing as he chewed and swallowed. "I thought you two were going to get down to it for sure, the way you attacked the guy."

My cheeks burned with a sudden rush of blood. "What does or doesn't happen between me and James is none of your business! You can't just go materializing into people houses, and bedrooms any time you feel like it!"

A sultry smile slid across Crixus' face. "You didn't seem to mind before."

I picked up another doughnut and winged it at him. "That's because I thought you were Mark! And by the way, what the fuck was that all about? Do you just randomly climb into women's beds pretending to be other people, or is mine a special case?"

He laughed, picking up the doughnut and licking off the chocolate icing. "I like fighting with you."

How the hell did he get his tongue to move like that?

"Seriously though," I said. "You got me in so much trouble it's not even funny. I owe you a hell of a lot worse than a doughnut."

"Is that what you call what happened in the attic? *Trouble?*"

Another wave of scarlet seared my cheeks. "How do you—"

"Demigod, remember?" He winked at me.

I snatched the doughnut out of his hand and stuck it on a napkin. "Bad demigod. No doughnut."

"Look, I can't say I blame you for being conflicted. But between you and me, I think you're better off with the cop."

I took a bite of doughnut to buy myself the time required to chew it. "I can make up my own mind, thanks."

"Really? Because to the casual observer, it looks like you're in love with both of them and are completely incapable of making a decision."

My hand itched with the need to throw something at him, but having just reclaimed my last projectile, I thought better of lobbing it at him a second time. "It's complicated."

"Hey, I know that better than anyone." Crixus pushed himself up from the table and sauntered over to Morrison's refrigerator. I slid a sideways glance over the sculpture revealed by his tight jeans and plain black t-shirt as he walked. Taller than Morrison, though not as tall as Abernathy, but equally muscled. He pulled out a gallon of milk, popped off the lid and chugged.

"Hey," I said. "This isn't even your house. You can't go drinking from the milk carton."

"The only thing your detective is going to catch from me is *awesome*, and I don't think he'd mind." He threw back his head and slugged down a few more gulps.

"Bring that over here," I said, chewing down a mouthful of chocolate glazed cake doughnut.

"Your wish is my command, *Lady Hanna*." He plunked the milk down in front of me, and I took it, filling my empty coffee cup.

"So did you follow me here just to torment me further? Or does your being here and robbing me of doughnuts serve an actual purpose?"

"I'm here for the wedding, of course. You're just a convenient way for me to entertain myself while I'm in town."

"What wed—" *Shit.* Shayla had mentioned a whole passel of

Greek relatives. Crixus, a demigod, would comfortably fit in the world of Nereids, nymphs, and satyrs. "You're related?"

"Distant cousin," he said. "I'm the unfortunate experiment between Zeus and a Gallic slave. The pantheon was falling out of favor by then. I think it was a revenge thing."

"Made you one hell of a gladiator though, I'd wager."

A nostalgic smile lit his face like sunshine. "It did."

The milk was colder in the center than it was around the edges, heated by coffee-warmed ceramic. The sensation reminded me of the times my grandmother pulled a mug warmed from the dishwasher to give me milk and cookies before bed. "How did you end up as Klaud's servant?"

Regret looked unnatural on a face that should have been carved in marble. "Hubris."

"Yours? Or others'?"

"Both. Demigod or not, I was the property of the man who owned my mother. He bet the emperor Nero that I was unbeatable. He knew nothing of vampires and at the time, neither did I."

"Your servitude was the wager?"

"Yes. Until my death, or his."

"But vampires are immortal." Sugar and fat began to congeal in a heavy lump in my stomach. I set down the remains of the third doughnut uneaten.

"Which information would have been useful *before* I agreed to those terms. I felt fairly certain I would outlive him by an order of magnitude, in the worst case. In the best case, I would have won freedom. My own, and my mother's. And a nice appointment for my master of course."

"And Nero brought in a ringer, I'm guessing?"

"That he did." Crixus snorted at the memory, apparently still chapped by it even now.

I pulled my knees up under my shirt. "Must have been one hell of a ringer to defeat a demigod. A vampire?"

"I have no idea what it was. Even to this day. It looked like a man, of course. Anyway, I lost, which is all that matters. I've been with Nero and Klaud ever since."

"That's a long damn time to be a servant. What's to prevent you from just walking away?"

"It was a blood oath. Breaking a blood oath is a very risky business."

"How so?" Before he could answer, my cell phone buzzed on the table. I glanced at the screen and felt my stomach do a death roll. *Morrison*. I thought about not answering, but then looked at the doughnut-laden table and felt a pang of guilt. "Not a peep," I warned Crixus, tapping the screen to answer the call. "Hey there."

"How the *fuck* did you do this?" Morrison's voice bore the tightly coiled tension of a spring. Conversations that began with this tone typically did not end well for me.

I tried to keep my voice as neutral as possible. "Do what?"

"Your apartment. I stopped by this morning to chat with the landlord and check out the damage."

"And?" I hoped the sound of the pulse rushing in my ears couldn't be heard over the line.

Crixus watched my face as he selected another doughnut.

"And there wasn't any." James Morrison, master showman.

I blinked at Crixus.

"Completely clean. The whole damn place. Spotless. Windows replaced. Antique banister repaired."

"Wow," I said, twirling my hair as if he could see the implied innocence of the gesture. "That is *so* weird."

"Weird?" Morrison barked. "No. It's not *weird*. It's fucking impossible."

"Maybe the damage wasn't as bad as it looked," I suggested. "The strobe light did make it pretty hard to see anything."

"Hanna, I know what I saw. I know what *you* saw. And, I'm

pretty damn sure you either know who undid this, or have a pretty good idea."

Many. None that I could share. A werewolf clean-up crew? Leprechaun luck? Unicorn magic? A satyr spell? "I was with you all last night. Remember? Whatever happened, I had nothing to do with it."

His silence often held more danger than his words. In this quiet space, the engine of his mind processed information into assumptions and theories often too close to the truth to be comfortable.

"We are going to discuss this further, Hanna. And when we do, I am going to ask you some difficult questions. You might want to start thinking about how you're going to answer them."

A sweat bloomed between my palm and the mug handle I discovered I was crushing in a white-knuckled grip. "Okay."

The line went dead. I dropped my phone and thumped my forehead on the table. "Shit. Shit shit *shit*."

"Trouble?" Crixus asked.

"Always."

"Cop catching on to your little secret?" Crixus grinned, a boyish dimple appearing in his smooth, tanned cheek.

"Little?" I raised my head from the table. "I don't think what I have going on here qualifies as *little* by any explanation. For example, I'm sitting at James Morrison's breakfast table with a Roman gladiator demigod, who has eaten six doughnuts to my two and a half. In the best case, he'll think I ate *nine* doughnuts for breakfast. In the worst, he'll add this to his list of questions to club me with at our next meeting. And that will be the easy one to explain away."

"Which is exactly why you should choose the cop, in my famously un-humble opinion. You choose him, you choose to stay human, and all this weird shit stops."

There.

He'd said it.

Had vocalized the very thought that had danced at the edges of my cognition since having accepted my soon-to-be ending position as Abernathy's gallery assistant. No more severed vampire heads in my luggage, no more gory battles, no more unicorns, or leprechauns or satyrs, or myths. No more secrets.

No more *Abernathy*.

The ache in my heart grew to encompass other faces. Other voices. It wasn't just Abernathy who belonged to this world. It was my brother, Steven Franke, his wife, Shayla, my new niece or nephew.

"It's not that easy," I said, rubbing the tension-taut muscle over my eyebrow.

"It could be. If you just—"

"Why did you come to my room?" The question sprang from some unknown source, freed only by my attention being focused elsewhere.

"I saw you wandering around your wing in Castle Abernathy. Shut away from everyone. Heard some of the things Abernathy said to you. Seems to me you're getting the short end of the stick. I thought maybe I should stop by and give you the *long* end for once." He waggled his eyebrows at me lasciviously.

Coffee-heated blood rushed to my cheeks. "It was a nice gesture and all. But you can't just go around pretending to be other people."

Crixus shrugged his bulky shoulders. "I only said what he *should* have said."

"If he can't say it on his own, it does me no good to have anyone else say it for him. I'd rather have an ugly truth than a pretty lie."

"If you say so." The rolling hills of muscle in his arms and chest tightened into sinuous bunches as he laced his hands behind his head.

"I do." I pushed my chair away from the table and took my coffee cup to the sink to wash it. "So how does it work when you need time off for a family function when you're the prize of a blood grudge? I can't imagine Nero giving you PTO or anything."

A hollow laugh escaped Crixus. "No, nothing like that. They came to town with me."

A cold chill slithered down my spine. Klaud and Nero. Here in Georgetown. My home. My post-divorce recovery ward. "They're not coming to the wedding too?"

"No, they won't be attending."

I froze with the dishtowel stuffed inside the mug. "They're in town because of the missing vampires, aren't they?"

Crixus met my eye and glanced away. "Something like that."

"Why do I feel like this is a really, really bad sign?"

"Because it is," Crixus admitted.

I rested my hands flat on the counter and allowed my shoulders to sag under the weight of this new knowledge. "So is war inevitable or what?"

Crixus rose from his chair and walked across the kitchen to stand before me in the arched cutout over the sink. "That depends."

"On what?"

He froze me in the alpine lake depths of his sapphire eyes. "On what you decide."

CHAPTER 21

"Why would what I decide have anything to do with the war?"

He leaned against the doorframe, somehow elevating it from a simple doorway to the hall of a Roman temple. "There hasn't been a mated alpha pair ruling the werewolf empire since the time of Anubis."

"Anubis. As in, the Egyptian god of the afterlife Anubis?"

"That's the guy."

"He of the jackal head?" I asked.

"Jackal…or *wolf*."

Images flashed across the slide projector in my mind, and with them, the notecards I had created to prepare essays for tests. I'd had a whole graduate theory class on Egyptian Iconography and Mythology. "Half man, half wolf, the dog of Egypt, weighing the hearts of the dead."

Surrendering his place in the doorway, walked over to where I stood at the counter. "The same."

"He was deposed by Osiris, or so the myth says."

"Also correct."

I called to mind all the imagery of Osiris stored in my

mental slide library. *A green skinned man. Green-skinned to represent both death, and rebirth. The living dead.* "He was a vampire," I said, slowly coming to the end of the trail of breadcrumbs Crixus had left for me. "He was killed by his brother, Seth, the embodiment of chaos, and his body cut into fourteen pieces and scattered across the earth."

"Which, as I suspect you know, would be a great way to make sure it took a very long time for a vampire to heal."

"Right," I continued. "Only his wife, Isis, gathered him together again. And the gods were so impressed by her devotion that they resurrected him, and made him Lord of the Underworld."

"And the balance of power has remained with vampires ever since," Crixus said, resting his elbows on the table. "Never has there been a pair powerful enough to unseat them."

"So was rulership passed down, then? From Osiris to Akhenaten?"

"Hadn't you guessed?" A broad smile split Crix's face. "Akhenaten *is* Osiris."

"Oh my God!" Akhenaten's otherworldly visage flashed through my head, merging with the images of Osiris still lingering there. He'd broken all the staid Egyptian canons of kingly depictions with his elongated features, exotic eyes, and odd proportions. And his wife, Nefertiti had been the subject of the most celebrated bust in all Egyptian art history. Were it possible for the powers of love and valor to be rendered down into unapologetic beauty, hers is the face that would emerge. "It makes perfect sense."

"I can't speak to Akhenaten's thoughts on losing the balance of power, but surrendering a thirteen thousand year reign doesn't go over so well with all the vampires."

"Sheesh. No wonder Nero's got his toga in a wad. He doesn't seem like the type to surrender power easily."

Crixus tapped the end of his nose. "The lady guesses well."

"So is that why you're here? To persuade me to choose Morrison so the vampires keep the crown?"

He was no longer in front of me, but behind me. Materialization, it seemed, put fast-moving to shame.

He pinned my hips to the counter with his, stunning me into immobility for a few breathless seconds by the size of what pressed against my back. "I can be *very* persuasive."

"Good God," I whispered.

"Only half." As quickly as the pressure had arrived, it evaporated. He sauntered away, that damnable mischievous grin plastered all over his face. "Never played with an heir before. I'll bet your body could do all *kinds* of things."

"*Played*? This is fun for you? Popping into people's houses, toying with their emotions, seeing what you can get them to do?"

He rewarded me with a self-satisfied smile. "You know what your problem is?"

Which one? "Please, Dr. Crotch, enlighten me."

"You need to have more fun," he said.

"Right." I blew hot air from my nose.

"I'm serious. Get out there. Play the field. Go on a vacation, drink a few dozen Mai Tais, dance your ass off in a club, pick up some local stud and ride him back to the dock." Here, he moved his hand like a jet ski skimming over the waves.

A sigh broke free from my chest before I could stop it. *God,* but that sounded nice. "Not likely to happen any time soon."

"Give it some thought."

"Right now, I'm giving thought to everything I need to be doing instead of standing in Morrison's kitchen chewing the fat with a demigod."

"Like showering?" A suggestive smirk notched his broad jaw.

"*No*. There will be none of that. And, by the way, it would be super creepy if you go all magically invisible so you can watch me. Don't do it," I said, wagging a finger at him. "Don't be *that* guy."

"Who says I have to be invisible? I could watch you—"

"*No*. There will be *no* watching. Got it? And probably you, Nero and Klaud should stay as far away from Mark as is superhumanly possible. In fact, if Mark doesn't kill you at the wedding, it will be a fucking miracle." Rinsing my mug, I set it in the draining rack next to the sink.

"Miracles, I can do. Demigod, remember?" He crossed his massive arms over his equally massive chest, the well-worn fabric of his tight black t-shirt looking like it had been painted on.

And well.

"Wait," I said. "Were *you* the one who fixed up my apartment last night?"

Genuine confusion crumpled his brow. "What about your apartment?"

"Never mind. Now, do me a favor and get gone so I can do the same."

"Your wish—" he bowed his head "—is my command. See you tomorrow." With an eardrum compressing *pop*, he was gone.

Or at least, no longer visible. I shuffled around the kitchen cleaning up our doughnut mess and scribbled a note for Morrison.

Thanks for the doughnuts. I took some extras to work with me for lunch. PS. Thank you. For all the things.

I marched back up the stairs and into the bathroom attached to Morrison's bedroom. He'd left an extra towel and washrag out for me, neatly folded in a stack next to the unused sink in his double vanity. His toiletries were neatly arranged around the one opposite, leaving its neighbor a blank canvas for my mental projections. Too easy, it was, to imagine my toothbrush cup, lotion, and face wash arranged around the naked sink, my blow dryer, curling irons, and brushes all tucked away in the empty drawers.

As easy as it had been to slide into Morrison's townhouse. As easy as it would be to slide into his life. Cooking dinners together in his kitchen. Sharing late breakfasts on the weekend. Lingering over coffee. Going back to bed together before venturing out for weekend grocery shopping. And our cart would be the cart to envy.

I let the fantasy play itself out against the Morrison-scented steam as I scrubbed myself down with his shower gel. Considering how strong Morrison's scent on me would be after sleeping in his bed and using his gel and shampoo, half of me hoped Mark hadn't yet returned from Scotland. The other half—well, I tried not to listen too hard to the other half.

She had a tendency to get us both in trouble.

I toweled off, dressed, and made the bed before applying makeup. Opting not to blow dry my hair at Morrison's, I threw the wet mass into a bun.

It didn't seem fair to leave so much of myself behind.

❧

My landlady was blessedly absent when I returned to my apartment. Only when I stepped in the door did I fully understand Morrison's contention.

My apartment was pristine. Perfect. Spotless. Wondrous to behold.

The carpets had been cleaned, the walls repaired, the broken banister perfectly restored. Even the antique leaded glass window that had last night lay in shards on the lawn had been replaced. Yet, no scent of fresh paint betrayed a hasty repair. No signs of construction or new materials could be spotted among the centuries old details of the house.

The damage was simply *gone*. As if it had un-happened. Could this have been Wallis's doing?

Would my landlady still have grounds for eviction if the damage had already been repaired? I didn't relish the thought of looking for a new job and a new apartment all in the same month.

Mark will help you.

"The hell he will. I'm done with the kind of *help* that man gives."

I shot a text to Steve letting him know he was okay to bring the cats back over at his leisure, adding a suitably peppy comment about his nuptials tomorrow.

A response came almost immediately, in true Steve style. *Well thankee kindly, doll! Will do! Oh, Allan said to remind you that he needs your shiny white arse at the gallery for your last bridesmaid's gown fitting sometime before the heat death of the universe (his words, not mine).*

Shit. I had kind of forgotten I had agreed to that. *Be there soon*, I texted back.

I schlepped my suitcase onto my bed, too distracted to unpack at present. Locking the door behind myself, I set off for the gallery.

My usual parking place had been usurped by a flower truck and several other unknown vehicles, so I parked around the corner and hoofed it down the street. The atmosphere inside the gallery was no less chaotic and crowded than the street had been. I stood slack-jawed in the doorway, taking in the transformed space.

Shimmering panels of fabric draped from the ceiling, strings of lights chased them across the room, creating a surreal celestial fairyland overhead. The walls, too, had been adorned with fabric panels to cover the exposed brick and adorned by garlands of flowers in shades of white, pale green, and Tiffany blue—the colors of the sea.

The main gallery space had been emptied of its postmodern white cube used to display paintings. Rows of chairs had taken their place. The aisle stretched out before me like an invitation I wasn't ready to accept. At its end, a triptych of an eight-foot canvas painted in seascape hues formed the altar in front of which my brother would be married.

"S'cuse me." A man carrying a crate of flowers brushed past me to continue adorning the satin beribboned chairs.

"Weww it's about bloody time!" I turned to find Allan darting his way through the steady stream of jostling bodies. "I'd ask you what took you so long if I didn't already smell 'im on you. Honestly, love, 'as he got a pecker made of platinum or somefing?"

"I didn't sleep with him!" I insisted.

Allan raised a perfectly plucked eyebrow at me.

"Okay, I *slept* with him. But sleeping is all we did. Except for the cuddling. And honestly, that doesn't even count really."

"Are dose rug burns?" he asked, eyeing my elbows.

"We wrestled a little," I added.

Allan shook his head. "It's no wonder, you bein' in heat and all. This place is going to be a bloody zoo, it is."

"Tell me about it," I said. "I think I met some of the wedding guests last night."

Allan took me by my elbow and steered me toward the stairs leading up to Mark's office. "How's that?"

"Oh, nothing much. I just got home from the airport to find a unicorn hosting a house party in my apartment."

Allan froze, his eyes as wide as the thick frames of his glasses would allow. "No 'e didn't!"

"By *he,* I can only assume you mean *Wallis.* And yes, my friend. Yes he did."

"Did he try to see your tits?" An unhealthy shade of scarlet flooded Allan's cheeks, lending him the appearance of an apoplectic rabbit.

"Sure as hell did," I confirmed.

"Fuck." Allan stomped his expensive loafer on the gallery's wood floor. "I might 'ave to kiww Joseph, you know that?"

"Why? What did he do? Wallis mentioned that he knew him—"

"When Joseph said he were arranging a special surprise for the weddin', I fought he meant a bloody car! Or one of those 'orrible singers. Not a fuckin' discount unicorn!"

"A *discount* unicorn? What the hell even is that?"

"Come on then. We can talk while we walk." Allan slid an arm around my shoulders and ushered me toward the stairs leading up to Mark's office and my desk.

Correction. My soon-to-be-former desk.

I stepped into Mark's office and gasped. "Oh, Allan! It's beautiful!"

He bustled past me to the filmy sea-foam green gown and held out the flowing skirt. "I still ain't sure I 'ave it long enough. It's all I could get done afore we had to take off for Scotland, and after fittin' your ball gown, I fink there's some room for improvement 'ere."

Like the gown Allan had made for the Spring Lambing mixer, this one had a fitted sleeveless bodice. But where the former had been a full-skirted ball gown, the latter dissolved into a flowing floor-length silk skirt layered with panels of chiffon. They caught the air as he slid the dress from the hanger, flowing like kelp caressed by an underwater current as he brought it over to me.

"Is it a bit too Li'il Mermaid?" he asked.

The skirt swam beneath my fingers like seawater. Too ephemeral and delicate to hold. "If it had sequins or a purple bra, it would be too Little Mermaid," I said. "This...this is delicious."

"As will you be when you're wearing' it," Allan said, securing the hanger back over the brass hook on the back of Mark's office door so he could begin work on its lacings. "Just try an take it easy on Mark, will you?"

"*Me*?" I asked, incredulous. "Take it easy on *him*? Are you serious?"

"He's under a lot of strain, love. Fings 'aven't been goin' well with Akhenaten, as I'm sure you can guess wif all the meetings. He's none too happy about all de vampires disappearing in Mark's realm. Then there's you. We'll need to assign you your own security task force just for de weddin'."

Chastened, I turned my eyes to the floor.

"And that's to say nuffink of your resignation, which has got him goin' off his tits."

"Bullshit," I challenged. "He accepted it without so much as a passing protest."

"Course he did, you daft lass! He's a four 'undred year-old bloody alpha male! He's been abandoned and betrayed more times dan you've changed your knickers. It's a defense mechanism."

"And not telling me about the last *heir*? Is that a defense mechanism too?"

It was Allan's turn to consider the wood floor. "You need to hear de whole story a'fore you condemn him for not tellin' you 'bout her."

"I'm all ears." I rested my hand on my hip, defiant and inviting.

"I told you, love. It ain't my place. My place is to get you fitted for dis dress, which task I couwd carry out much easier if you'd take off your shirt and pants and let me have my way."

"Seems like a lot of men have been saying this to me lately." I kicked off my converses and gave him my back while I shrugged out of my t-shirt and shimmied out of my jeans. "I thought you'd be immune to my charms."

"Immune, yes," he said, pulling a length of yellow tailor's tape from his suit coat pocket. "Patient, no."

A yelp escaped me when he popped the clasp on my bra. "Allan!"

"I need to see this wifout straps." He unzipped the bodice and held the gown out for me to step into. "And let's not pretend like I didn't strap you into a pair of stockin's and garters at de state dinner."

With hands covering the ladies, I stepped into the pool of silk, and raised my arms above my head as Allan drew the dress up my body and began fastening an innumerable row of buttons. "Wouldn't a zipper be quicker?"

"So would paint by numbers, love. Do think Da Vinci would have gone in for 'at?"

I held my breath as he reached my ribs. "Point conceded."

"There!" He stood and walked around the front of me and frowned. "You've lost weight! Where are your tits?" He stalked over to me and peered down my bodice.

I clapped my hands over my chest before he could perform any kind of archeological excavation. "I've been under a lot of stress."

"Shit. This corset is going to be de hardest part to take in." He ran his hands down my ribs and tugged the stiff fabric backward.

"I ate doughnuts this morning!" I offered, remembering. "Like, three of them! That could help, right?"

"We might have to stuff you," he said, looking over me with an assessing eye.

"I have some...inserts." I cleared my throat, glancing around to make sure no one was there to overhear us. "You know, just for special occasions."

"Bring a couple pairs of socks," he advised. "Just in case."

"Fine. Any preferences on the hair?"

"Wear it down." He reached beneath the skirt to shimmy the corset higher up my back. "Wild and wavy. Big."

"The *big* part is a guaranteed," I said. "Beachy waves? Or organized waves?"

"Beachy. And wear the corset I got you for de other gown."

I gave him a thumbs up. "You got it."

He walked around behind me and began the complicated process of unfastening me.

"How are Steve and Shayla doing?" I asked. "I haven't seen them since I've been back."

"Steve is ducky as ever. Insisted 'e wanted a kilt as Mark and Joseph would be wearin' them, and them being part of the wedding party and aww."

"Shit. I hadn't even thought about that. Are we doing a rehearsal or anything?" I asked.

"Naw. We'll pair up bridesmaids and groomsmen tomorrow mornin' and give a few last minute instructions. Should be pretty simple beyond that."

I folded my arms across my chest as the gown pooled at my ankles, then stepped out. Allan whisked it away and returned it to its hanger.

I slid back into my bra and pulled on my jeans and t-shirt. "And Shayla?"

"I had to let her wedding gown out. As well as Helena's, for 'at matter. It's been so long, I'd forgotten how quickly werewolf pregnancies progress."

"Oh God. *Helena*. I had completely forgotten she's knocked up too."

"I fink Steve wanted Scott Kirkpatrick as a groomsman, and we needed a bridesmaid to match. It sort of made sense, you know?"

"Works for me," I said.

"Mark will be back later today. In case you were wanting to see him." Allan flicked a glance over his shoulder.

"Actually, I think I should get out of the way. It seems like the arrangements are pretty well in hand, and there are a few things I should take care of before the wedding tomorrow."

"Whatever you say, love." Allan guided a filmy sheath over my gown. "But do me a favor?"

"Anything," I promised.

"Don't *sleep* wif the detective tonight. A werewolf weddin' ain't considered a success wifout at least three deaths, and I'm guessin' you'd prefer 'is weren't one of them."

CHAPTER 22

Morrison's knock tattooed my door with the same pattern I'd come to know, dread, crave, and love. The first time I'd heard it, I'd spilled coffee on his lap. The second, he'd brought doughnuts, and a handful of orgasms.

But I'd eaten his doughnuts earlier this morning, and sleeping with him had been strictly forbidden me by a millennium old werewolf.

How times had changed.

I opened the door to find him leaning against my doorway, groceries hanging from his wrist, a brown paper bag tucked under his arm.

"What's in there?" I asked, nodding toward the groceries.

"This is a Serego Alighieri Armaron," he said, grabbing the bottle with the grocery-laden hand and holding it out to me like an offering. "And these," he said, shaking the bags, "are the makings of an antipasto platter."

"Bastard." I took the bottle and opened the door wide. His jeans-clad ass drew my gaze by magnetic force as he sauntered into my kitchen and set the bags on the counter. He navigated my space as easily as I had his earlier this morning, pulling down two wine glasses from the cabinet over the counter and opening the drawer below it to select a bottle opener.

I perched on a stool in front of the counter while he poured rubied liquid into both of our glasses.

"Might want to let it open up for a few minutes," he said.

I took the glass he slid over to me and swirled the contents, watching the scrim of burgundy slide across the swell and dissolve, again, and again.

Morrison dumped olives, marinated artichokes, caramelized garlic, and capers into separate bowls then turned his attention to the cheese.

The man brought me *cheese*. I tried not to think about how it would probably be a perfect room temperature by the time I'd fucked him on the kitchen floor.

He laid a slab of aged Parmesan on a plate and anointed it with a smear of thick golden honey. "It's supposed to be excellent with the Armaron. Oops, almost forgot." He reached into the bag and withdrew a can of white albacore tuna, which he opened and divided among the three bowls on the floor. The three sets of eyes that had been watching his preparations with abject fascination turned their attentions to this unexpected gift. "Thought they should have a little something special if we were going to," Morrison added.

On second thought, we'd have time for a go on the floor, and against the wall. Parmesan holds beautifully, after all. "Looks wonderful," I said.

A tumbling handful of figs and silky slices of prosciutto completed his masterpiece of a plate. "Should we do this here? Or on the coffee table?"

"Both," I said.

"What?" he asked.

"What?" I repeated. "I mean, sorry. Let's sit at the coffee table. More comfortable."

We each grabbed a couple bowls, balancing them in the crooks of our elbows while we held our glasses and plates, unwilling to make two trips even over such a short distance.

He picked up his glass and held it out to me. "Cheers?"

"To what?" Lest I clink glasses to a cause I didn't support. A girl couldn't be too careful these days.

"To cheese. And food. And you."

"I'll give you two out of three." We clinked and sipped. The aroma of figs and licorice tickled my nose before the wine stroked my tongue with deep, raisiny resonance. My throat warmed as the liquid burned its way to my belly. "Whoa. This packs a punch. What's the percentage on this stuff?"

"Fifteen, I think." He swirled his glass and inhaled the bouquet before taking another sip.

"Mee-ow." I let another bolt of warm liquid velvet slide down my throat.

"I like it when you make animal noises." Morrison reached out and tore the crusty end piece off the baguette, and, knowing it was my favorite, offered it to me.

I took it and we built our plates in silence. It had always been so with us—appetites assuaged first, questions asked later.

"I didn't have time to check if your fridge had been replenished along with the rest of your apartment. I took a chance you might need dinner," he said, building himself a bite of prosciutto, honeyed Parmesan, and baguette.

"Very thoughtful," I said, following suit.

In fact, my fridge hadn't been all that great before I'd left for Scotland. The mostly disappointing contents had indeed been returned to their non-leprechaun-invaded and mostly empty state.

We chewed together in silence for the space of several moments.

"Actually, there's something I wanted to ask you."

"Goddamn it," I said, plopping a goodly wedge of Cambozola

back down on the cutting board. "When will I ever learn that your food always comes with ulterior motives?"

Morrison picked it back up and ferried it to my plate with a cheese knife.

"Hanna, what happened here last night," he said, "what's *been* happening as long as I've known you. It's not—it doesn't—"

Offering him no assistance whatsoever, I paired the new cheese acquisition with a fig and set my total focus to enjoying the silky, salty, piquant creaminess.

"Things have to make sense," he said, finally able to distill his point. "Everything has an explanation. A *logical* explanation."

"Not everything does." A truth I had to be taught again and again.

"That's where you're wrong." Morrison turned on the couch, angling his body to face mine. "If you wait long enough, even the most inexplicable events can be traced back to a single decision. Some seemingly unimportant detail you overlooked. *Everything* has a beginning, and an end. And if you're patient, the pieces come together. They always do."

"You're talking like a detective." I leaned forward to pick up my glass of wine and take a healthy swallow.

"I *am* a detective."

A wave of trepidation rippled through my rapidly filling belly. "I'm aware."

"You're not, though. Those are the rules, and they apply universally. With one exception."

I gave him back the words he'd so often given me. "My boss?"

"Your boss. *Nothing* about him makes sense. I followed the facts. I followed the patterns. And I was *wrong*."

"Happens to the best of us." I myself had been wrong about Mark at least a dozen times. Maybe more. A feeling I had not altogether become comfortable with.

"You don't understand," Morrison insisted, scooting closer to me. "I am *never* wrong. Fifteen years in homicide, and every time I've locked down on a suspect, their guilt has been proven without a shadow of a doubt. Except one."

"My boss," I repeated.

"Your boss. And you know why?" His hazel eyes surged with some unspoken revelation.

"Enlighten me," I said far more casually than I felt.

"Because he doesn't follow human patterns."

My breath froze in my lungs. I pushed myself up from the couch and aimed myself toward the kitchen.

"Where are you going?" Morrison called after me.

"To get the wine." I brought the bottle back to the table and refilled both our glasses, picking up my own before handing his to him.

"This won't change the questions I came here to ask," he said, taking it.

"And it won't change my answers. But we're lushes, and there's no reason we shouldn't enjoy the wine."

We clinked glasses again over this sentiment.

"As I was saying," Morrison paused to take a sip. "Your boss doesn't follow human behavioral patterns."

"He's eccentric. You won't find me arguing that point." I took a sip from my own glass.

"And I was willing to accept that," Morrison added. "Until you."

"Me? What about me?" Why did it feel like I was asking this question too often lately?

"*You.*" Morrison reached forward to construct another bit. Manchego cheese this time, but with a smudge of orange fig spread and a thin slice of spicy capicola. He'd always been a rebel.

"I used to be able to read you," he continued. "I used to know when you were lying. When you were stalling, bluffing, holding back. I used to be able follow your thread. Put you together. Take you apart. All your pieces made sense."

"I'm pretty predictable." And I was. A creature of habit and most of them bad.

"*Used* to be. You don't follow the patterns, Hanna. You don't make sense. What's happening here—" he gestured around my apartment "—doesn't make sense. Not anymore."

I sat quiet in the space made perfect by a source completely unknown to me. Morrison was right. As usual. "I don't have an answer for that."

"That's the same thing as saying you do, but you don't like it." Morrison wiped his fingers on the super elegant patterned paper towels I had supplied by way of napkins.

I did the same, not knowing what else to do. "Then I guess there's nothing left to say."

Morrison lifted his glass from the coffee table, skewering me with that intense, green-blue hazel gaze. "Why won't you tell me what's happening?"

I drained the contents of mine, a warm barrier against his cold questions. "Because I can't."

Well, shit. Damned if I didn't sound like—

"You can, but you won't." Morrison reached out and captured my hand in his. "*Please,* Hanna. Just tell me. It won't change anything. Nothing you can tell me will change what I feel for you."

A loud, unexpected laugh erupted from my mouth.

"What?" Morrison asked. "What's so funny?"

"Nothing. You just have no idea what you're saying."

"What? You're a serial murderer?"

Not yet.

"I'm something worse," I said.

"Stop this, Hanna." Morrison now gathered both my hands in his. "Stop taking on his guilt. I don't care what he's told you."

At this, I finally understood what the word *hysterics* really meant. "He hasn't—" a painful laugh seized my abdominals "—he hasn't told me anything. Never does."

Morrison's expression bore genuine concern. "Fuck *me*. I shouldn't have brought the wine."

"Believe me, I would if I could. And the wine was fabulous. Don't be sorry." I rested a hand on his knee, feeling beneath my palm the muscles of his thigh attached to the rounded bone. Such a wonder, he was. So beautifully made.

He brought a hand to the back of my neck and pulled me to him until our foreheads touched. "Why won't you be with me?"

Because my fucking you could drive my boss to murder the first para/super natural who crossed his path, resulting in a war capable of consuming every last life on the planet.

"I just...my feelings are too complex. It's not fair to—" My words stopped the second I saw Morrison's face.

He looked as if he'd been slapped. Eyes wide. Cheeks pale. "You're in love with him."

A ton of bricks fell from the sky and landed on my chest, each one extracting its own weight in flesh. "I didn't say that."

"You didn't need to." A sardonic smile stole across his lips. "Now this, *this* makes sense. Why you lie for him. Why you stay." His laugh matched my own for bitterness. "Shit. All this time, I'd been gauging your actions against what you might feel for me. Your pattern *does* make sense."

Hearing him talk this way ground the last of my heart to dust. "Don't. Please don't do this."

"I didn't do this. *You* did." He pushed himself up from the couch and slipped on his shoes.

I slid across the couch and reached out to capture his hand. "James, please don't go. I want you here. I do."

He peeled my hand away from his body as if it was a leech. "Then tell me what happened here last night."

My heartbeat marked every second as it passed, thundering in my ears like a metronome from hell. “I can’t.”

“Goodbye, Hanna.”

The closed door to my apartment was a gunshot, marking the end of the life I knew.

CHAPTER 23

Clad in silk and chiffon, standing beneath the artificial heaven of twinkling lights and swirling fabric, on the day of my brother's wedding, I contemplated murder for the first time.

Was it possible to kill a unicorn?

I added this to the long list of questions someone, anyone, had yet to answer for me.

Were they like vampires? Slow healing but impossible to kill? Or was it more like a werewolf proposition? Capable of sustaining massive damage unless you steal the core?

I might yet find out.

There, buried muzzle deep in Steve and Shayla's four-tier wedding cake, was Wallis. The same unicorn who had destroyed and magically restored my apartment, was now eating my brother's wedding cake.

Arms folded against the considerable cleavage Allan's gown had architecturally created, I crept up behind the offender's rounded white haunches and delivered a stinging slap.

A sudden jet of warm, cotton candy-scented air sent my riotous pile of curls flying a second before the blizzard of glitter erupted toward me. Too late, my hands flew up in front of my face. I stumbled backward, tripping over my own dress and falling hard on my ass. As if in a snow globe, the world around me became visible by gradual degrees as the sparkling flakes settled on my skin, my hair, and the floor. At the end of my fourth sneeze, a wad of glitter-caked snot flew into my palm. I shoved myself to my feet and grabbed a monogrammed napkin off the nearby table. "What *the fuck* was that?"

"You fucking startled me." Wallis's rainbow-colored mane tossed against his muscular neck as he turned toward me. Frosting and fondant decorated his muzzle instead of the cake. White crumbs fell as he spoke.

He turned and resumed eating, his horsey lips making rude smacking sounds.

"You...you *farted* glitter on me?"

"What did you expect," came the mumbled reply. "I'm a goddamn unicorn."

"Ugh!" I danced around the gallery, brushing glitter out of my hair, shaking it out of my dress, slapping it off my skin. "That's disgusting!"

"It's fucking magical is what it is." He turned away from the cake, his golden hooves echoing across the wooden floor as he licked the last of the frosting from his lips and belched. But instead of a burp, the tinkling sound of babies' laughter filled the gallery.

"So *that's* what that sound was! You piece of shit! Do you have *any* idea how much trouble you've caused me?"

"No, but I've got an idea of the kind of trouble I'd *like* to cause you." His thick pink tongue swiped the last of the frosting from his velvety muzzle.

"Do you bleed rainbows? Because I'm just about ready to—"

"Hanna! 'ere you are! I've been—" Allan stopped short, his small eyes growing wide behind their glass walls. "Cor blimey, love! I know it's a weddin' an all, but I fink you might've gone a bit over de top wif de body glitter."

"*I* didn't wear any body glitter," I said, cutting my eyes toward Wallis as I continued batting it out of my hair.

"Oh, shit," Allan said, following my gaze. "What de 'ell did you eat?"

"He ate the wedding cake!" Quite unsuccessfully, I attempted to scrape glitter off my arms with my fingernails. "That's what he ate."

"You try being the only sucrose intolerant unicorn in a species that spins sugar into magic!" A sheen misted his large brown eyes. "Do you know what they eat for breakfast in Unicornland?

"Cotton candy!" Wallis sobbed. "Cotton fucking candy. And for lunch, it's jelly beans. And dinner—" his voice grew thick, choked with tears. "They, they gave me...hay. Hay! Just because I was *different*." Fat, pearlescent teardrops slid down his long, elegant face. "They all laughed at me. They called me names."

"Oh, Wallis." I rushed over to him, wrapping my arms around his broad neck. "I'm so sorry."

"Hanna," Allan coughed.

"It hurt so much." Wallis inhaled a long, wet sniffle.

"You poor thing," I said, stroking his flank.

"Show me your tits," came his hoarse whisper.

I drew back, looking him in the eye. "What did you just say?"

"It would make me feel so much better." He batted his long equine lashes at me. "Really it would."

"You son of a bitch!" I said, the realization dawning. "The laughing, the name calling. You stole that from Rudolph the Red-nosed Reindeer!"

"He's my cousin," Wallis said. "Isn't that close enough?"

"Look, you," Allan said, grabbing Wallis by the ears. "I'm going to call the caterer and have another cake brought. And you're not going to touch it. You're going to carry de bride down de aiswe. You're goin' to keep your mouf shut, and be a good unicorn, if you do right the rest of the time you're here, I won't *report* you. You understand?"

Wallis' eyes widened. "I'll be good. Promise I will. Just don't report me, okay?"

"We'll see." Allan released Wallis's ears as he pointed a stiff finger down the hall. "Go see Joseph 'bout your weddin' gear."

The sound of hooves clopping against a wood floor echoed across the gallery until Wallis was out of sight.

Allan pressed his forehead against the wall. "If we get out of this weddin' alive, it will be a bleedin' miracle."

"In the meantime," I said, taking a dramatic step back to admire his ensemble. "You look fantastic."

He wore a fitted black jacket over a white button up shirt and black vest. Below this was a kilt of red, green and blue tartan. Thick white socks came to just below his knee interrupted only by the laces of his black ghillie shoes. Hanging at his waist, the traditional tasseled Scottish *sporran* swayed in time with his panicked breaths.

"Breathe, Allan," I said, completely unfamiliar with being the calm-ee in this scenario. "It's going to be okay."

"It's not!" he insisted. "In a few minutes 'is gallery is going to be full of werewolves, satyrs, nymphs, and God knows what else!"

"You forgot Crixus." Who definitely fell under the *what else* category.

"Bite me ballocks! 'Es here too, then?"

I nodded.

"Mark's goin'ta kill 'im you know. After what he done at the castle. Gonna skin him alive and wear 'im like a scarf."

"I'll take care of Mark and Crixus," I said. *Somehow.* "Just go make sure Steve and Shayla are ready."

Allan closed his eyes took a deep breath, the unflappable

mask of professional confidence dropping back into place. "All right, then," he said, giving my arm a squeeze. "Showtime."

MARK AND I MET AT THE TOP OF THE AISLE, HIS DARK EYES DRINKING me in from head to heels just as I'd hoped they would. Draped in Allan's sartorial masterpiece, I felt bold enough to meet his gaze.

"Hi," I said.

"Hi," he answered.

We stood opposite each other just out of sight of the throng of seated guests, their excited buzz making a hive of the gallery. He offered me his suit coat clad arm as we shuffled to our place in the processional line. Paired up by height—or so Allan said—we were to be the caboose.

Kirkpatrick and Helena were in front of us, disparate height notwithstanding in consideration of their mated status. Pregnancy had tacked on a good thirty pounds since the last time I'd seen her, her rounded butt a hypnotizing juggling act beneath fabric the same pale green shade as mine.

Allan had met my shocked expression with the revelation that werewolf gestation periods were roughly equivalent to all wolf gestation periods. At forty days pregnant, Helena was more than halfway through, and Shayla wasn't far behind.

"Nice sparkles," Mark said, giving me a quick sideways glance.

"I don't want to talk about it." I fixed my eyes straight ahead, trying to prevent little bursts of light from reflecting from my cheeks by keeping my head still.

We took a few steps forward and paused, waiting for Allan's nod to signal our turn to walk.

My lack of breath had nothing to do with a corset this time, though I was able to reuse the expensive contraption Allan had laced me into for the Spring Lambing social at Castle Abernathy.

No.

Dusted by blue rose petals, the narrow expanse of floorboards between the chairs choked with creatures from both sides of the families whispered to me.

What if this were your wedding? The aisle seemed to ask me. *And all these people were here for you? Your mother would be here. Just like she would have been if she knew her son was alive.*

"I didn't have a choice," I said.

"What?" Mark asked, ducking his head to listen above the swelling violin version of Lionel Richie's "Hello."

"I—er didn't have a choice. About the dress. Allan made it before we left for Scotland."

"Neither did I." Mark glanced down, and I made the mistake of following his gaze. "Haven't worn a one of these things in ages."

Oh. God. Mark Abernathy in a kilt. He was an Iron Age savage, a warrior, a crusader, a *king*. The muscle-bound Laird on a thousand paperback book covers.

Heat flushed my cheeks as a sharp, acute wave of nostalgic longing rolled through me.

Mark steadied me, his large, warm hand easily spanning the small of my back. "Easy."

But nothing about this was.

Allan nodded, and then we were walking.

I felt eyes from both sides of the aisles roving over my face, my breasts, my hips, and my ass.

"I'm going to have to kill half the wedding guests," Mark mumbled out the side of his mouth.

"Bad manners," I whispered.

"Don't care. You're still my assistant."

"Until 10:00 PM," I reminded him.

"Plenty of time." He nodded toward the werewolf side of the aisle, attempting to smile, but mostly bearing his teeth.

Steve's grin, on the other hand, shone like the crescent moon against the painted panels behind him. My brother, radiantly, stupidly, happy.

I forced myself to keep walking when all I wanted was to stop and cement this memory for all time. Like Mark and Allan, he wore a dark jacket, vest and kilt, his calves impossibly narrow in their socked tubes.

Unable to contain myself, I broke from Mark and squeezed Steve in a tight hug before shuffling to my assigned spot behind Helena in the line of bridesmaids.

Helena's face was round as a pie plate as she turned to me, tears streaming down her cheeks. "I just love weddings. Don't you?"

"Not especially," I said.

She blew a smoochy kiss to Kirkpatrick, who caught it, and placed it somewhere that made me stifle a gag. Though I didn't know how it was possible, Kirkpatrick looked less…less—gingery. His pale face less freckled. His nose not as piggish as I remembered.

Mating agreed with him.

The musicians quieted, only to take up again, switching from Lionel Ritchie to the Beatles' "Across the Universe."

To Wallis's infinite credit, he bore Shayla down the aisle with the silent grace I had once imagined all unicorns possessed. Yards of sapphire satin from Shayla's gown spilled to one side of Wallis's white flank as she rode sidesaddle. Her cobalt blue hair had been swept up into a pile on the top of her head, curly tendrils escaping to fall around her neck and shoulders. Allan had taken full advantage of her ample cleavage, selecting an empire waist to accommodate her swelling belly. The silk ribbon tied beneath her bosom mirrored the color of my own gown. Her wide green eyes glowed with happiness, the vintage siren red lipstick the perfect compliment to her wide grin.

Married.

My only brother was getting married.

My nose stung as I bit my lip to stave off the eyeliner-compromising tears.

A giant, broad-shouldered, white-bearded man stepped forward from Shayla's side of the guests and helped her slide down from Wallis's back.

Zeus, I presumed?

Allan emerged from behind Mark and stood in the center of the painted triptych. "Who gives 'is woman in marriage?" he asked.

"I do," came the thundering voice.

"Fank you," Allan said. "Everyone may be seated."

The titan nodded, turned, and winked in my direction.

I looked over my shoulder but found only a decorative spray of flowers. Sure enough, Zeus had winked at *me*. As he seated himself, my eye came to rest on the man behind him.

Crixus.

He gave me a charmingly crooked smile.

On the off chance telepathy could be found in the catalog of his powers, I sent him the following message: *Try anything funny in front of all these people, and I'll make you sorry you can't die.*

Wouldn't dream of it, arrived the prompt reply. *There's always later.*

Mark's twitching jaw was visible at twenty paces.

Shit. *Giraffe. Giraffe giraffe giraffe.*

Allan shot me a warning glance. "Right, then. We're all gavered 'ere today..."

His words washed over me as I stood and tried to smile instead of think. And yet, thinking was all I could do. *Could I really leave this*? This gallery, these people, this world? Steve would still talk to me, I was certain. But would Allan?

Would Mark?

Travel, I had promised myself. Travel and art and all the cheese I could eat. My life would be so full of all the amazing things that I wouldn't even have time to miss this place. More importantly, the things I would *not* miss.

Vampires in my bathtub. Heads in my luggage. Leg-humping werewolf suitors.

Heartache.

"I now pronounce you *wolf and wife*!" Allan announced with a flourish. "You may kiss de Nereid!"

Steve cupped Shayla's face in his knobby-knuckled fingers and planted a solid kiss on her lips.

The crowd of wedding guests shot to their feet, stomping, whistling, hooting and hollering, united, however briefly, by this shared joy.

Steve and Shayla rushed up the aisle, the guests filing in after them.

Allan stuck his fingers in his mouth and whistled twice. Once audibly, once at a decibel that caused only half the crowd to duck and clap their hands over their ears. "Listen up, you lot! We've got to get dinner tables set up in 'ere. Everyone in the lobby untiw we're ready." He nodded to Joseph, who began ushering people toward the door.

Crixus lingered near the back of the pack. The strange, strained expression on his usually arrogant face dug an acidic pit in my stomach.

CHAPTER 24

"To the bride and groom!"

Despite the fact that Steve and Shayla had already done their honeymoon getaway departure, glasses rose at every table. Some made contact, many others missed. Not surprising, considering this was about the seventy-eighth toast of the evening.

Droplets of red wine fell on Mark's white shirt sleeve like rain as an expansive lavender-skirted bum tumbled into our assigned table. "Oh, my dear! I am *so* sorry!"

Mark helped to untangle her from a chair and helped her back to her feet while I steadied the table's towering centerpiece.

"Goodness," she said, straightening the flower-assaulted hat perched precariously atop her floof of graying hair. "I don't have the head for wine I once had."

I returned the heavy silver scissors to the purse that had exploded across our table at her arrival. "Nothing to worry about," I said, handing the purse over to her. "We've all been there."

After all, no one wanted to piss off one of the Fates. Shayla's aunt or no.

"You *are* a lovely girl," she said. "I can see why Shayla likes you. Even if you are destined to—"

I held up a hand. "I don't want to know. Whatever it is. I...I like surprises."

Lipstick flecked her dentures when she smiled. "I dare say you won't be disappointed, then." She weaved away, bumping from table to table like a lurching purple bumblebee.

"I don't know about you," Joseph slurred, consulting his twentieth glass of scotch like the Delphic oracle, "but I get tired of all these obscure, vaguely threatening prophesies."

"You call 'at a prophecy?" Allan's speech was slower than usual, and losing the distinction of an accent. "De old twat doesn't know 'er ass from 'er elbow."

"Shhh!" I held a finger to my lips, feeling a little booze loose myself. "We've come this far without an apocalyptic battle. Let's just be nice. Okay?"

This comment drew a piqued look from Mark, who occupied the chair next to mine. His posture was slack, his body radiating a delicious mix of soap, and scotch, and warm, salty skin. Somewhere in the course of the evening, he'd lost his coat along with the top few buttons fastening his crisp white shirt. Through the enticing "v" of the open fabric, I stole glances at the shadowy ridge where his pectoral muscles sloped upward from his sternum.

And oh, the trouble that kilt was causing.

Slumped down in his chair, his long legs haphazardly shoved under my seat, that damnable plaid fabric brushed the spot just above where the rounded muscles of his thighs met up with his knee cap. The darkened cave between them left my fingers craving to cartoon-walk right up into that magical cave of manly wonders.

"Hanna's right," Mark said. "We should—"

"Wait," I interrupted. "What did you just say?"

Mark's dark brows gathered over his eyes. "I said we should—"

"No," I said. "Before that."

"Hanna's right," he said in his very own distinctive *I'm humoring Hanna* tone I had grown to know and mostly resent.

"Oh God," I said, affecting a full-body shudder. "That was so good for me."

"I could do better," Abernathy promised, his lips curling in a lazy, cat-like smile.

"Well," I said, clearing my throat. "I think I'm going to go get a Tide stick to take care of that stain."

Mark caught me by the wrist as I pushed myself up from my chair. "Hanna, I don't care about the shirt."

"You may not," I said, "but I do. And I'm your assistant for another two hours, remember?"

"I remember." The playful smile vanished from his lips.

"Not to mention I spent a bloody millennium cuttin' it to fit them mile-wide shouwders of yours." Allan lifted his glass to his lips.

"Cigar?" Joseph reached into his pocket, producing three, long fat tawny sausage-sized rolls.

"Don't mind if I do," Mark said, rising.

Allan followed suit, taking a cigar from Joseph and examining it with bright-eyed interest. "If I didn't know be'er, I'd say someone 'as a fixation they ain't dealt with yet."

"Trust me friend," Joseph said, clapping Allan on the back. "If I had the urge to play the skin flute, you'd be the first to know. We'll be outside," he said over his shoulder.

"I'll find you," I said.

Pushing through the tables and mingling bodies, I reached the stairs and loped up to the landing outside Mark's office where my tidy desk sat.

My desk.

Would Mark hire another assistant after I left? He hadn't really wanted one in the first place. But that was the curse of providing excellent service. Though initially resistant, Mark had conceded territory to me. First, his schedule, then his tasks, then his filing, his phone calls. Lately, he'd taken to malingering at my desk until I gave him something to do.

Who would tell him what to do when I was gone?

Picturing another girl at the workstation I had set up filled me with an instant, murderous rage.

"Quite a party."

I jumped and spun to find Crixus leaning on the railing at the top of the stairs. Having forgone any kind of uniform formality, he wore his ubiquitous plain black t-shirt and ass-worshiping jeans.

"It sure is," I said, shuffling through my desk drawer in search of the Tide stick. Unsuccessful, I began rifling through my pencil cup, stopping when my fingers closed over something smooth and cool.

"Clancy!" I crowed, looking at the silver flying pig letter opener that had opened much more than letters during my time at the gallery. Strange to hold in my open palm something that had once been planted deep in a werewolf heart.

It had been thoroughly scoured and sanitized of course.

I imagined myself at a different desk. A purely administrative desk for some CEO or other, managing his mundane calendar appointments. Picking up his dry cleaning. Doing his lame-ass expense reports.

"You looked awfully good on Abernathy's arm," Crixus said, sauntering over to one of the chairs opposite my desk.

"Yeah?" I asked idly.

"Looked pretty happy, too," he added, slouching into a chair, knees splayed in the posture of a man with testicles roughly the size of grapefruits.

"That was my fake happy face." I put Clancy back in my mug

of pens and pawed through the shallow drawer in the middle of the desk. "Where the hell is my Tide stick?"

"All due respect, I don't think it's his shirt Abernathy is concerned about losing." That damn dimple appeared in his cheek as grinned at me.

"What gave you that impression?" I did my best to sound casual as I pulled open my emergency snack drawer, rifling through cans of EZ Cheese, buttery club crackers, phosphate-rich meat sticks, and several half-eaten bags of chips.

A girl had to have her options.

"His face," Crixus said.

"You're going to have to give me some more detail on that." I said, fully aware I was doing the uber-pathetic *you really think he likes me!?* info pump.

"In any given room at any given time, he's both watching you and watching everyone around you and looking like he's already calculated twelve strategies for killing everyone in it if the so much as sneeze in your direction." Crixus stretched his arms over his head, lacing his fingers behind his skull like a hammock.

"So?" I said. "He's probably always calculating strategies for killing everyone in any given room whether or not I'm in it." Ducking down behind the desk, I squirted a dollop of salty, processed spray cheese on my tongue. Desperate times, and all that.

When I poked my head above the desk, I found Crixus wearing an expression of bemusement. "That's the most pathetically in love motherfucker I've seen in two millennia on the planet."

My stomach engaged in a spontaneous death roll, releasing a swarm of manic butterflies into my chest. "You look pretty good for your age," I said, hoping to change the subject.

"*Yeah* I do." Beneath the body-hugging fabric of his t-shirt, his pecs began an alternating flex-off.

"As charming as that is, did you come up here purely to annoy the ever-loving shit out of me, or does this little chat have a point?"

"Yes," he said to both. "You just seem like you don't have any neutral parties helping you make your decision is all."

"How very magnanimous of you," I said.

"One of my many sterling qualities." At this, he scooted his hips toward the edge of the chair as if to suggest his *most* sterling quality lay smack between his powerful thighs.

"I'm sure." I slammed closed the last drawer of my desk and collapsed into my chair out of desperation, officially calling off the stain stick search party.

"How about a list?" Crixus suggested. "You could make a list of all the things you like about Abernathy and the cop, and whichever one is longer, that's the one you bang for life."

I cocked my head at him. "Why are you making all the sense right now?"

"I have my moments." Picking up my pad and pen from the pencil cup, he pushed them across the desk at me.

"All right," I said, tapping my pen against my teeth. "We'll start with Abernathy."

Crixus raised an eyebrow at me.

"I'm working alphabetically." Dividing the page into two neat columns, with Abernathy at the top of one and Morrison at the top of the other, I scribbled for several silent moments.

"Okay. Let's have it," Crixus said when I'd put my pen down.

I cleared my throat, attempting to sound as clinical and impartial as I was capable of. "Abernathy," I said. "Plusses. Has forearms I want to lick."

"Is that so?" Crixus glanced down at his own, road-mapped with thick veins and tawny dunes of sloping muscle.

"Is protective," I added, moving on before I could stop to ogle. "Is handsome and brave and strong and wise and also adorably grumpy."

"I'm already bored with this game." Crixus sat up in his chair and crossed an ankle over the opposite knee. "Minuses?"

I glanced down at the paper and the one item listed in the "minuses" column. Because really, it was the source of all the other things that bedeviled me on a daily basis. "Is a werewolf," I said.

"But *you're* a werewolf," Crixus pointed out most unhelpfully.

"I'm a werewolf *heir*," I said. "There's a big difference."

"What's the difference?"

Only, the question hadn't come from Crixus.

It had become from behind me.

In increments too slow to measure, I turned around in my chair.

There, leaning against the door jamb of Abernathy's open office, was Morrison.

I'D REHEARSED THIS CONVERSATION A MILLION TIMES IN HEAD. The one where, sitting next to Morrison on the couch, steaming mugs of tea between us on the coffee table, I patiently and gently explained to him that I was the carrier of DNA from an unbroken and ancient line of staggeringly powerful werewolves. At this point in my mental conversation, Morrison usually did one of the three things. Throw himself out the window, throw *me* out the window, or call the nice men in white coats to come and take me away.

Which is precisely why we'd never had this conversation.

Now he knew.

Personal experience had taught me that *knowing* was a far shot from *believing*.

Looking at his face now, I searched it for any clue as to

where on that scale Morrison was currently camped. I found only that stern, impenetrable cop face that gave nothing away.

"Well this is awkward," Crixus said, looking for all the world like he wanted to reach for a bucket of popcorn.

"James, I—" I began.

He held up a hand to silence me. "This actually explains a lot."

"So, you...I mean, you're not..." Try as I might, I could find no concise way to ask him how he was doing with the revelation that the human race coexisted with a vast and sometimes murderous array of creatures.

"I'm a homicide detective, Hanna," Morrison said. "I've seen some shit out there that would make this news look like a sing-along with Mary Poppins."

"Mary Poppins," Crixus said, rocking back in his chair. "I would totally hit that."

"Ditto." Morrison crossed the room, taking the seat next to Crixus's and sliding it several man card-retaining feet away before sinking down.

A wave of sweet, clear nostalgia swept over me. It had been in exactly this spot when, on my first day of the job, Morrison had come to question me about Helena's murder.

He sat across from me now in that same, hunch-shouldered concentration. "I do have a few questions."

"Everything's real," I explained pre-emptively. "Vampires, werewolves, witches, satyrs, centaurs...unicorns." This last I pronounced less than enthusiastically, picking at a glitter fleck on my arm.

"What is he?" Morrison jerked his chin at Crixus.

"A pain in the ass, mostly," I said. "But also a demigod."

Morrison was quiet for a moment. I could almost see the wheels turning behind his hazel eyes. That powerfully analytical brain of his weighing, sifting, sorting.

"About this heir thing," Morrison said. "What exactly does that mean?"

With slightly less gentleness and patience than I had imagined, I gave him the whole scoop. With sprinkles. Abernathy and Joseph, Oscar Wilde, London, the peace pact, the severed heads, the werewolf vampire war, the state dinner, my near strangulation at the hands (did ghosts even have hands?), Klaud, and Nero.

"Jesus," Morrison said, dragging a hand down his face.

"Yeah," I said. "I know. But nothing happens until I—"

The happy buzzing downstairs ceased with a sudden, startling rush, the sound disappearing so quickly and completely that my ears rang in the thick silence.

Crixus, Morrison and I all shot out of our chairs and flew down the stairs.

When we reached the bottom, we saw why.

A perfect circle of party guests, their varied faces all wearing identical expressions of shock and disbelief. At the circle's center, Allan lay on the floor. His face ash gray. Eyes closed. Mouth open. Limbs stiff. Half-smoked cigar still clutched in his bluish fingers.

"I found him in the alley," a tall, heavily muscular man with cobalt blue hair—Shayla's side of the family—said.

"Were there others?" I asked, panic rising like acid in my throat.

"No," the man said. "Only one."

My heart dropped into my shoes, my stomach clenched in a sickening twist as I rushed over to them, jumping back when I touched Allan's cold, waxy skin.

"Is he—" The words refused to leave my mouth.

"Not yet." A woman with raven black hair and impressive collection of beaded necklaces and bracelets slithered through the shocked crush, coming to kneel at my side. "But he will be if we don't counter the potion in time."

"A potion?" I asked, my face feeling like a slab of dumb meat.

"Yes," she said, already digging into a crocheted handbag. "But the longer we wait to administer this, the more he is to stay this way."

I stood, finding Crixus's eyes as he spoke the one word that appeared with perfect clarity in my head.

"Nero."

CHAPTER 25

Everything in the room took on an alarming brownish sheen as a cold sweat broke out over the back of my neck as I swayed on my four-inch heels. Crixus managed to snag me before I fell face-first onto the gallery floor, ushering me to one of the tables and easing me into a chair.

Morrison appeared shortly thereafter with a glass of water. "Drink," he said.

I drank. I swallowed. I stood.

Impatiently gathering the folds of my skirt, and kicking off my heels, I made a beeline for the stairs.

"What are you doing?" Morrison asked, hot on my heels.

"I'm going to go get Mark and Joseph."

"No," Crixus and Morrison said in unison.

"Yes," I said.

"You don't even know where they are," Crixus added, not far behind.

"You're right," I said, over my shoulder as I clomped up the stairs. "But I'll bet you do."

Crixus froze in place for a beat, and I knew I'd hit pay dirt.

He caught up to us on the landing as I grabbed my purse, my keys, my Taser (ahh, memories), and Clancy.

"You are out of your fucking mind, lady." Crixus placed the leathery palms of his warrior's hands flat on my desk and looked me dead in the eye. "You can't go up against a horde of angry vampires by yourself."

"As much as I don't want to say this, I agree with the demigod," Morrison said. "Let's at least get some back-up or—"

"Back-up?" I laughed bitterly. "You gonna call some of your detective friends? Explain the situation?"

Morrison glanced away.

"Anyway," I continued, "we go busting into Nero's lair with a rag bunch of werewolves and forget about any kind of negotiation. We're talking a complete and total bloodbath."

"But—" Crixus began.

"Did you *see* Allan downstairs?" Every speck of fear and sadness and desperation I'd been tamping down, exploding into violent life. To my extreme irritation, my throat clenched as tears stung my eyes. "Mark and Joseph are probably frozen and completely helpless somewhere in the clutches of a mad Roman emperor vampire. We don't have fucking *time*."

"Do you think you're just going to waltz in there and ask Nero politely to give Abernathy and Joseph back to you?" Crixus demanded.

"Nope," I said. "I'm going to get some of whatever our witch friend is brewing and you're going to magic me in there. Or however the hell it is you travel from place to place."

"Why would I do that?" Crixus asked, watching as I gathered anything that even remotely looked like a weapon.

"Because somewhere deep down in that shallow, self-serving heart of yours there's a slightly less shallow and self-serving heart that wants to do the right thing."

The closest expression to fear I'd yet seen darkened Crixus's arrogant, irritatingly handsome face.

"Please." I looked him in the eye, marshalling every ounce of pleading I could.

"Okay," he said. "But once I get you in, you're on your own."

"Deal." I reached across the desk and offered him my hand. He stared at it for the briefest second before he took it and squeezed.

"I'm coming with you." Morrison, who had been strangely quiet during this whole conversation, came to stand at my side. Again, that wave of nostalgia swelled in my heart. He'd been wearing almost the exact same thing as the day I'd rear-ended him on my way to first interview with Abernathy.

The slightly rumpled button-up shirt. The off-the-rack slacks that never fit him quite right but always managed to show off his ass. And his expression. Dogged and determined despite his lightly rumpled golden brown hair and shadowed jaw.

"Why would you do that?" I asked. "You hate Abernathy."

"Yes." Morrison turned to me, his hands on my shoulders, his face an odd mixture of tenderness and anger. "But *you* don't."

"OH GOD." PANTING, I FELL TO MY KNEES IN THE HALLWAY OF Nero's super-secret mountain lair, Morrison moaning at my side in a similar posture.

As it turned out, spontaneous orgasms were a side effect of materializing—Crixus's method of poofing us from one place to another.

After having briefly stopped at Morrison's house to improve our small arsenal, Crixus had stood in the kitchen, holding his arms out as if hoping for a hug. "All right," he'd said. "Hop on."

"Excuse me?" Morrison, various weapons strapped to his body and an expression of horror strapped to his face, looked from me to Crixus and back again.

Not that I was much to look at.

In a pair of Morrison's drawstring sweatpants, a Kevlar vest, borrowed t-shirt, and an anti-bite collar he had fashioned from scrap leather and duct tape, I looked like I belonged on a street corner with a THE END IS NEAR sign.

"I can't transport you if I'm not touching you," Crixus explained. "And the more of you I'm touching, the easier it is for me to do it."

"I call middle," I had said, marching to him.

"Actually, it works best if I'm in the middle." Crixus tugged me over, and tucking me under one powerful arm, pressed me into his side.

Morrison had taken a step backward.

"James," I snapped, panic washing over me anew. "We're wasting time. Get your ass over here and spoon this man. We have werewolves to rescue."

And finally, he had.

"You breathe one word of this to anyone and I'll—"

But then his words had stopped because time had stopped. Every single cell of my body experienced a simultaneous reorganization. Like when a rollercoaster's sudden drop sends your stomach lurching upward as the rest of you is coming down, only times a thousand and ending with being pulled through the Universe's anus.

Backwards.

With a deafening *pop,* we had tumbled into being in a dark, musty hallway.

And promptly blew our wads.

Well, one of us, anyway.

"Not cool." Morrison, who had regained his ability to stand, glanced down at the wet spot on the front of his trousers.

"No one's going to see it," I said. "It's too dark in here anyway."

Or so I hoped.

"Ugh," I said, tugging at the thick, heavy cowl around my neck. "I fucking hate this thing."

"Do you hate it more than dying?" Morrison asked.

"No," I said. "But did you have to rub it down with garlic?" I sniffed at myself and stifled a gag. "I smell like a pesto burp."

With a hand against the clammy stone wall, I got to my feet, taking in my surroundings. Whether it was my unusual journey, or the torches—yes, actual by God burning tar sticks—lining the walls, I felt like I had spooled back into the middle ages.

The same strange feeling of déjà vu I'd experienced at Castle Abernathy descended over me. "Where are we?" I asked.

"Nero's summer house." The flickering light changed Crixus's face, stripping from it any trace of levity or playfulness. Hardening the angle of his jaw. Turning his eyes to black sapphires.

"But the walls, the torches…" I trailed off.

"He likes to evoke a mood," Crixus said.

Boy did he ever. He'd captured *creepy castle dungeon* all the way down to the mysterious dripping noise somewhere beyond sight.

"This way," Crixus whispered.

Morrison and I exchanged an uncertain look and followed him down the hall. When we reached the dark space between two torches, he reached out and grasped my hand.

Of all the intimacies we had shared, this had never been one of them. Even as fear for Abernathy pierced my heart, I felt the warm strength of Morrison's grip. His lifeline and mine, so near each other if only for a moment.

His other hand, I was certain, was already on the butt of the gun strapped to his ribs in a well-worn leather holster. I had informed him that the only way to truly kill a vampire was to remove its head, but also that they healed slower than a thorazined sloth.

This information had been the impetus for his bringing the

guns in addition to several hastily made stakes he'd fashioned by snapping the handles off several unassuming garden tools.

For my part, I ran a hand over the small pouch tucked neatly into my bra. Within it, the potion promised to unfreeze Abernathy. Even as we had left the gallery, color had begun to return to Allan's cheeks, if not much else.

Crixus paused at the center of the hallway and pointed to a wide wooden door on giant, rusting hinges. "They're in there."

"*They*?" I asked. My heart beat so hard that I would have sworn I could taste my own pulse. "There was no mention of a *they*."

Crixus's eyes took on a strangely haunted quality. "Nero likes to keep his prisoners in the nursery."

"The nursery?" At that second, I couldn't decide which would be scarier. A room full of wailing infants, or neophyte vampires.

"Fledglings," Crixus said. "But don't worry. They sleep until midnight when they're that young."

I pulled my phone from the pocket of my borrowed sweatpants. 11:45. Fucking fantastic.

"We better get moving," I said. "Not much time to waste."

Morrison and I traded one last glance as Crixus reached into the pocket of his jeans and produced a large brass key.

"Nero gave you a key?" I asked.

"It's my job to clean their coffins," he answered, turning the key with a deep, metallic click. He looked at me, and I understood that I was to be the one to open the door.

"Wait." Morrison grasped my wrist and pressed into my hand the thick, cool handle of one of the stakes. "I'm going in first."

He pushed the door open with his non-dominant hand, it treating us to the customary Vincent Price film slow-motion creak.

Morrison swept in, keeping his back to the wall, aiming his

gun first to the right, then to the left, then checking behind the door. Wordlessly, he nodded and motioned me in.

Looking behind me, I discovered Crixus had already vanished, the motherfucker.

I blinked and moved forward, allowing my eyes to adjust to the darkness.

Then abruptly, the darkness vanished. Lights bright enough to sear my retinas flooded the room.

I took a step backward, my arm instinctively flying up to cover my eyes.

"What the fuck?" Morrison said.

Dropping my arm down, I blinked away white-blue bursts still flashing behind my eyelids. When I could begin to make out the shapes before me, my jaw dropped to the floor. Glossy black coffins on pedestals, neatly lined up in perfectly calibrated rows. Four across, four deep. Glittery signs at the foot of each bore carefully stenciled numbers, 1 through 16.

On the right side of the room, double stone staircases with ornate wrought iron railing led up to a small landing where a door presumably granted entry to more pleasant places in Nero's dungeon/castle/chalet/summer house.

Through the door, stepped Joseph Abernathy.

Relief washed over me to see him well and alive but was quickly replaced with hurt and disbelief when I saw the expression on his face.

Disdain. Triumph. Amusement.

"Joseph?" Even as I said his name aloud, some little scrap of hope that people could change, and stories could end happily dissolved permanently.

"Your detective is even more intrepid than I thought," Joseph said, fixing us with a dazzling grin.

Morrison, gods bless him, said nothing. He only moved closer to me while training his gun straight at Joseph's chest.

"You..." I stammered. "And Nero? Why?"

"Someone has to rule after the war is over."

The war.

With these words, something clicked and several windows in my mind aligned. "The dead vampires. The heads. *You* put them there."

"Yes," Joseph said. "It's only a matter of time before Nero stirs his forces to attack and with you and Mark out of the way—"

Joseph stopped short, coughed and a bright red bubble of blood erupted from his mouth. Shock widening his eyes, he pitched forward over the railing, landing with a terrible crunch on the stone floor several yards to our left, a long silver blade smoking in his back.

"If it isn't Hanna Hawvey," a strangely resonant voice boomed. I glanced back up at the landing to find a man standing where Joseph had been seconds earlier.

It only took a moment to convert memories of marble busts into living flesh before me.

Nero.

In the statues I'd studied in my Roman art history classes, Nero had been the original Neckbeard. The man on the landing did nothing to disabuse me of that notion. A wavy strawberry blond mop roosted on his head and made an odd doughnut from his sideburn down below his chin and up the other side. Rounded ears like jug handles sat low at the edge his jaw, his chin sloping inward to the small pouch of a mouth beneath a prominent nose. Acne pocked skin and small, eerily light eyes. Apparently, vampirism had restored him to his most vital state, but couldn't provide him with the kind of untouchable perfection so often associated with that condition.

He still wore the purple robes of an emperor, but they were covered by dark spatter marks and appeared to have at one point been a moth buffet.

"Sowwy about that," he said, glancing over the railing at

Joseph's motionless body. "*Someone* was supposed to dispose of him *befowe* you awwived." With this, he cast an irritated glance over his shoulder where Klaud looked, his pale face ghostly in the gloom.

"Apologies, Your Excellency," Klaud said, bowing.

"Take your pwace," Nero ordered.

A chastened Klaud hurried down the stairs and across the room.

"Who's that creepy fuck?" Morrison asked through the side of his mouth.

"Standard henchman," I whispered back.

"I suppose you'we wondewing what aww this is about," Nero said, sweeping a small hand grandly over the rows of coffins.

Certain historical accounts suggested that Nero's congenital defects might have included a speech impediment, but not that he was the oratorical equivalent of a slightly deranged Elmer Fudd. The effect compromised his ability to instill fear considerably.

"I suppose you're right," I said, flicking a nervous glance at Morrison, who looked exactly as gobsmacked as I felt.

Nero cleared his throat. "I brought you hewe, because I want you to pway a game."

"A game?" I repeated.

This too, I remembered from my Roman art history seminars. Nero's love of sport. Toward the beginning of his reign, those games had been mostly athletic in nature. Wrestling matches. Chariot races. Toward the end, the only racing was between two men trying to see who could expose the other's looping bowels or slippery purple liver to a crowd just as bloodlusty and mad as Nero was.

"What kind of game?" I asked, feeling like I'd drunk a quart of motor oil all of the sudden.

With that, Nero pointed toward the other corner of the room, where, much to my dismay, I discovered Klaud holding a slim dark remote. He depressed it as overly-dramatic TV game show music flooded the room.

"Wewcome to...." Nero paused as riotous lights flew around the now darkened room like a rave. "Deaw, or no Deaw!"

"You have got to be fucking kidding me." Morrison's face switched from blue, to green, to magenta, to gold as the strobes circulated. "Why doesn't he just try to kill us like a normal villain?"

"He loves games," I said, leaning toward his ear. "Also he's batshit crazy."

All at once, the strobing ceased and a single spotlight dropped onto Nero, who held a long, skinny microphone a la 1989 "Price is Right" Bob Barker.

"In one of these coffins," Nero bellowed into the lollipop-sized mic, "is Mawk Abewnathy."

Strange how the mere mention of that name made my heart leap in my chest.

"You have thwee guesses to find the coffin he's in," Nero continued. "If you guess correctwy, you aww get to weave unharmed! If not..." He trailed off, leaving the insinuation in his wake.

"How do I know you'll let us go?" I asked, glancing meaningfully at Joseph's still-smoking body on the floor below Nero's landing.

"You don't," Nero said, glistening lips drawing back to reveal the pearly tips of his elongated canines. "But what awtewnative do you have?"

I looked to Morrison and read the same thought already forming in my head in his eyes.

Nero had a point.

And anyway, if I *did* guess correctly, at least I'd know which coffin Abernathy was in. I might even be able to get the potion to him in time.

"I'll play," I said.

"Oh goody!" Gripping the microphone in one hand, Nero clapped it against the palm of his opposing hand like a delighted child, the sound amplified into thunderclaps. "This is going to be evew so much fun!"

Aware of both the clock ticking toward midnight and Abernathy in his frozen stupor, I looked at the coffins, reaching into the ether for some kind of guidance. Some kind of sign.

"Number four," I said.

By the irritated grimace on Nero's face, I gathered that I had been supposed to wait for some kind of formal invitation to make my first guess.

As any seasoned game show host would, Nero recovered quickly. "Show us coffin numbew fouw!"

Dour and dusty, Klaud shuffled over to coffin number four with maddening slowness.

I held my breath as he open the lid.

"Fuck!" My heart sank into my guts as a pale, blonde vampire popped up, her gold sequined dress throwing off sparks as she gave us a toothpaste ad grin, fangs and all. She handed an envelope to Klaud, who, somehow managing to move *even* slower, brought it to Nero.

Nero opened it and drew out a card.

"Hannewore Harvey, if you weave right now and agree to mawwy a human, you wiww receive wifetime protection from aww paranormaw cweatures, a house in the Hamptons, a check for a miwwion dowwars, and my personaw cowwection of Van Gogh paintings. Deaw," Nero said, his eerie gaze catching mine, "or no deaw?"

Klaud had done his homework. I had to give him that.

"No deal," I said without hesitation.

I felt Morrison stiffen at my side.

Nero's small mouth flattened into an angry line. "Aww wight," Nero said, regaining a measure of his contrived TV show host brightness. "What's youw next choice?"

Heart beating in my throat, I scanned the coffins once again, willing my mind, my heart to know which one held Abernathy. "Number ten," I said.

Once again, Klaud shuffled over to it, pushing open the lid.

A stunning redhead in blue sequins sat up, handing over her creamy envelope with a sultry gaze in Morrison's direction.

My heart sank from my guts straight through to my shoes.

Klaud brought the envelope to Nero, who opened it with a smugness that made me want to drive my knuckles into his already sunken mouth.

"Hannewore Hawvey, if you weave wight now and agwee to mawwy a human," he said, continuing the obvious theme, "you wiww weceive a wifetime suppwy of cheese from Wa Fromagewie in Pawis, fwee airwine tickets fow anywhewe in the worwd fow the duwation of youw naturaw wife, and entwance into any Awt Histowy PhD program at the univewsity of youw choice. Deaw," Nero asked dramatically, "or no deaw?"

I contemplated this for exactly zero seconds.

"No deaw…er…deal," I said, drawing a look of consternation from Morrison.

An orchestral version of the *wah waaaaah* music when a game show contestant selects the wrong option crackled through the speakers

Nero's left eye twitched as he tossed the envelope aside. "Fine," he said in the exact tone of a wife whose husband has just asked her if she minds if he goes to the strip club with his buddies. "You have one wast choice."

I took a deep breath and closed my eyes, mentally blocking the lights, the music, the pageantry. Sinking down, down, out of my mind and into my body, I forgot trying to figure out which coffin held Mark.

There, in the nameless, wordless, wild part of myself I'd been fighting. The part of me I had denied, degraded, concealed, and rejected.

I asked the wolf.

What returned to me was a rush of gratitude so intense I almost began to cry. Abernathy's scent flooded my nostrils, his essence firing across my brain like a rain of lights.

I opened my eyes, meeting Nero's leering gaze with one of calm certainty. "He's in number thirteen."

Nero's face crumpled into a mask of pure, murderous rage. "That's not faiw! You'we not supposed to have any powews untiw *aftew* you mate with an awpha!"

"I…I didn't know I did." I said, honestly just as surprised as Nero was.

"Wiar!" he accused, stabbing the microphone in my direction.

"Like *you're* one to talk." I clapped my hands over my mouth. The voice hadn't come from me. At least, not the me I had been for the past twenty-eight years. No. This came directly from the quiet, eternal, unafraid part of me that I had apparently woken up just now.

"*You*." Nero exhaled the word like a poisonous fume. "You insowent swut!"

"But you—" I began.

"I. Changed. My. Mind." Nero stomped his sandal-clad foot with every syllable. "Kwaud! Kiww them!"

"With pleasure." Klaud moved with the same, shambling, hesitant gait common to horror movie villains as he rejoined Nero on the platform before reaching into his pocket and producing a brass bell.

One quick flick of Klaud's wrist, and all the coffins began to creak open.

"Cover me," I said, catching the slightest twist of a grin from a cop who had probably never used these words in real life.

Racing over to coffin thirteen with Morrison close behind, I threw open the latch, and nearly fainted. Abernathy's pallid face stared up at me, eyes open wide, mouth a gaping "O" of shock.

Looking at him, I knew what I was seeing was the precise moment when he realized his father's betrayal.

"Hanna." Morrison's voice curved upward like a question. "Hurry."

"I am!" Fumbling madly inside my shirt, I dug into the leather pouch, my fingers slippery with sweat. They closed over something cool and hard. A small vial with the tiniest of cork stoppers. It nearly squirted through my fingers as I pulled it free, panic slamming into me like a freight train when I fumbled it back into my hands inches before it exploded on the stone floor

"*Hanna*." Morrison was louder this time.

Thumbing off the cork, I tipped the greenish liquid directly into Abernathy's open mouth.

I waited, frantically searching his face for any of the signs the witch had given me that marked the draught taking hold.

Nothing.

Cold, creeping fear flooded my heart. It had been too long.

"Please," I said, placing my hands on either side of his frozen, pallid face. "Please come back." Hot tears leaked down my cheeks, washing the taste of salt and crypt dirt into my mouth. "I love you."

Hearing myself say these words out loud for the first time only made me cry all the harder.

"I don't care if you ever love me. I don't even care if you *like* me. Just let me sit outside of your office, and file your papers, and just…just be *near* you."

My tears fell from my cheeks to his, darkening tracks down the chalky surface of his cheekbones and jaw.

Through the fringe of my wet lashes, I saw the tiniest twinge of rose at the very center of his ashen lips. It stayed only there for a moment before flooding outward, moving from his face down his neck.

Abernathy's horrifically guttural, shuddering inhale was the most beautiful sound I'd ever heard in my life. The terrible, pained rasping of a man who had just kicked his way to the surface after inhaling a lungful of water.

And then I was hauling him up by the forearms and slapping his broad back and suppressing a whoop of pure joy.

"Hanna—" Abernathy's voice sounded like he'd gargled with broken glass. His fingertips were still cool to the touch as his hand molded itself against the side of my face. "I—"

The first gunshot boomed in my ears, deafening and sudden. I looked up from Abernathy's coffin to find Morrison with his back to us, the blond vampire from Coffin Number Four twining herself around him Bride of Dracula style as he tried to get a clear shot at Klaud.

"Stay here. You're no good to us until you have your strength back." I offered him what I hoped was a reassuring smile.

Unstrapping a stake from the makeshift utility belt Morrison had fashioned for me, I hauled back and cracked the blond vampire with enough force to send her flying face-first into a concrete wall.

The gunfire ceased as Morrison stared at me in open-mouthed amazement. "What the fuck was that?"

"I don't know," I said. "But I like it." Attempting to twirl the stake like a baton for affect, I almost clubbed myself in the face.

And all was once again right with the world.

"We have to get him out of here," I said.

"How?" Morrison asked.

All around us, coffins continued to creak open, their largely female occupants sequin-clad, licking rubied lips as they languorously stretched long, silky limbs like Barbies escaping their boxes. Worse, the door behind Nero and Klaud had opened, legions more of neophyte vampires spilling down the stairs.

The nerve-sizzling adrenaline I'd experienced evaporated as

quickly as it had come, and I felt the familiar grip of cold, pure dread.

Abernathy tumbled out of the casket, landing in a heap at my feet.

I could see the intensity gathering on his face as he tried to transform, tried to become the version of himself both dangerous and deadly. Instead, he only managed to sprout strange patches of fur on the backs of his hands and an exceptionally unfortunate mustache.

"Give me a weapon," he growled, dragging himself to a standing position against the coffin.

To his credit, Morrison reached into his belt and handed over a stake and the deadliest of the wickedly curved hunting knives in his arsenal.

Abernathy took them, anchoring the knife in his belt and clutching the stake in his palm. The other hand, he offered to Morrison, who blinked at it as the horde began to close in.

"If we die," Abernathy said. "We die standing."

Morrison closed his hand over Abernathy's and for a moment, I thought my heart might just swell up and explode in my chest, killing me before any vampire would have time to reach me.

"We die standing," Morrison repeated.

When the deafening *pop* sounded, I thought for the briefest of seconds that Morrison had punctuated this statement by resuming his shooting.

"How about we don't die at all?"

I spun around to find Crixus leaning against the coffin Abernathy had recently vacated.

Several of the vampires glanced nervously at each other, as if perplexed by this unexpected development in the program.

"Cwixus!" Nero screamed in rage. "You are bound to Kwaud by a souw debt. If you betway him, you wiww suffer etewnaw towment!"

Echoes of Crixus's gladiator past collided with his present as he squared his shoulders, turning to Nero and Klaud as if seeking the thumbs up or down that would save or damn the life of his opponent.

"Only if he survives," Crixus said.

The same door Morrison and I had so tentatively entered burst open precisely at that moment. In one of the most surreal moments of my life—definitely saying something, given the day I'd had—Wallis the unicorn came thundering in, pausing on the landing to rear up on his hind legs and whinny a screaming war cry that dropped the entire room into silence.

Which he promptly ruined by opening his mouth.

"Who's ready to get shanked, you undead motherfuckers?" he asked, brandishing his horn at the vampires nearest him.

Crixus gave us a "what you gonna do?" shrug and the action resumed.

Wallis, mowing his way through the crowd, all rainbow mane and golden hooves and "yeah, you like that bitch?" as he skewered hapless vampires with his golden horn.

Morrison, unloading clip after clip, aiming for the necks.

Crixus, broadsword in hand, lopping off head after head.

Abernathy, still unable to transform but slitting throat after throat and tossing the bodies aside like discarded husks.

And me, with my handle-stake, cracking skulls the other four had missed.

I was sweating, panting, more exhausted and exhilarated than I'd been in my life when I saw that someone else had joined Klaud and Nero, bending close to the emperor's ear. A smile that could peel paint curled across Nero's face. He nodded to his guest, who disappeared back through the door. Klaud gave his bell a short, sharp ring, then followed.

The vampires froze in place, fangs bared, hands like claws still reaching for our necks.

"As entewtaining as this wittle show has been..." Nero

trailed a stubby finger along the railing. "I have a new offew to make you, Hanna."

Abernathy, Morrison, Wallis and Crixus, gore be-smattered and breathless, all looked at me.

Wiping a spatter of something off my cheek with the shoulder of my shirt, I pushed a stray clump of matted red hair out of my eyes. "I'm about tired of your games," I said.

Nero stepped aside dramatically to reveal Klaud, pushing someone through the door before him. With one hand fisted in his captive's hair, and the other holding a blade to his throat, he pushed him into the spotlight.

Time hung frozen, horror collapsing my throat.

It was Steven Franke.

CHAPTER 26

One of Steve's eyes was swollen shut, his cheek purple and puffed with a bruise. Crusted blood ran from the corner of his mouth and stained the Ramones t-shirt he had changed into for his and Shayla's official exit from the reception. His hands were bound behind him, his ankles wrapped in a silvery chain.

"Steve!" I could scarcely squeeze his name from my throat before it contracted in a sob. I lurched toward the stairs, only to be dragged back by Crixus.

"Don't," he whispered low and gruff in my ear. "This is a game, remember? You want to keep him playing."

"Suwwendew," Nero said, eyes gleaming with insane glee. "Ow he dies."

"S'okay, doll. You got bigger trout to tackle." Steve coughed, sending a fresh gout of blood down the front of his shirt. "No matter what happens, you were the best friend a guy could ever have."

"Fweind?" Nero asked, glancing from me to Steve. "Does he not know?"

"I know your face looks like a foot." Steve's split lip gapped as, even now, he smiled.

Klaud tightened his grip on Steve's hair. "Now is not the time for levity, I assure you."

"In a way, this is vewy poignant." Nero turned to face Steve, the crown of his head ending a good three inches before Steve's chin. "Teww him, Kwaud. I want to see the wook on his face. What's weft of it, anyway." Nero snickered.

"Hanna is not your friend, Mr. Franke." Klaud's blue eyes bored into mine even as his lips brushed Steve's ear. "She's your sister."

Despite the swelling, I could see the emotions twisting Steve's face into a mask of pain. "My…I have a—"

Steve's words ceased as the blade of Klaud's dagger sank into his sternum with sudden, brutal force. One pink tear leaked from the corner of Steve's blackened eye. Klaud released him, Steve's long, lanky body crumpling to the ground with a sickening crunch.

We all stood there, frozen in shock and grief, the room silent until Nero yawned and stretched. "Bowwwing," he sang.

I stared at him, my body beginning to shake.

The pure distillation of every ounce of pain, horror, grief and fear I had never found the strength to give voice to welled up out of me until it was no longer a scream, but a *howl*, boiling up from the depths of my soul.

All around me, vampires fell to the ground, clutching their ears as they writhed.

"The heir!" one of them groaned, contorting in agony.

"She's real!" another cried.

They began peeling off in droves, scampering toward the nearest exit like spiders on their broken, twisted limbs.

"Get back hewe!" Panic made Nero's face almost boyish as he watched himself being deserted by the very beings he'd created.

Still, I couldn't stop. The howl amplified, bouncing off the soaring ceilings, filling the room. Filling the world.

Beside me, Abernathy surged like he'd been plugged into an electrical socket. A ripping, primal growl tore free from him, effectively ending my banshee wail as at long last, his body began its violent transformation from man, to wolf.

"That's what the fuck I'm talking about!" Wallis galloped through the thinning crowd, donkey-kicking the remaining vampires, spinning like a mechanical bull to repeat the process.

Moving into the sea of migrating bodies, Morrison continued picking off vampires, his gunshots echoing in the hall we'd come through to access the nursery/crypt in the first place.

With a sudden *pop* Crixus was no longer standing next to me, but at the top of the stairs to the landing. Moving faster than I had ever seen him, Klaud broke for the door.

Nero took one look at Abernathy racing up behind Crixus and followed Klaud, his tattered purple toga flapping in his wake.

I came unstuck then, aware that I, too, could move. Could act.

Leaping over vampire carcasses, I launched myself at the stairs and found Steve at the top of them in a crumpled heap.

"That was pretty badass." Klaud's dagger shivered in Steve's chest with his quick indrawn breath. Smoke coiled up from the place where it met his t-shirt, rising in a thin column toward heaven.

"Yeah?" I asked, coming to kneel gently at his side.

"Yeah." He smiled at me, teeth rubied with blood.

"I HAVE A *SISTER*."

"You sure do," I said, squeezing his clammy palm.

"I have a *family*." He pronounced this word with such awe,

such pure wonder that a fresh wave of tears spilled over my cheeks.

My mind flashed back to a different night. A night when I thought Abernathy might be a murderer, and where a sleek, tawny golden wolf had followed me into the dark. There, he had put himself between me and a thing that wanted me dead, and nearly died himself in the process. That night, I learned that werewolves could heal from horrific wounds.

On another, I had learned that the presence of silver makes that healing all the harder. On another still, that powerful werewolf blood can assist in that process.

But Allan was nowhere to be found.

Come back. I willed the thought out to Abernathy.

"I have to get this out," I said, glancing at the dagger's jeweled handle.

"Sure thing, sis." Steve's chest rattled through a wet cough. "Unstick me."

I stood, positioning myself directly over him so I could withdraw the blade at the same angle it had gone in. "Ready?" I asked.

He nodded, his good eye falling closed to join the one already swollen shut.

Gripping the handle, I pulled with every ounce of my greatly waning strength. I felt it slide free, squeaking slightly when the blade cleared the bones of his sternum. Tossing it aside, I immediately pressing both palms over the wound and applying all my bodyweight.

"You're like King Arthur." He grinned me again, a fresh stream of blood leaking from the side of his mouth.

I felt a hot rush seeping through my fingers with every beat of his good, kind heart.

"Rest, Steve. I need you to concentrate on healing."

"We'd just gotten to the hotel," Steve said. "That honeymoon suite you booked for us at the Windsor. Shayla sent me out for ice." His voice took on odd faraway quality, like he was talking to me from the other end of a tunnel.

His pulse weakened beneath my palms, the beats coming farther and farther apart.

"Steve?"

Oh, please, God no. Not him. Not my brother.

Powerful blood.

Several times that night, I had startled myself and others with a show of unexplainable strength.

The dagger glinted in the corner of my vision. Before I could lose my nerve, I picked it up and slashed my hand, pressing my wound to his.

Closing my eyes, drawing a breath, I sank.

Down. Down beneath my mind. Beneath my panicked, useless thoughts. Down to the foreign and familiar presence there.

This time, I didn't just feel her.

I *saw* her.

Her coat like burnished copper. Eyes of topaz and emerald. The creamy sleekness of her muzzle. Ageless and boundless. Wild and wise.

Heal him. Please, please heal him.

Fire kindled in my heart, burning its way through my chest, down my arm, into my palm.

Into Steve.

I felt it pouring into his chest. Felt it mending, binding, sealing.

"But the ice machine was broken—" Steve said, taking up directly where he'd left off.

With a whoop of joy, I gathered my brother's bony torso to mine, sobbing and laughing, nearly sick with relief.

Helping Steve to his feet, together we limp-walked side-by-side down the staircase and out to the hallway. Steve, who'd been brought in via vampire and not via demigod teleportation, steered us out to the main hall.

In great contrast to the artificially archaic dungeon basement, it looked like nothing so much as a mountain lodge. Which, of course, it was. Deep leather couches. Woven rugs. Cathedral ceiling with exposed wooden beams.

There, at it's center, a sight that banished what feeble happiness had taken root in my heart.

Abernathy, Crixus, and Wallis standing over the prone body of Detective James Morrison.

"HE'S NOT DEAD," CRIXUS SAID, CLEARLY SEEING THE NAKED PANIC on my face.

Steve and I hobbled over to them where I slid Steve onto the couch and took in Morrison's milk-pale skin and bloodless lips.

With one finger, Crixus peeled back the collar of Morrison's shirt. There, in the smooth patch of skin where his shoulder met his neck were two neat puncture wounds.

I dropped to my knees, my palm against his cooling cheek. "We have to do something," I said, glancing frantically from Abernathy to Crixus, to Wallis as I scrubbed spattered blood from Morrison's neck with a scrap of the borrowed t-shirt that still carried his living scent. "He's a detective. And he solves murders. And paints and he cooks wonderful food and he can't be dead. He can't." Hot, salty tears leaked from the corners of my eyes, pooling in the corners of my mouth. "Isn't there anything we can do?"

Abernathy, still in wolf mode, aimed his muzzle toward Morrison and sniffed. When his golden eyes caught mine, the news I read in them wasn't good.

"But," I sobbed. "Is there any way to—"

Werewolf, demigod and unicorn all shook their heads.

I choked on watery inhale. "But in the movies if—"

"The whole *killing the one who made him* thing?" Crixus asked.

"Yes!" I said hopefully.

"Myth," Crixus said. "Vampirism is a lot like herpes."

"You would know," Wallis mumbled.

Crixus pointed a warning finger at him. "You better shut your horse mouth before I shut it for you."

"What does this mean?" I asked, refocusing their attention. "What's going to happen to him?"

Crixus glanced at the ornate grandfather clock in the corner. "In about twenty-two hours, he's going to wake up very confused and very hungry."

"I'll call Akhenaten." Abernathy settled himself on his haunches, his tail curling around his gigantic paws. "They'll at least help him acclimate."

I pushed a lock of hair away from his waxy forehead. Never in a million years would I have predicted what strange roads we'd travel the day I rear-ended him. He loved me. He had died for me. And now he would live forever.

I knew in that moment that whatever happened after this night, wherever my life took me, Morrison would always be part of it.

"Klaud and Nero?" I asked, pushing myself to my feet. If the gore painting Abernathy and Crixus was any indication, they hadn't faired well.

"Dead," Abernathy said.

"*Dead* dead." Crixus added. "Along with his followers."

"The ones who didn't quit this bitch, anyway." Wallis flicked his tail in a gesture reminiscent of a self-initiated back pat.

"Speaking of not dead." Steve peeled up his t-shirt to reveal his bony, fish-white, but perfectly intact sternum. "Check out the patch-up job Hanna did."

Wallis whistled through his teeth. Because who even knew unicorns could whistle. "His narrow ass looks showroom new."

"Right? And a good thing too. Because I," Steve said, flexing his long, lean arms, "am a remarkable specimen."

Abernathy and I shared a look of pure, unfettered fondness.

Hands on my knees and every part of my body screaming in protest, I got myself to my feet. "What will you do?" I asked Crixus. "Now that you're free."

"Funny you should ask that." Crixus grabbed one wrist with the opposite hand, reaching upward in a sympathetic stretch. Even smattered with gore, his tight black t-shirt managed to show off the abdominal perfection beneath. "Someone at the wedding was talking about this new program the Bureau of Supernatural Affairs is launching. Kind of like a bounty hunter gig for rogue paranormals. I thought I might check that out."

"Sounds promising," I said.

"How about you, Wallis?" I asked. "Back to Unicornland?"

"Fuck that shit," he said. "I'm going to Vegas."

CHAPTER 27

With Steve restored to his honeymoon, Crixus off to explore his new career, Wallis off to annoy a new city, Morrison safely installed in his new vampire training academy, Allan on the mend, and Abernathy engaged in heavy vampire-related damage control, I returned home to my own little nest.

I was met at the door by the warm, furry feline satellites of Stewie, Stella, and Gilbert, who were somehow more life affirming than the breath in my lungs.

"Hi guys!" I greeted. "Mommy is going to snuggle the shit out of you just as soon as she gets the vampire guts out of her hair."

Three sets of eyes followed me as I cleaned out the overloaded food bowls I'd left them pre-wedding and replaced it with fresh—first things first—before peeling off my crusty clothes and dropping them directly in the trash.

After about eleventy-seven rinse and repeats, I exited the shower in a cloud of steam, scrubbed, shiny, and almost human.

Almost.

No sooner had I belted my silky green robe when three short raps rattled my front door.

My stomach flipped as my helpful brain spooled back to the final scene in a horror movie, where, inadvisably triumphant, our heroine discovers that dead is an extremely subjective state subject to much interpretation.

Nero? Klaud? Joseph?

On quiet feet, I tiptoed over to my door and applied my eye to the peephole.

Mark. Andrew. Abernathy.

Showered, shaved, and wearing his standard uniform of a button up shirt and illegally well-fitting trousers.

I didn't bother checking myself in the mirror as there wasn't a damn thing I could do about my wet hair and scrubbed-shiny face. Also, he'd seen me looking worse.

Much, *much* worse.

With trembling hands, I slid open the chain, flipped the deadlock, and opened the door.

"I thought you were—" was all I had time to get out.

Abernathy pulled me to his chest, his arms wrapping around me so completely that his hands rested on his own biceps. His chin rested on the crown of my head. With my ear to his chest I witnessed the unseen drama of his wrestling for control of his own breathing, the thunderous rhythm of his heart.

We stayed like that for an immeasurable space of time, breathing each other in in total silence. Then his fingers migrated to my neck, his thumbs on the upward thrust of my jaw as he slowly, deliberately rested his forehead against mine.

He pulled away from me then, his whiskey-colored eyes burning down into mine as the words escaped him on panting breaths. "I thought I'd lost you."

For perhaps the very first time in my life, I didn't feel the need to drag more words out of him, or add a stream of my own. I only waited.

His hands tightened on either side of my face.

"What you did…charging Nero's house like that…it was absolutely insane," he said.

Shoulders sinking, my eyes sank to the planks of my hardwood floor as I prepared myself for the imminent lecture. About how I put myself and him, and pretty much the whole human and paranormal world at risk with my poor life decisions.

"I owe you my life, Hanna," Abernathy said.

I glanced abruptly up at him, finding his eyes glowing with unshed tears.

"I was in the dark, and you found me. You found me, and I love you. I love you, Hannelore Harvey. Every moment. Every day. Since the first time I saw you. I loved you then. I love you now. I'll love you always."

I opened my mouth, but he pressed the pads of his fingers over my lips, effectively ending the possibility of my ruining the moment with a joke.

"*Ruith ri mo thaobh.*" The syllables sounded silk over stone.

Cocking my head at him, I moved his hand away from my mouth. "Are you sure you didn't sustain some sort of head injury?" I asked. "Because you are making zero sense right now."

"It's Gaelic," he said, his hand closing over mine and pressing it to his heart.

"What does it mean?" The rushing, primal pulse thundered in my ears with my heart's every stunned and wondrous beat.

"Run by my side." His fingers stroked my temples, his gentle grip making it impossible for me to look away.

The image came to me at once and complete. Wolves in a pack, running together. Neither owning or being owned. Free but choosing the same course, each finding a common speed. A common purpose. A common life.

"If this is about protection—" I began.

"It is," he said. "*My* protection. I need you, Hanna. You're everything good, and light and true. You're my breath, and my life. Be my mate, Hanna. For now and for always, run by my side."

We stared at each other then, our breaths the only measure of time's passage in this uncharted space.

"Mark Andrew Abernathy," I said, reaching up to place my hands over his. "I would run by your side to the very ends of the earth."

With these words, it was decided.

A thousand times I had imagined what would happen in the moments after I made my choice. A thousand times I had been wrong.

In my imagination, he had been hot, hungry, and demanding.

The man standing before me now looked ready to collapse with relief. Relief, yes, and wonder too. Uncertainty still haunting the edges of a face so hopeful it nearly broke my heart.

"I'm sure," I said, answering the question writ large on his face.

We had in our history an entire galaxy of kisses. Some tender. Some urgent. Some passionate. Some painful.

This one was different.

Me, tasting him with my already blooming powers. Drowning in the pure, chemical loveliness of him. And his scent. *His scent*. Like wind. Like earth. Like rain. Like air. Like every single thing on this planet that causes life to be. I drank him in deep greedy gulps with each one of my now heightened senses.

Mouths fused and hands busy, we freed each other from the layers separating our bodies. Him, pulling the tie on my robe and letting it fall from my shoulders. Me, unbuttoning his shirt, his belt, his pants.

We fell to the bed together, skin on skin, writhing and

grinding as if every cell in our bodies could merge in perfect fusion.

He left my stinging mouth to drag his lips down my neck, my collarbone, my nipples, stopping to taste every part with quick, feathery flicks of his tongue.

Ready, so much more than ready, my body jerked when his hand slid between my legs. The slippery warmth he found there eliciting a groan as I came violently against his palm.

He brought his hand to his mouth licking his fingers. "Gods, how you taste." Kneeling before me, he pushed my knees apart, appreciative fingers trailing down the insides of my thighs before gripping my hips. "Please Hanna," he said, that one word unstitching me at once and forever. "I can't wait any longer."

"Don't," I panted. "I need to feel you. All of you."

But he did wait.

He hesitated there, on the threshold that would divide the life I had known from the life I would yet live. My past and our future.

Abernathy tilted my chin up to face a gaze of such intensity, I might have burst into flames had I endured it on our first meeting. Eyes that had seen death, had known life, had killed and nearly died for me, now anchoring me as he pushed into me for the very first time.

He came to rest fully within me, the pressure of him like a discovery. A previously unknown place where *we* were possible.

He began to move. Slowly at first, acquainting himself. Acquainting me.

With each stroke, the delicious friction seemed to build on itself, multiplying within me until, half mad with the need for more, I began arching my hips up to meet him.

"Oh, God, Hanna." Abernathy's voice seemed to dissolve with the same pleasure turning my insides into molten sugar.

Sounds came from me. Unfamiliar, animalistic, hedonistic

sounds. They found their answering call in Mark, matching me cry for cry.

Profane, holy, primal and perfect were the words we spoke to each other.

When I thought I might die from the incomprehensible intensity, Mark scooped a hand under my thigh, turning me over. With one hand buried in my hair, he angled my face to retain eye contact as he drove into me from behind.

And what a vision he was. Savage and beautiful in equal measure. His abdominals flexing, chest tensing, dark locks of hair falling in his smoldering eyes. Each increasingly desperate thrust rode in like a wave, breaking over me, breaking *in* me, until I broke with it.

Bucking and shuddering, I screamed his name as I came utterly undone.

His teeth bared, Abernathy buried his face in my neck, his teeth gently nipping the skin in mutual conquest as he lost himself within me. Those quick, hot pulses which forever marked me his.

Which marked us mated.

Abernathy's face rolled toward mine on the pillow. He patted his chest, and obediently, I snuggled into it, smelling the living salt of him.

"So what happens now?" I asked.

"We sleep," he said in a voice already drugged with satiated pleasure.

"I mean, how does this whole werewolf thing happen? Am I just going to like sprout a tail one of these days? Should I invest in elastic clothing? Oh! And what about babies? Do werewolves have litters?"

"Are you that eager to bear my loin-fruit?"

I could literally *hear* the smile in his voice.

"No," I said. "Especially since you just called it *loin-fruit*."

"Transformations usually happen with the onset of an

emotionally inciting incident." Abernathy repeated this with the patience of a man who had clearly said it many times before. "Litters are unusual but not unheard of."

"You know," I said, my breathing having returned to something like a normal pattern. "You never finished telling me about Lily."

"Must we always have these conversations when I'm naked and just had my mind blown?" Abernathy flopped an arm over his eyes.

"I mean we're mated now so you probably should be able to tell me about your long dead love." With lazy fingers, I traced the sloping line of his clavicle.

"Hanna," he sighed. "You *are* my long dead love."

In the silence that followed, a choir of crickets broke into spontaneous chorus.

"Come again?" I pushed myself up on my elbows, gazing down into his passion-slackened face.

"Some heirs are more powerful than others. They can accept the responsibility of that power, or can turn away from it and live a normal life." To my great alarm Abernathy's sleepiness was increasing in direct proportion to my curiosity.

"And if they elect to live a normal life?"

"They eventually die and the cycle begins again. Just as it did with you." In silence thick with meaning, I let this sink it. "You were born a warrior," Abernathy said around a cavernous yawn. "But tonight you chose to accept that destiny. And I will always fight at your side."

Nuzzling my face into his neck, I breathed him in. This man, this being who I had alternately feared, and wanted and loved.

My destiny. My mate.

At his side, the one place I forever wanted to be, I finally gave in to exhaustion.

"Come with me."

Aroused from the best sleep of my entire life, I awoke to find Abernathy standing before the window, his naked silhouette limned in silver.

"I thought I already had." Dreamy and slack-limbed, I dropped back down to my pillow like a shot bird.

"Come with me *outside*," he said.

"But we're naked," I answered, my eyes still closed.

"That's kind of the point." I felt the bed depress as he sat down next to me, his fingers dancing up my spine.

Shivering, I sat up. "But what if the neighbors see?"

"They won't," he said. "Promise."

So it was like that, wearing not one stitch of clothing, I followed Abernathy down the shared hallway of the old Victorian home that had once been my mental ward after a terrible divorce.

"Are you ready?" he asked, holding out his hand.

"Ready for what?" With one arm across my breasts, the other covering my lady-bits, and my eyes everywhere at once, the only thing I was ready for was to crawl back into bed.

"To run." In that light, with that expression on his face, Abernathy didn't look like a 431 year-old werewolf. He looked like a ten year-old little boy.

"You want me to hold your hand and run naked down the street."

"That's what I want." He grinned at me, teeth white in the moonlight.

"But my feet—"

"Trust me," Abernathy said.

I did.

Pulling in a deep breath of sweet night air, I realized for the first time that I could smell the pollen, the bird feathers and twigs in their nests, the sleeping flowers, the sprinkler wet pavement and chlorophyll rich grass.

Fueled by this olfactory revelation, I relinquished my modesty and gave Abernathy my hand.

Before I even knew what I was feeling, the world became a blur around me. An impressionistic painting punctuated with lights and sounds and smells, flashes of detail too small to see with the naked eye.

I glanced downward, perplexed not to feel pavement biting into my feet.

Because I no longer had feet.

Delicate russet paws flashed out before me, the elegant forelegs attached to them swift and sure.

I was a wolf.

As I had when it came to mating with Abernathy, I had envisioned in great detail what my first transformation would be like. The B-movie low budget version of bulging pockets of skin and cracking bones, sweating, swearing, and screaming.

There was only bliss.

Bliss and terrific speed, my mate a dark blur beside me as we raced past the edge of town and into the foothills. Into a whole new world of scents. Pine, and beetles and moss and dead leaves.

Joy as I had never known suffused my entire being as we broke into a clearing. We loped to a stop, padding through soft grass to find the edge of the cliff overlooking the city. Lights scattered like glowing confetti on the stretch of land below.

Then there was only Abernathy.

Abernathy against the obsidian shards of the mountain, the sky, and the moon.

THE END

ALSO BY CYNTHIA ST. AUBIN

Tails from the Alpha Art Gallery

Love Bites

Love Sucks

Love Lies

The Witches of Port Townsend

Which Witch Is Which?

Which Witch Is Wicked?

Which Witch is Wild?

Which Witch is Willing?

The Case Files of Dr. Matilda Schmidt, Paranormal Psychologist

Unlovable

Unlucky

Unhoppy

Unbearable

Unassailable

Undeadly

Unexpecting

From Hell to Breakfast

Unraveled

Also available as Box Sets...

Disordered

Dysfunctional

&

The Complete Case Files of Dr. Matilda Schmidt

Volume I

Volume II

Volume III

Jane Avery Mysteries

Private Lies

Lying Low

ABOUT THE AUTHOR

Cynthia St. Aubin wrote her first play at age eight and made her brothers perform it for the admission price of gum wrappers. A steal, considering she provided the wrappers in advance. Though her early work debuted to mixed reviews, she never quite gave up on the writing thing, even while earning a mostly useless master's degree in art history and taking her turn as a cube monkey in the corporate warren.

Because the voices in her head kept talking to her, and they discourage drinking at work, she kept writing instead. When she's not standing in front of the fridge eating cheese, she's hard at work figuring out which mythological, art historical, or paranormal friends to play with next. She lives in Texas with the love of her life and a surly cat named Patches.

Cynthia loves to hear from her readers. You can find her here:

Visit me: http://www.cynthiastaubin.com/
Email me: cynthiastaubin@gmail.com
Join my Minions: https://www.facebook.com/groups/Cynthiastaubins/

Subliminally message me: *You were thinking of cheese just now, right?*

And here:

Ingram Content Group UK Ltd.
Milton Keynes UK
UKHW012204200323
418888UK00015B/392/J